BLOWING UP

BLOWING UP

Biff Mitchell

BLOWING UP

DOUBLE DRAGON

Preface

Smile. No scowl ever lifted the mood of those doomed to continue.

The following stories appeared first in these ezines and literary journals:

A Touch of Time (Rose & Thorn Literary Journal, 2011; Ginosko Literary Journal, 2013)

Sleeping In Ditches (Otis Nebula, 2012)

Surfing in Catal Hyuk (Projected Letters, 2018)

These Eyes (Strangelet Literary Journal, 2014)

Still Life with Sax and Muse (Rose & Thorn Literary Journal. 2014)

Still Life with Muse and Rain (Punchel's, 2012)

Driving to the End of the World ('Nonymous Magazine, 2014)

WHAT YOU ARE ABOUT TO READ

Sleeping In Ditches

Near the close of the 21st Century, God
commanded, "Hey Noah, I want you to build a
canoe."
"But Lord," said Noah, "shouldn't that be an ark?"
"No," said God, "there's not that much worth
saving."

***

By evening and day I'm the man of the hour, the life of the party, the wit, the insider, the compleat schmooz rider. I'm the water cooler sage, the lunchroom rage; everybody wants to hear me, everybody wants to be near me, everybody wants to absorb me through that huge umbrella of thought that surrounds me, bouncing away everything I don't want to know.

There's a lot of crap out there, and shit falls out of the sky, but not on me. I'm the source of my own crap and people respect me for that. I'm like the faucet I can't turn off. Wordsworth's spontaneous overflow without the meter. I'm a damn flood.

At night, I sleep in ditches.

Not the same ditch every night. I have favorites and sometimes I like to try something new. I've slept in ditches full of needles and condoms and barking spiders. I wear two wide swatches of red on my back from a slick of bubbling something-or-other at the bottom of a ditch by a chemical plant.

9

I've seen small things flitter and flap in the darkness around rusted tin cans while they debated whether to leave me alone or eat me.

But it's not all bad.

I woke once in a ditch with immaculate new suburban ranch-style houses with carved lawns on one side and a field of sprawling swamp and early morning animal sounds on the other. In a clearing by a stream banked with yellow and blue flowers, an army of bulldozers pointed right at the swamp and its animal noises. I felt like I was on the cusp of something wonderful and nascent. Soon, I thought, those bulldozers will turn God's land into something useful for his children. Yes, I believe in God. His outline glowed in the aura surrounding those formidable machines—his tools built by man in his power's image.

The grass in that ditch was long and thick and made for comfortable sleeping. Right by my head, the biggest most beautiful dandelions opened with brilliant bursts of yellow and orange, their leaves vibrating with the deepest green I'd ever known. There was grandeur in those flowers. Their beauty was irresistible. I reached out…and I ate them.

***

She took a long slow swallow from her champagne glass and it was erotic the way her throat undulated with the swallow, but she was well into her seventies and I'm not that liberal-minded. Besides, I think downing her glass of bubbly may have had something to do with her being impressed with what I had to say. I get this a lot at dinner parties.

Yes, I go to dinner parties. I love nothing more than a free meal in a friend's home, friend or not. I wear my best for these occasions because dinner parties are all about appearances, even in the things we say. And I have a lot to say.

She wore a red gown with black lace dangling over where her breasts may have been at one time. She wore black gloves. Her face was surprisingly wrinkle free and she had a youthful glint in her eyes. Then, her throat, though still erotic…suddenly lurched, and lurched again. She was choking. The woman beside her (her granddaughter, who was young and beautiful and had been eyeing me for most of the evening) slapped her grandmother on the back, hard. That seemed to do the trick and as the old woman reclaimed her composure, she glared at me and her youthful glint turned to fire, my cue to continue.

"Nature needs to be pushed," I said. "Without some sort of imbalance or conflict, nothing happens. Everything stays the same forever and then it all just disappears out of boredom. So we're doing Nature a favor when we pump her full of garbage."

The man beside me with the thick glasses and a paunch spilling over his chair told me that nobody was doing anybody a favor, least of all nature, by dumping garbage into the oceans …

"…but," I corrected, "it's not just the oceans, it's the air and the soil. We need to maintain a balance; we need to fill them all with the things we took from them." I paused for effect and noticed the old woman was just about to ruin my train of thought by speaking. "Think of it, think of its simple cyclic beauty," I said. "We take raw materials from the land, air and seas, mix them into entirely new materials that might take Nature billions of years to create—things like all-season tires and chrome bumpers—and then we feed them back into nature in their new forms …"

The man with the paunch coughed out a laugh.

"… and those new materials mix with the raw materials to create something even newer. And a stronger, more robust Nature evolves in the process."

The old woman, whose throat was obviously still irritated from the choking (and whose granddaughter had just winked at me), scratched out something about overloading the environment before it had a chance to adapt and then we all die, to which I replied wisely, "The happy gambler is the one who embraces the concept of losing with grace and dignity."

Around the gathering, heads nodded agreement. Somebody always nods agreement. It's what keeps the plastic corks in the champagne bottles cooling in ice-filled silver buckets the length of the table.

***

Yes, I thought, hours after the party, she'll have that same glint in her eye when she's her grandmother's age. I watched the condom swirl in the toilet and disappear, my contribution to the environment.

12

Then I left her place to find a comfortable ditch.

***

The company kitchenette is the 21st Century's answer to the Greek amphitheatre where philosophers met to stare at ideas. I would have made a great Greek.

I was sticking a meat pie, all wrapped in shiny plastic, into the microwave and thinking how the true worth of a man's life is not measured as much by his acts—all of which are subject to anybody and his dog's opinion—as it is by the amount of garbage he creates during his life. A man's pile of garbage is something you can measure, and the less biodegradable the better because we need to leave monuments so that aliens will know we were here.

But we weren't talking garbage on this particular day. We were talking Free Will. One of the junior managers said something about everything being pre-determined so what did it matter if we were good or bad because we were doomed to heaven or hell even before we were born.

"Hell is where everybody chews gum," I said. "And the saliva tastes like it came from somebody else's mouth."

The junior manager looked confused.

"I'm talking about God's hell," I explained. "He owns it all."

I had a feeling that I still wasn't getting through to him. "You see," I said, "God gave us Free Will.

We do what we want and he just stands back and watches. Everything after that is just pure chance because there's nobody in charge."

He still wasn't getting it, and the administrative assistant with the low cut blouse and magnificent cleavage wasn't getting it either. "Life isn't a path," I said. "It's a maze, and we should all be happy to be lost."

Ah...I was sure I was getting through to them now. "That's what Free Will is all about, being happy to be lost."

They stood with their beautifully wrapped microwave dinners in their hands, saying nothing, just feeling the full force of my words.

I have that effect on people.

***

Hell has its eyes set on me
An' it's takin' me away
Hell has its eyes set on me
An' there ain't no runnin' away

Hell's lips are kissin' my ass
An' it's catchin' up to me
It's comin' right outta my past
Makin' this what I've done to me

- from a 21st Century Ballad

***

14

The young man with the orange spiked hair spoke with a slight lisp through lips pierced with a dozen silver rings. He said something about his rage and how he wanted to scream into every sewer in the city because there was no intelligent life above ground.

"You might awaken things you don't want to meet," I said. Sleeping in ditches gives you these insights. He said that he would gladly give his life just to be heard by a single human being. A young woman with bright green hair and rings dangling from her eyebrows and nose offered to die as well.

"It's when people listen to you," I said, "that your life is most in danger."

The young lady pointed a finger wrapped in black mesh that seemed to be some sort of glove traveling the length of her arm and disappearing into her black sun dress. She accused me of having said the exact opposite last week. "The problem here," I said, "is that you've obviously gotten today mixed up with last week."

While she thought about that, I changed the subject. "Have you ever thought about why we're here?" This got their attention. The young man forgot about his death wish and the young lady stopped thinking. "It's something I think about a lot when I look up at the light bouncing off the bottoms of iron oxide clouds."

The young man asked if I was talking about the ultimate purpose.

"There is no the ultimate purpose," I said. "There're lots of ultimate purposes, as many as you can count, and none of them more ultimate than the others. We waste so much of our lives looking for the ultimate purpose that the search itself mistakenly becomes our ultimate purpose."

The young man said something about that being OK with him, but the young lady wondered how there could be more than one ultimate purpose.

"Because they all turn out to be ultimately wrong," I said. The young lady picked her nose quickly and asked if I really believed that.

"Check back with me next week," I told her.

***

I was stung one day taking a piece of European chocolate away from a wasp with whom I was sharing a ditch. The pain was like a tiny pocket of steam trapped under my skin and looking for a way out. It was such an interesting feeling that I encouraged the wasp to sting me again. It didn't feel the same the second time so I squashed the wasp and ate the chocolate.

***

I went to an anti-abortion rally that had free home cooking. I shared a picnic table with a group of women who made a point of showing the hair in their armpits. Some had tattoos on their thighs and backs. They were talking about how much gas their SUVs ate. I, of course, knew the truth about this.

"God put oil in the earth for us to use," I said. "The more gas we use, the closer we bring ourselves to God's purpose."

A spandex-coated woman with muscular arms twice the size of mine asked me what the hell I was talking about. Before I had a chance to answer, she leaned toward me—all testosterone and sweat—and asked if I was really an anti-abortionist, or was I a baby-killer.

"Overpopulation is the baby-killer," I said. "But we need to populate the earth at an alarming rate so that we outnumber the insects before they finish eating our crops and then turn on us. This is why God lets women get pregnant."

I slept in a hospital that night. It wasn't quite as elegant as sleeping in a ditch.

***

I just wanna punch you in the face
Wanna smash and batter you all over the place
Ain't no such thing as a savin' grace
So hold on buddy while I punch your face

- from a 21st Century Ballad

***

I was eating burgers and fries in a fast food restaurant after waiting over an hour for a family of four to leave, praying the whole time they would leave their leftovers on the table.

They did…proof that God sometimes smiles through the odds.

The youngest, a girl with blonde bangs and a permanent pout, had eaten one fry and nothing else.

Her soft drink was pristine, her burger still resplendently wrapped. Her parents had threatened repeatedly to cut her chat time, but she kept muttering something about mad cows.

I have thoughts about mad cows. I think I'd be mad too if somebody slaughtered me, stuffed me with food coloring and preservatives, pounded me into patties, fried the crap out of me, shoved me into a bun soaked with thick sauce and half-hearted vegetables, and served me up to some pouty little bitch who didn't even have the grace to eat me because she was afraid to join the army of zombies that mad cows are creating to get revenge on the human race for feeding cows to cows.

But…that's another story. On this particular day I was sitting in a fast food restaurant chewing on a cow and thinking that, if the company kitchenette is the 21st Century's amphitheatre for staring down ideas, then the fast food restaurant, besides offering designer food for the masses, is the mirror into ourselves. It's what we've become. A tribute to our ability to reconstruct reality and believe whatever we want. In fact, I like to think of modern civilization as a fast food restaurant.

They're like schools where we can get to the kids before they've had a chance to be corrupted by non-productive spending habits. For instance, if a child spends five dollars on a bag of bean sprouts at a farmers' market, who gains? The farmer. And maybe his family. Maybe even the guy who rents the stalls at the market. But that's it. Now, that same five bucks spent in a fast food restaurant supports entire industries: the beef industry (along with the regulatory government agencies), the trucking industry, the advertising and public relations industry, the fast food furniture industry, the building industry, not to mention all those high school kids working in fast food joints who need to be exploited so that they can afford to buy iPods for their pirated music.

And you might say that the bean sprouts are better for the kid than the burger, fries and pop, but what the hell, who wants to live past their ability to go deeper into debt? Which is one of the dangers we face when we eat foods that haven't been carefully screened by marketing managers and prime time television.

***

My burger's got E. coli and it's gonna take me down
My girlfriend's got ebola and she's wearing a black frown
My doggie's got the canine flu and his piss is turnin' brown
There's a germ on my finger tip
Doin' a flip
He's really hip
A sensational hit
In a world where everyone's sick
And I got the I'm-afraid-to-eat-touch-drink-smell-or-fuck-anything-cause-it's-all-out-to-kill-me blues

- from a 21st Century Ballad

19

***

In 1918, the worst pandemic in history cancelled attacks between allied and German forces because flu was killing so many men in the trenches that there weren't enough to properly feed into the machine guns. Anywhere from twenty million to a hundred million people died from flu that year, more than all the deaths in all the wars, plagues and train crashes in history.

Some people say the human race is no better than flu...that we're a virus threatening to spoil the universe and if aliens ever find out about us, they'll cure us right out of existence.

I have a theory about this.

Viruses never turn on themselves. They may be suicidal, but they're not homicidal. They kill their host by accident and excess and take themselves down in the process, but they never turn on themselves.

We do.

We kill our own kind. We kill our host. We kill ourselves. We kill everything that's killable. We kill our children and our mates. We kill for pleasure and recreation. We kill because it feels right and we kill when it feels wrong. We kill for our gods. We kill for nations and governments and ideals. We kill because voices in our heads tell us to kill. We kill for profit and prophets. We kill to even the score and then we kill because there's nothing else to do. We kill because it's in our nature and we're damn good at it.

Trust me. No aliens are going to mess with us. They'll wait till we're finished killing and then they'll explore our garbage.

***

I feel so useless I could die
I'm drinking rubby 'stead of rye
I got no place to go
An' I got no one no more
But that's OK with me
Cause buddy can't you see
I just wanna punch you in the face

- from a 21st Century Ballad

***

Tonight I'm sleeping in a ditch that's almost a piece of Christmas. Yes, I believe in Christ. All of them. Especially tonight. When I entered this ditch, I found a red plastic bag just lying in here and it had a six-pack of beer and two cigars in glass tubes inside. One of the beers was smashed but, like I said, I believe in all of the Christs and I'm thankful for the other five beers.

The moon is full tonight, bright and clear and precise around the edges. I don't see a cloud anywhere and the grass in this ditch is long and packs down comfortably and dry because there's been no rain for a few days. I have a cardboard box for a pillow.

There's a new housing development growing from the woods a few blocks away and the air is scented with the rich aroma of machine oil and tree blood. There's a pinch of carbon monoxide in the air to remind me of the interconnectedness of all things human, if only in our fate.

Fireflies ignite the air with streaks of light. I grab one and use its ass to light my cigar. Then I eat the fly. The smoke from my cigar reminds me of my beginnings, whatever they were. I down a beer in one long non-stop guzzle that almost drowns me in the rapture of the moment and I belch mindlessly under a perfect chemical night sky.

These Eyes

I've given myself a week to live. I think that's a reasonable timeframe. One week.

It's going to be tough. I just received another call. From her. Like nothing's happened. Like everything's normal. It shook me the first time she called. It shook me a few minutes ago. Tomorrow at 7:29 PM, it'll shake me again.

She talks about ordinary things: "Did you find that clicking sound in your car?"

I try to keep my answers short. I get a feeling that she only has so long. About ten minutes, including the silences, those wordless seconds when we're likely more connected than when we're talking, when all we can do is feel each other's presence. "Do you still think about me?"

"Yeah. I do."

"Did you get the new air conditioner installed?"

Deliberately drawing out the silences, savoring the closeness that comes from knowing the other is waiting, as though we become real knowing someone is waiting for us.

I'd like to say I waited my whole life for her, but I didn't. She was sprung on me out of the blue, something I would never have seen coming because I really didn't need—or want—it at the time. But suddenly she was there and going back to the way things used to be was...well, I've given myself a week.

I was on my way to the Cedar Tree Café for a hazelnut coffee, something I'd been thinking about all morning, mentally savoring the sweet nut taste and the hot cream-thick liquid. My agent had just called with great news; my latest book had just been picked up by a publisher of photography books with some of the biggest names in the field on their list. Mine was a book with a hundred and twenty images of shopping carts that had been abandoned around the city, pictures of shopping carts left on curbs, stashed under verandas or pushed over the banks of ravines. I had a picture of a cart that someone had lugged up to the top of a billboard advertising the city transport system.

It was a three-year project with thousands of images pared down to the essential. I used the carts as a metaphor for the sense of abandonment that runs through industrial/digital society, but I won't get into that now. Maybe later.

It was a big step forward. I was excited. I was on top of the world. I was in a hurry. I didn't see her as I rounded the corner. She was right in front of me, standing there with a vacant look in her eyes, something I noticed at just about the same time I walked into her hard enough to knock her off her feet, hard enough so that her ass hit the ground about the same time her head hit the door—the metal rim of the door. I should have turned around and headed back to the studio right then.

But I didn't.

I was stunned motionless. She lay on the sidewalk, slumped against the door, her plaid skirt pushed up revealing slim legs with black leggings. There was a couple on the other side of the door looking through the glass at her. They couldn't open the door with her lying against it and I could see the struggle in their eyes: wait until she's not against the door before opening it, or risk hurting her more by opening the door so they could ask, "Are you hurt?"

And, yeah, I just stood there like a frozen turkey until she lifted her hand up to me. It took a few seconds to sink in: *She wants me to help her get up.* Her eyes were a deep brown that created an earthy aura around her eye lids. She didn't seem angry or hurt, not even flustered. She seemed amused, calm. I thrust my hand out clumsily, missing her hand by a good few inches. She grabbed my wrist and pulled herself up, almost pulling me down in the process. Not that she was heavy, it just took me by surprise. I was suddenly face-to-face with her. She was beautiful, with brassy brunette bangs bouncing off her shoulders and cutting sharply across her forehead. She reminded me of pictures I'd seen of hippy women during the 60s: no lipstick or makeup or other fakery—just natural beauty. A black turtleneck suggested college girl from some other period. I didn't see a purse. She was smiling.

The couple at the door were outside now. The woman asked, "Are you alright?"

She ignored the question, still smiling, looking straight up into my eyes. I think I was blushing as I stammered out a barely coherent apology, gesturing with my hands, lusting for a hazelnut coffee, in a hurry, rounding the corner...but, oh my god, she was beautiful.

"You're Steven Glen, aren't you?"

She knew my name.

This wasn't as much a surprise as it might seem. My work had been exhibited around town for several years and I'd been interviewed by newspapers, television and regional magazines. I wasn't a celebrity, but I wasn't invisible.

I nodded yes.

"I saw your exhibit at Ingrid Mueller's Art + Concepts two months ago."

I nodded yes.

"You're very talented."

I nodded yes.

"You don't talk much do you?"

I nodded..."I'm so sorry. I didn't see you until..."

"It's OK. I'm all right. Back of my head's a bit sore, is all." She rubbed her backside. "Sore butt too."

My god, she was beautiful. I was feeling a bit woozy from just looking at her. "I was in a hurry, not thinking. Just got some good news."

Her smile widened. "And your good news was?" She seemed cheery and relaxed, but for some reason, I couldn't shake that image of her eyes just before I knocked her down, the vacancy. There was something almost chilling about it.

But she was so beautiful.

I bought her a coffee—hazelnut, of course. She loved it. I told her about the book, how it as a big step for me. In fact, that's all we talked about: me—my books, the shopping carts, my exhibitions, my artistic vision. Whenever I asked her about her own life, she turned the talk back to me, and I let her. Ego: that slippery plain of victories leading to ultimate defeat. I should have pressed her but I was on a ME high with a beautiful woman, and less than two hours later we were at my place, in bed, naked.

Yeah, that fast. I should have known something was out of whack. But I was on top of the world. I was invincible. Nothing could bring me down.

Her name was Heather. Heather Smith. Although I'm still not sure if that was her real last name. I'm not even sure if that was her real first name.

While we were drinking the coffee, I asked her, "How would you sum up your life?"

She said, "I'm the seed pod that fell into the river and was carried out to the ocean. How about you?"

And, of course, I blabbed on about myself, never bothering to ask what she meant by the seed pod, and that was the closest she ever came to saying anything really personal about herself other than to talk about her current mood, how things went at work, where she'd like to dine out.

Her moods were always the same: tranquil in a disquieted way, as though something was rumbling under the surface. She was a graphic artist for a company that produced educational software. My sum total knowledge of her work: the graphics have to be meaningful. But I did know if the day went well, fast, slow, or challenging. In the time that we were together, we never dined at the same place twice and in all that time she never failed to take my breath away.

She moved in the day after we met. The last thing in the world I wanted was a roommate; I didn't even want a relationship, didn't want the complications. I was so close to having everything I'd always wanted. I needed to focus on the book, on the exhibition for the book launch. Plus, there was the commercial photography—the weddings and portraits—to pay the bills. My life was too busy for a relationship. I thought about this while I was waiting for her to show up with her things and I made up my mind that I was going to tell her that we should wait a bit. This was too sudden. It wasn't like me. I'm sorry but...

I answered a quiet knock on the door. She stood in the hall wearing blue jeans and a dark gray sweater, a suitcase in each hand. She took my breath away.

"Just two suitcases?" I said.

"I like to keep things simple."

I kissed her and she walked through the door into the rest of my life.

Two suitcases.

***

Living with a woman was something new in my life. I'd had women stay the weekend but this was different. It was an adventure. Physically, she didn't put much of a dent in my apartment. We shared my dresser, and the closet was less stark. Cosmetics, brushes and hair products appeared in the washroom along with a cherry red bathrobe and matching towel. We moved the couch to the middle

28

of the room, closer to the TV, which I started watching more in the evenings. Things materialized in the refrigerator: yogurt, tofu, plastic containers of bean sprouts. All-in-all though, she made as much an imprint as a hotel guest.

But she brought a certain color and texture to life in the apartment, as though I'd turned the settings of my life to black and white and she re-set them to color.

My apartment was no longer just a place to eat, sleep, shower and catch the news; it was a place to live and create memories with color and texture. I looked forward to going home and finding her waiting for me. Seeing her on the couch or strolling out of the kitchenette or just hearing her calling out from the washroom: "Be out in a minute." I never tired of her beauty. In fact, I never really got used to it—like it was something I could never define or understand. Like her.

Just like her.

***

We ate together, usually in the dining area, with music in the background and candles in the foreground. Sometimes we ate in the living room and watched TV. Conversation was sporadic. We didn't talk much and when we did it wasn't for long. I talked about my book, my exhibitions, plans for my next photo project, problems with my commercial work. She talked about things in the news or asked questions about my work, my artistic vision, my hopes and fears.

Weekends we got out of the apartment, starting with the Farmers' Market early Saturday morning. She loved the Market: the stalls with fresh produce, the crafts (which she adored but never bought, not even letting me buy them for her), the exotic foods (her favorite was mild chicken samosas), the buskers juggling bowling pins or staging puppet shows. She never once became impatient because a line was stalled by people stopping to talk or someone just stopping to take in the movement and noise. She blended well into crowds.

After the market we took to the sidewalks for some window shopping or drove into the country where I'd take pictures of barns and ponds as backdrops to her beauty. Sometimes we'd go to a mall where she'd admire everything and buy nothing. She loved the shopping experience but wasn't into accumulating things, except for the odd piece of clothing.

No matter what we did, though, her conversation focused on what was happening around us: "Oh look! A puppet show!" "Can you get the water lilies in just behind me? What kind of lens do you need for that?" "How do you think I'd look in that red dress?" She lived in the immediate.

We didn't go to church on Sundays. Sunday was our stay-at-home-in-bed-and-make-love-all-day-long day. Conversation was mostly me telling her over and over how beautiful she was, how perfect she was, how much I needed her.

***

30

After a couple of months, I stopped doing portraits. I needed time to work on proofs for the book and re-write captions and the artist statement—a sprawling twenty-page monument to ambiguity, which I eventually pared down to a few pages. I needed time to start my next project: abandoned toys. These were pictures of toys, like play kitchens, play houses and pedal cars left on curbs for trash day, or left at the back door of the Salvation Army store. I had a rough concept about what I was doing, something along the lines of shedding the tools of our youth, learning to let go as part of the growth process. Something like that. I was having a hard time focusing and I can't say that it was her fault. It was my fault. I couldn't stop thinking about her, day and night, even when I was with her. Yeah, even when I was with her. I think most people think about other things when they're with the ones they love because they're right there with you, where you just feel them and think about other things.

In my case though, she'd be right there, lying beside me or sitting across the table from me, and I'd be wondering about her, wondering about her day, wondering about her past, about who she was and what she was doing when she wasn't with me.

Wondering about why she was with me.

***

"So what meaningful graphics did you do today?"

"Mostly boring ones."

"Boring? How so?"

"Just boring. Visual representations of boring material."

"What kind of material?"

"Really boring material."

"You're not going to tell me anything about your job, are you?"

"Did you find out about that clicking noise in your car?"

***

We'd been together almost six months when I first noticed it. By that time I'd cut my commercial work down to almost nothing, taking occasional jobs to pay rent on the apartment and studio. She took care of all the other expenses, and the publishers had given me a generous advance—something unheard of for a still not-so-well-known photographer.

I spent my days roaming the city looking for cast-away toys—snooping around alleys, frequenting dumpsters, scouring the early morning streets on trash pick-up days. I'd finished the work on the shopping cart book. My next exhibition was a few months away, in conjunction with the book release.

I was at the studio, going through pictures I'd taken of her over the weekend. On Sunday we'd gone to the college campus, to the geology building, where they'd painted the walls in one of the stairwell alcoves with a lifelike forest motif. The alcove stretched up three stories with towering rainforest trees. The predominant color was deep green. She was wearing blue jeans and a loose red blouse, the first time I'd seen her wearing a bright color other than her bathrobe. It was raining lightly that day and she had a red umbrella. There was a long bench built into the wall at the base of the forest mural. She lay down on the bench with the umbrella open beside her. The contrast of colors was breathtaking. I took almost a hundred pictures.

I'd just deleted the ones that were definitely a no go, leaving me with ten images to process. In three of them, taken in succession, she was looking straight into the lens, smiling seductively. The bright irises spread a light brownish tint over her eyelids and the hollows of her eyes. Even looking at pictures of her caught my breath. I zoomed in on her eyes. The screen turned monochrome brown. My chest began to tighten with excitement as I leaned forward to let myself be lost in those eyes. And that's when I saw it.

I wasn't sure what I was looking at, only that it triggered a cold flash across my back and froze me like in those moments when you wake up feeling threatened by something you can't define but and you know that if you move, it'll pounce. It was the vacancy I'd seen in her eyes the first time we met, but it was more—like a pit descending into bottomless nothing, a complete absence of…I didn't know what. I jerked back, fearing I'd be sucked into something from which I'd never return.

I sat at my desk, sweating, cold, shaken, fingers trembling. My thoughts tripped over explanations that might make sense of what I'd seen.

33

After a few moments I calmed enough to lean forward into her eyes and confirm what I'd just seen but it was gone, if it had ever been there. It could have been stress, change of lifestyle, anything.

I spent the next couple of hours working on the remaining pictures. Nothing out of the ordinary happened. In each of the pictures she was beautiful and her eyes took my breath away without swallowing me whole.

I didn't mention any of this to her.

***

"As a photographer, there's something I find really odd about you."

"What's that?"

"You don't have any pictures."

"Pictures?"

"Yeah, pictures…family, travel, childhood, school. How come you have no pictures?"

"Well, hun, as a photographer, you weren't around then to take them."

***

I started losing it. Whatever I'd seen in her eyes wouldn't let go. I went through hundreds of pictures, burrowing into her eyes as she sat on the edge of the fountain by City Hall, zooming into her eyes as she smiled under a black moustache at the dollar store, digging deep into her eyes as she waved to me high in the air from a swing at the playground across the street— searching her eyes in picture after picture.

But it was gone. I tried to chalk it off to imagination. Stress. A disagreeable lunch. I tried to doubt what I'd seen, distrust my eyes, but that look in her eyes when we met hovered over me. I remembered the chill I'd felt.

***

I started an obsessive campaign of picture-taking, catching her while she ate, watched TV, slept, showered, dressed and undressed.

"Steven?"

"Yes?"

"I'm undressing."

"I know. And I'm taking pictures."

"Steven?"

"Yes?"

"Why are you taking pictures of my eyes while I'm undressing?"

***

I put over a thousand images through every Photoshop routine I could think of, including a barrage of special effects like fish eye, sepia, duo tone, HDR, everything I could think of. I varied the resolutions, hues, temperatures, white balances, color saturations, brightness, sharpness, densities.

Did I mention I was obsessed?

***

I decided it was time to talk to her about it. We were eating authentic Mexican food in an authentic Mexican restaurant with authentic Mariachi music in the background.

"I know I've been acting weird lately." I was on my fourth Corona

"Oh, you noticed?" Sometimes she could be a bit of a shithead.

"Yes, I did."

"Steven." She leaned forward, looking me straight in the eyes. "There's something wrong."

"Yes?"

She reached over the table and took both my hands. "When you're not taking pictures of my eyes, or working on my eyes on your computer..."

"Yes?"

"You stare."

"I stare?"

"Into my eyes, constantly. Like you're looking for something."

"You have beautiful eyes. I..."

"Steven. This is a nice restaurant. Don't make me pour a bottle of beer over your head." She squeezed my hands tightly as she talked. "I want it to stop...the whole eye thing. It stops."

I nodded yes.

"Give me your word."

"I promise. I'll stop. No more eye fixation."

***

For a while, I managed to reign in the eye fetish and pay more attention to her as in: "Nice to see a man who appreciates his woman undressing for the camera." I immersed myself in my abandoned toy project and scoured the streets looking for toys left on the curbs for trash day or tossed beside dumpsters. Gray drizzly days were my favorite, with the rain adding a bit of the old sparkle to the colors of the toys, now contrasted so vividly with their drab surroundings and suggesting the magic they once cast on the children who owned them.

I was picking up more commercial work. My book release was a month away, and I was almost ready for the exhibition and launch.

She seemed to be more excited about the exhibit than me, talking about it incessantly, asking me if I was excited, telling me how beautiful the prints were. Her favorite was of a cart sitting in snow up to its lower tray. Behind it, a field stretched into a narrow line of trees. Behind that, a black storm-filled sky stretched across the horizon moving with a precision edge into a sunny cloudless sky. The play of light between the storm and the clear sky was surreal and foreboding. The cart was about thirty feet into the snow and, strangely, there were no footsteps leading out to it, as though it had just appeared there.

Things were looking good.

For the time being.

**

"I know hardly anything about you."

37

"What's my favorite pizza?"

"Sausage."

"What's my favorite color?"

"Brown. Chocolate brown."

"What's my favorite food?"

"When you want a break from health food…steak, medium rare, baked potato with sour cream, and broccoli with cheese sauce."

"What's my favorite song?"

"But, what's this…?"

"Indulge me. What's my favorite song?"

"These Eyes."

"Most men wouldn't be able to answer those questions."

"So?"

"So, you know me better than most men know their women."

***

There're two schools of thought about balance. One claims that the purpose of our lives is to attain a state in which everything is completely in balance and then keep things that way until we die. This is a kind of spiritual approach. The other claims that it's just fine to work towards a state of balance, but then we need to find ways to throw everything into chaos again so that we can start over trying to achieve balance. This would be an evolutionary approach with the rationale being: if things are always in balance, nothing happens—nothing goes forward, nothing goes backward. We have stasis. No progress. No evolution.

I guess I'm one of those people who need to evolve.

Things were too good between us. It was driving me nuts. Who was I to have this perfect relationship with this breathtakingly beautiful woman who never complained, who wanted the same things I wanted, who treated me like everything I did and thought was essential, who never told me how to live my life and who arrived on my doorstep devoid of historical baggage?

These were the kinds of crazy thoughts I was beginning to have. On the one hand, I was afraid to push things; on the other, I couldn't resist the urge to push.

I started investigating. Google, LinkedIn, MySpace (after all, she was a graphic artist), Facebook, Twitter, online directories and dozens of other cyber ways to stalk a person were all dead ends. I couldn't find a single pixel of her on the Internet.

Of course, it didn't take long before she noticed that I was acting crazy again.

**

"My brother and I used to love toasted peanut butter sandwiches dipped in tea with lots of milk and sugar for breakfast."

"Peanut butter is good for growing bodies."

"Mom used to pack salmon sandwiches for lunch. Every day. And a banana. And Kool-Aid."

"The salmon would explain why you have such a strong heart."

39

"What was your favorite breakfast when you were a kid? Let me guess…bran flakes."

"Why would you say bran flakes?"

"Um…I don't know. Just a wild guess."

"Did you get around to taking the car in about that clicking noise?"

***

"You look tense tonight, Steven."

"Got something on my mind."

"Sounds serious."

"It is."

"How serious?"

"Really serious."

"You just put half an inch of salt on your baked potato."

"I like salt."

"With a bit of potato on the side?"

"Who are you?"

"Who do you think I am?"

"I don't know."

"Is this why you were taking all the pictures, tracking me all over the internet?"

"Tracking you? What…"

"Browsers have this thing called histories. You were searching for information on me day after day. You even searched for things like demonic eyes. I'm guessing in relation to me."

"You knew all this? Why didn't you say anything?|

"I was hoping you would either find whatever it was you were looking for, or come to your senses."

"I need to know about your past."

"You need to get over this obsession."

"But why can't you just tell me…"

"OK. I was raised on a farm. I came to the city. I met you. Happy?"

"Is that true?"

"No."

"Then...?"

"Do you love me?"

"Yes. Of course I…"

"Then just love me."

***

But I couldn't just love her. I pushed it like picking a scab trying to heal over a major artery.

We were home, drinking wine, watching a Seinfeld re-run, eating homemade guacamole. I felt like I was sitting beside myself, watching myself reach for the remote and turning the TV off, watching as I turned to her.

"Tell me about your past."

"You don't want to know about it."

"I have to know about it."

"I don't want to talk about it."

"Where did you come from?"

"I told you…a farm."

"You told me that wasn't true."

"Maybe I lied about it not being true."

"What was it I saw in your eyes?"

"Probably your imagination."

"What are you hiding from me?"

41

"Nothing that should mean anything to you—to keeping us together."

"But I have to know."

"Maybe I don't want to know."

"But you do know."

"I just want things to stay the way they are."

"Things will stay the way they are, but I'll know. I have to know what you know."

"What I know—and all I have to know—is that I love you and I want things to stay as they are." She stood up and walked slowly to the window. She stared towards the park but her eyes seemed focused on something far away, lifetimes away. It was a sad stare that flushed me with guilt. I should have backed off then. I should have put my love before my curiosity and gone to her and held her and told her everything would be all right. Just like in the movies. But I didn't. She stood by the window for a few minutes before turning to me. Tears glistened on her cheeks. "The truth is, Steven, I don't know. I remember my job and the people I work with, but that's all. I went home after I met you and packed some things. As soon as I arrived at your door, I forgot where I'd come from. At work, I sort of floated through each day listening to people talking about things I should have known about but didn't. I played along with them. It happens less often now. But, Steven, I can't even remember the things they used to talk about. All I remember is you. And what we have. And I don't want to lose it."

"But you have to remember."

***

42

Finally, she remembered.

I came home late one night. She was sitting on the couch. I said something about being sorry for missing supper but she ignored me. The hair running over her shoulders was like a chocolate waterfall. Even the back of her head thrilled me. I walked quickly to the kitchen to see what I'd missed eating by candlelight.

There was nothing. Not even the smell of cooking. Evening sun cast a surreal aura over the kitchen. There was a note on the breakfast table. I picked it up and read.

Steven dearest,

I remembered. Thanks, Steven. We should have left it alone like I wanted. Just left it alone.

As for what it is: no, you don't get to know that. At least not yet. I'll be in touch. Oh, and sorry for the blood stains on your couch.

Love always,
Heather

The calls started a week later.

***

When I think of it now, I got home at around close to eight that night. The blood on the couch was still slightly warm. Maybe it was 7:29 when she pushed the butcher knife into her stomach, maybe that exact moment when her soul fled her body.

43

Maybe that's why she calls every night at that time. I'll ask her about that next week. It's the kind of thing I should ask face-to-face.

One week.

I think that's a reasonable amount of time to talk myself out of this. Though I can't see that happening, and it's going to be tough waiting through those seven days. But like I said, I have a solid objective within a reasonable time frame. She's waiting for me. She knows.

And I need to know.

Still Life with Sax and Muse

It was a quiet afternoon at Molly's Cafe. Outside, gray rain sliced through the air like tiny hatchets. Behind us, a lone sax player ground out something bluesy with all the gravel and grit of a break-hardened heart. Across from me, Jo's eyes, as usual, were green, a green that could feed forests.

She wore a black turtleneck with matching black tights divided by a red swatch of tartan skirt. I tried to keep my eyes on her eyes, but the green threatened to swallow my soul and toss me around in the tides of her green forever. I focused my eyes on a couple of dust motes arguing about semantics and existentialism somewhere in that distance between her green eyes and her long legs, those legs that flowed up into an unimaginable playground, into … I refocused my eyes on the dust motes.

"Do you like my sweater?" she said.

"Huh?" I said.

"Do you like my sweater? You haven't taken your eyes off it. Are you thinking dirty thoughts again, you pathetic literary pig?"

Damn dust motes, arguing right in front of her breasts.

"Oh, uh … yeah. Nice sweater." The plan was to be cool. "I've always liked large sweaters," I said.

The plan wasn't working.

The two dust motes were cooler than I was.

She smiled. "You're blushing, pig."

"Something caught in my eye."

"And it's cutting off your air supply, goat?"

"Yeah, that's it," I said. "Air supply."

"How's life … boar?" she said.

"I haven't slept in three days," I said. "I drink too much. I can't write anything anymore. I dream about grabbing spoons and stabbing people. I found God rummaging through the bottles and boxes in my medicine cabinet. He looked hungry and confused. There's a dead rat in my refrigerator. It sees everything. Its whiskers quiver. It asked me where I go." I slumped my head. "I don't know where I go." I looked up past Jo's black sandals and black forever legs and dazzling tartan and past those damned pretentious motes and into the deep green seas of her eyes. "Other than that, I'm fine. And you?"

"I made love to John Lennon last night."

I nodded. "Big night."

The sax player winked at the empty tables around us and dove into a toe-snapping rendition of So What.

Jo put a cigar to her lips and lit it with a snap of her fingers. She puffed deeply and exhaled Hurricane Castro into my face. I breathed in the smoke and felt every hair on my body go bongo in the Congo. Her lips parted slowly and she said: "Then we talked about the third brick from the left."

"Which is?"

"Just another brick until you mention it."

"There's a dead rat in my refrigerator."

"Does my sweater display my breasts to advantage? I don't want one looking more intelligent than the other."

I curled around this thought. "I find them very similar."

"You what, trite verbalist?"

" ...," I said.

"Tongue-tied spelling bee reject," she said.

I had a thought.

I expressed it: "John Lennon?"

"Yes. He stabbed me in the side of my dawn, comma lizard."

"Did I mention ... there's a dead rat in my refrigerator?"

"I'm going to become a veterinarian and devote my life to things with four legs or more. Does your rat need help?"

"Yes, I think it does."

"What exactly does it need?"

"A second chance."

"Do you find my breasts fascinating?"

"Huh?"

"You're staring at my breasts, shallow imagist."

"What ... what is the sound of wax melting?"

"How are the people in your life?"

Uh ha.

Trick question.

But I can handle it. "Alive," I said.

"Alive?" she said.

"Except for the dead ones."

"Dead?" She puffed on her cigar and blew half of Cuba into my lungs. [Thank you.]

"Not alive," I said.

She thought about this.

I thought about this.

She nodded.

I nodded.

I tore the tablecloth off the table and ate it.

It tasted like …

… plastic.

I said: "The dead rat in my refrigerator asks questions I can't answer."

"We all have our dead rats," she said.

"How's work?" I said.

She puffed on her cigar and blew Jamaica and The Cayman Islands into my face. I surfed in green water. "Imagine a bored labia …" she said. "… waiting for a bus in the middle of a prairie. With no bar in sight."

"So … things are getting better at work."

"New management."

"What are your dead rats?"

"Mundane symbolists," she said. "Like you."

"Do you keep them in your refrigerator?"

"Yoko was pissed at me," she said.

"Yoko is pissed at everything," I said. "In a sublime sort of way."

"It doesn't matter. I didn't care."

"Of course," I said.

"Would you like me to take my sweater off, banal sentence arranger?"

I blinked.

She winked. "Perhaps I could take my sweater off and we could discuss my bra."

I gulped. Was she serious?

I said: "God looked so desperate in my medicine cabinet, as though he expected something

48

that never happened. It made me sad, so I went to my refrigerator."

"Big mistake," she said.

"How's that?"

"Never do anything right after seeing God," she said. "Especially when he looks that bad."

Outside, the rain spread acid waste over the cars and pigeons. I had tears in waiting for every piston and wing.

No.

Not really.

I have no tears.

Not even for myself.

She said: "Are you feeling sorry for yourself, maudlin moralist? Thinking about crying for the cars and the birds?"

Damn, she's good.

"Is God in your medicine cabinet?" I said.

"No, he's between my legs."

"He looked like he had something to say," I said. "But he was too busy rummaging ... just rummaging around ... to do anything other than look confused."

"Do you want to know what God is doing between my legs?" she said.

"The rain is our only contact with the fate of our sky."

"The rain is dead," she said. "The sky is dead. The rain is our only contact with the death of air. Why are you staring at my toes, lecherous linguist? Do you want to suck them?"

"Huh?" I said.

"Suck my toes?" she said.

My face sloshed with blood.

She said: "Hah!"

She said: "Hah! Hah!"

She said: "Hah, frightened little adverbial toilet!"

I blushed deeper.

She said: "Have you read any good books?"

I said: "There's a good book?"

"It resides on a shelf …" she said " … reserved for one good book. Do you think about me when you masturbate?"

I gulped. "And where is that shelf?"

"Wherever you keep it."

"There's a dead rat in my refrigerator."

The sax player took off his shirt without missing a note and winked at a table full of nobody. He had talent.

She said: "Do you think the sax player has talent?"

I said: "He lacks audience."

"This room lacks ambience," she said.

I looked around. Empty tables. Afternoon light drifting through the skylight. Harsh light for a bluesy sax. Small stage. Just big enough for an audience-depraved sax. Depraved. Like in the song poem. The bongo song poem. The bongalongo songo poem. Dipdooling bonga …

"Grammar slut," she said.

"I wrote a poem once," I said. "It had words arranged boldly on white space, announcing their presence, if not their meaning."

"Did it rhyme?"

"Nothing rhymes."

"Yeah, right."

"Nothing rhymes."

"Yeah, right."

"Nothing rhymes."

"Fucking transformational syntactical bongalongo songo dipalongo boo bipi diddly bump ....

... bump."

"Exactly," I said. "Boppa loppa bang." I said.

"Boppa loppa bang," she said.

"Boo bop," I said.

"Bop," she said.

We were standing, standing in the groove of the smooth green ever green of her eyes dancing in the space of the boppa boomalongo of the ...

"There's a fucking rat in my refrigerator. It's dead."

"Refrigerators are not good for rats," she said.

We shimmied and shook as her green eyes swallowed me in the greenness of my own lies and blindness. My teeth vibrated. I ate the table.

"Hungry?" she said.

The sax player swallowed the air around him and sprayed broken hearts and bus stops into the blue void of empty tables while Jo and I danced everything green and good in a universe of bop dilop.

"Boop," she said.

"Biddly boppa," said I.

"Bop diddly boop diddly diddly boop," said the sax.

"Boop boppa boop," she said.

"Boop," I said.

"Poppa poppa boop." said the sax.

"There's a dead rat in my refrigerator."

Jo sat down, legs and all. Sat down and said: "My ears have teeth. I've trained them to kill your tongue."

"Nothing rhymes," I said.

"Lingo egoist. Feeling sorry for yourself?"

"Do you have a dream?" I said.

"I'm dreaming now," she said.

"Do you have another dream?"

"Only when I'm awake," she said.

"I have a dream," I said.

"Forget it, verb dweeb, my playground is beyond your leer."

"Any plans for the weekend?" I said.

"I'm going to read a story about a man whose life means absolutely nothing. Nothing ever happens to him. Nobody knows him. Even death forgets him."

"Does he live forever?"

"No. He dies," she said. "Life forgets him."

"Shouldn't he go somewhere in between?"

"Get your mind out of there, filthy word bucket."

"I was thinking about buying a new suit of armor," I said. "You know, something to keep out the cold shafts of my insecurities. They glare at me through the peep holes of curtains and the stale looks of passersby."

"I think we're getting somewhere, cliché clincher."

"I think I'm the man in the story you're going to read."

She nodded. "No one can handle life," she said. "It kills us all."

"There's a dead rat in my refrigerator."

"Shall we sit?"

The sax player went silent. He waited.

Jo waited.

I thought.

I had an idea.

I said: "Yes. Let's sit."

We sat facing each other. The sax droned something slow and Blue in Green. The table was gone. It was in my stomach. Drums swished in the distance. Odd. Suddenly, the distance between us was less than a trillion miles. There was no border of table. There was no fence of table. There was no prison of table. We were free. Unrestrained.

She said: "Before you can chew, you must bite."

The dust motes stabbed each other with logical palette knives screaming ontological bullshit. They were killing each other with concrete abstractions. I had an idea.

"Premature focus kills art," I said.

"Premature ejaculation kills a good time," she said.

"There's a ..."

"Yes, I know," she said. "In your refrigerator. A rat. Dead. What are the fifty-seven ways you would suck the index finger of my left hand?"

"I thought there were fifty-eight."

"After one," she said, " ... there's no difference between fifty-seven and fifty-eight. They don't exist."

"I can't write anything anymore."

"You never could write."

"But I used words."

"No," she said. "Words used you."

The sax player shot three bars of Flamenco straight into the hearts of the dust motes. They died painfully. But they never stopped arguing. Their mote corpses still blocked the view. I cried.

"Stop your damned wailing, spineless symbol spinner … it's only mote morte."

I laughed.

She said: "Stop your damned hysterics, clause clown … they're still arguing."

I stood up and ate my chair.

"Now you have no excuse," she said.

"Now I have no excuse," I said.

I walked through the empty air of an eaten table and stood directly in front of her. I bent down on one knee, staring into the emeralds surrounding her irises. The sax player's head blew off his shoulders and stuck to the ceiling. He winked as the room exploded with unresolved meaning. The sax didn't miss a beat.

"You must bite …" she said.

I reached my hand toward Jo. Her eyes ate my soul. My fingers were inches from her knee. My brain spun inside my skull like a dryer full of starched dreams.

"Before you can chew," she said.

I touched her knee and she disappeared.

Surfing in Catal Hyuk

It would be impossible for anyone to lead a more ordinary life than Bobby Parker, whose life was ordinary to the extent that the more you saw him and the more you knew about him, the less you would remember him and the less you would think about him.

He was pizza without toppings. Bran flakes without milk.

He lived for seventy-two years, the average allowable age for a married white male in his particular milieu. Two hours after his funeral, Libby, his wife of thirty years, was deep in a game of bridge. When her best friend, Laura Jenkins, who'd arrived at Bridge Night late because she had just returned from her grandfather's funeral in another town, said: "I'm so sorry, Libby, dear," Libby, who'd done badly in the first round of play replied without taking her eyes off her cards: "That's OK, Laura. I think I'll do better this round." And she smiled so sweetly, like a little darling.

Within days of his death, even his children, Roxanne and Leo, had difficulty remembering his face but then they wouldn't have remembered it when he was alive, five minutes after talking to him.

Here's what Bobby Parker looked like: his face was sort of round in a kind of square way that wasn't so much long as it was short and nobody seems to recall the color of his eyes. He wasn't tall but he wasn't squat. His weight was right on the money. He dressed in clothing appropriate to the occasion and he never mixed pink and gray. He may have been losing hair but one thing is certain: his hair was dark brown.

Or was it light brown?

But one thing is certainly certain: Bobby Parker worked for thirty-five years in an accounting firm. He wasn't exactly an accountant, more like just a clerk, doing clerking things that involved forms and files and filling in blanks. At the beginning of his career he had a rubber stamp that he could apply to those forms. He loved that rubber stamp. At some point before he retired, he stopped using the stamp. Nobody at the firm remembers that stamp. Nobody at the firm can recall a form needing the application of a rubber stamp. Nobody at the firm remembers, recalls, recollects, reflects upon, or reminisces over Bobby Parker. This was true one minute after he left the firm on his retirement day. This was true for the entire thirty-five years that he worked for the firm.

The fact that he received a pension check at the end of each month is probably proof for the existence of God, or at least a remarkably successful test bed for payroll software. In fact, everything that happened to Bobby Parker from the moment of his birth was anticlimactic in the way that turning off a tap stops the flow of water, but might allow a continuous drip.

***

When Bobby Parker was five years old he lived in a small rural community close enough to the city to smell the smog on humid days but too far from the country to see the occasional cow munching grass behind a wire fence. On one particular day a certain number of days after his fifth birthday, Bobby Parker was walking along a sidewalk thinking about nothing in particular.

Oh, this and that, his thought train went.

Ahead of him lay the community's busiest intersection. One of its traffic signals was malfunctioning. When it turned red, it turned red in every direction. When it turned green, it turned green in every direction. Fortunately, the community's busiest intersection saw only a handful of cars on Sunday afternoon and this was Sunday afternoon. Unfortunately, a car was approaching the intersection and the driver was thinking more about being stopped than he was about driving in a manner that would ensure that he wouldn't be stopped. The driver's name was Ted Jenkins, the father of Laura Jenkins, who would one day be Bobby Parker's wife's best friend. Ted Jenkins was worried about being stopped by the police because he'd just finished a day of fishing and drinking, and his quota of downed beers far exceeded his quota of caught fish. In fact, after he'd run out of bait without catching a single fish, he'd just watched the fish jumping in the middle of the lake as he drank the entire twelve bottles of beer in his cooler.

He was traveling a tad over and then a tad under the speed limit. His car wound just over the centerline, and seconds later, a tad over the right shoulder. For about three seconds out of every minute Ted Jenkins kept his car traveling perfectly in the center of his lane, so perfectly in fact, that he could very well have won safe driving awards for each of those three seconds. But then he would have flunked the urine test.

Ted Jenkins was about a mile away from the intersection. Bobby Parker was less than a block away. The light facing Bobby Parker was red at the moment, which meant that it was also red for Ted Jenkins. Bobby Parker was whistling something. It might have been a show tune; it might have been a hymn; it might have been a few bars from song he'd heard on the radio. It didn't matter what Bobby Parker was whistling because now he was less than half a block from the intersection and the light was red again which meant it was red for Ted Jenkins who was so involved with trying to win safe driving awards three seconds out of every minute that he didn't even see the light, even though it was now easily within view.

For no reason other than to change the rhythm of his movement Bobby Parker began to skip. He wasn't very good at skipping but neither was he the world's worst skipper. He had about as much chance of winning a skipping award as Ted Jenkins had of winning a safe driving award every three seconds but Bobby Parker's skip was satisfying to himself and he rarely ever tripped and fell. Today for some reason he skipped somewhat slower than normally and this somewhat slower pace brought him to the intersection at the exact same time that Ted Jenkins arrived at the intersection smiling and nodding to all the people lined up along the road applauding him for winning his safe driving awards three times a minute.

Fortunately for Bobby Parker he was on the sidewalk as Ted Jenkins was experiencing three seconds of fame in the exact center of his lane. He nodded appreciatively to Bobby Parker who stopped skipping to wave to him, and then he crossed the center line and smashed head-on into the pickup truck that would have killed Bobby Parker if Ted Jenkins hadn't stopped Bobby with this nod and the truck with this car. Ted Jenkins died instantly, but since Laura Jenkins had already been born, she would still get to be Bobby Parker's wife's best friend one day.

***

As a fifteen year old Bobby Parker was pretty much like any other grade ten student at Chester C. Chester Memorial High School. He had a locker, books, pens and pencils, and he wasn't going bald yet. He had his own homeroom desk that he shared with four other students of grade ten Math during the day. But then he would be butt-warming other chairs in other rooms, and some of them would undoubtedly be the homeroom desks of other students, so it was just fine with Bobby Parker that other students would use his homeroom desk…if this were something that would ever occur to him to think about.

It wasn't.

Chester C. Chester Memorial High School had been built more than a hundred years ago in the days when buildings were built to last more than a hundred years, when builders built with a sense of craftsmanship and bricks were cemented into place with thoughts of permanence occupying the minds of the builders: This brick I am cementing in place will still be here more than a hundred years from now. And although the wooden floors had dulled with age and there were cracks and dents, they were still level more than a hundred years after they were laid, glued and nailed. Chester C. Chester Memorial High School was about as solid and permanent as a building or anything else on the planet could be.

Which was the exact opposite of Bobby Parker. His presence was about as solid as a rat's fart and as permanent as free beer. He was never chosen to be on a team. Teachers never thought to ask him questions. The students on either side of his locker could never remember his name, nor could they have described him in terms other than: "Oh yeah...that kid. Yeah, I think he was wearing a sweater, or something."

He had the substance of ant breath on a windy day.

And then one day his fifteen minutes of fame finally closed around him with all the potential of an obscure sonnet written on river water. On this day Bobby would, for the first time in his life, stand up before an entire class and talk about his summer vacation. He'd spent two weeks working every night and all through his weekends, every lunch break, every study period. He'd even waked up half an hour early each day to work on his fifteen-minute speech. In it, he described how he mowed the lawn twice a week (making sure not to bump into the dwarf pines with the mower), how he had long meaningful talks with this dog, Rex (while the dog laid on its back all summer staring at him as though wondering who the kid was who wouldn't shut up for five minutes and let a heat-pooped dog get some rest on a summer's day), and how he even stayed up (omigod) right up till 9:30 one night. And that was where he'd ended his speech because it just don't get any better than that, no sir.

Bobby was ready for his fifteen minutes of fame. He hungered for it. He'd acted it out in his mind over and over again like a telemarketer selling garden benches to apartment dwellers all day, five days a week, week after week. Each enactment was the same. He took his position in front of the room. A hush fell over the class. Every eye and every face turned toward Bobby Parker. No one spoke a word. No one thought a thought. Even Corey Burke, the school bully, softened and awaited Bobby's words. And then he began speaking and his words flowed from his mouth like syrup waltzing out of a tuba, and then sentences flicked from his tongue like verbal spikes of rap music and the excitement built in his delivery and the eyes of his classmates widened as their mouths opened and tears poured out of Corey Burke's eyes. His teacher closed her eyes to enjoy the beauty of words measured perfectly with yardsticks of meaning and emotional content. And by the time his voice carried his listeners to the brink of that canyon from which inspiration overflows into life, he swooped in furiously with the grand finale: "And I stayed up until 9:30 one night." Corey Burke wailed. Cynthia Wortman fainted. Charley Davis' head slumped onto his desk, his brain suddenly too heavy with thought to fight gravity. His teacher slipped into an intellectual coma and would never open her eyes again. And then, one by one, they stood and applauded, first politely, and then in a frenzy. And Bobby glowed. And then he bowed and returned to his seat, side-stepping through a double row of admirers.

That was the plan.

Unfortunately, Bobby was the only student at the bus stop that day and, as always happened when he was the only person at the bus stop, the bus didn't stop. Bobby missed his bus and was late for school. English was the first class of the day. He was to be first up to speak. The teacher didn't even notice that he wasn't there. She asked if Gretchen Kidder was ready to speak and Gretchen took her place at the front of the class right where Bobby was supposed to be standing and right at the time when he was supposed to be standing there. Gretchen Kidder stood in the spotlight of Bobby Parker's fifteen minutes of fame. She bathed in the glow of his moment of recognition with words about summer camp and swimming and horseback riding and canoeing and…and then her hair curled and the skin on her face glowed red and melted as her head separated from her body and flew into the blackboard behind her. It stuck there with its deep black eyes registering nothing. Her right arm, all covered in flames, thudded into the board beside her head. Her legs evaporated.

She didn't do any of this alone. About the same time that she was spreading herself on the blackboard and evaporating all over the spot where Bobby Parker was supposed to have had his fifteen minutes of fame, the rest of the class was doing pretty much the same thing. Arms and heads were popping off all over the room. Skin, which is mostly water, was boiling and fizzling and turning into smelly air. And only a few yelps managed to escape through the furious speed of the heat, which filled the room in less than a second and mixed the bodies of children and one teacher with the parts and pieces of desks and chairs and pens and notebooks and chalk. Everything in the room became part of everything else in the room, all the bits and stuff of everything mixed in steam molecules and barely identifiable classroom shrapnel to create what could only be called school mush. Within seconds, even the solid objects like chalk and wood were beginning to evaporate as though they were made of water. And then all that blazing school mush turned its fury on the walls and ceiling and blew them apart.

By the time Bobby arrived, fire trucks and police cars crammed the street in front of Chester C. Chester Memorial High School, their lights flashing red and blue as firefighters and police officers scurried and scrambled, screaming orders and moving hoses and equipment into place.

But it was too late for Bobby Parker's class. Corey Burke had missed his chance to cry. Cynthia Wortman would never get her fainting debut. Bobby Parker's teacher would never know what it was to be comatose with emotion. Gretchen Kidder's father, a firefighter, stood, arms hanging by his sides, yellow coat open, yellow hardhat under his arm, eyes wide and unbelieving, staring at the unbreakable building burning with all his daughter's parts sizzling into black tar. He screamed. And then he screamed again. And he screamed and screamed. And then he ran like a bolt of screaming yellow rage right past the police lines and around the fire hoses and right through the flaming doors and into Chester C. Chester Memorial High School, and twenty-five minutes later, when the entire structure collapsed because the supremely-crafted wood slats in the ceilings and floors had dried like tinder bombs, there was nothing left of more than a hundred years of Chester C. Chester Memorial High School, there was nothing left of Gretchen Kidder's father except the same black tar his daughter had become.

The explosion, apparently, had been caused by a new furnace installed right under Bobby Parker's class a few days before to replace the one that had heated the school safely for more than a hundred years.

***

In his last year of high school (in the new Morton L. Kidder Memorial High School named after Gretchen Kidder's firefighter father, who'd selflessly given his life trying to save his daughter when the Chester C. Chester Memorial High School burned down) Bobby's history class went for a tour

64

of the Stanley B. Burroughs Cemetery which was chock full of famous people, albeit dead, but famous, nonetheless. There was Wilma R. Randall, the town's first woman to go to college and graduate, and there was Jimmy H. Johnston (aka JJ) who ran for federal office and although he didn't win because of a fatal heart attack halfway through his election campaign, there was never any doubt in anybody's mind that he would have changed the course of national affairs for many years to come if he'd just lived a little longer. And there was Lawrence O. Billings, (aka Larry O) who unofficially broke the world's record for the total number of nonstop jumps over a park bench from a dead start—meaning without a running start – his total number of jumps being one hundred thirty-two and a half (On the last jump, his left foot brushed the lower part of the bench, but he cleared the top and he didn't fall on his face, but in fairness, he called it a half jump.). The record was unofficial because when Larry O and his sponsors—one of them federal office candidate Jimmy H. Johnston, who had two more days to live before his heart stopped jumping its own personal benches—for all their efforts couldn't find out where to register Larry O's feat and soon learned that nobody anywhere in the world had ever tried anything like it. Unfortunately, before they could invent a new world record classification anywhere, Jimmy H. Johnston keeled over halfway through a campaign speech and died and Larry O tripped on a bench while trying to break his own record and cracked his head open on a slab of pavement. The only place his one hundred thirty-two and a half jumps ended up being registered was on his headstone, which read:

Lawrence O. Billings
1925 – 1952
World Bench Jump Champion
132 ½ Jumps
June 4, 1952

There were a lot of great people in Bobby Parker's town and they had all been planted in a graveyard worthy of their greatness. Stately Dutch elms spread their magnificent foliage like giant green sorrels endowing the grounds with a sense of classical art like something out of a Rembrandt or a Turner, something hazy and ancient suggesting midsummer grandeur. And the grounds were impeccably manicured by Glen Boson, the caretaker, who many thought was older than the yard's oldest tenant. No one, not even the town's oldest living resident, Selma Hartt, could remember Glen not being the caretaker of the graveyard and everyone was certain that he had always been old and wrinkled, but also spry and strong. He dug the graves with a spade, tended the flower gardens on his knees and mowed the lawns with a push mower.

Every day after his usual chores, he toured the yard with a bottle of Windex and a roll of paper towels and he washed the pigeon droppings off the headstones, and what a splendid array of headstones they were, a rich blend of time-stamped sandstone, alabaster, granite, marble, feldspar, and serpentine. There were mausoleums and obelisks and plaques;

there were headstones in the shapes of crosses, pointed arches, rounded arches, square slabs, rectangular slabs, and double hearts...all inscribed with names, dates and epitaphs. There were flower gardens and a three-tiered fountain that bubbled and dripped quietly all through the summer. There were benches and a wooden case with a map of the grounds even though the entire graveyard was visible no matter where you stood inside its wrought iron fence.

Sometimes the mysteries hidden behind the graves winked as you walked by.

The Stanley B. Boroughs Cemetery reeked of mysteries and history, stories and questions peeking out from behind the inscriptions on headstones, like the Brown family, both parents and three children all dead on the same day; or suggested by the homage paid to the dead, like the Wilburs, three generations of skyscraping obelisks and the most recent, Eddy R. Wilbur, a plaque in the ground with his name and death date. One entire section on the North end of the cemetery housed almost all new graves, each with the same date of death, which was the same day the Chester C. Chester Memorial High School had burned down.

Every year Marilyn Pringle brought her grade twelve history class to the cemetery for a tour. She knew every prominent site by heart and had even read and memorized the obituaries of almost everyone buried there. Not only could she tell you that Duncan T. Wilson died in a car accident at the age of twenty-nine in 1978, she could tell you that he was survived by his wife, Sara A. and his daughter Donna M., and that he would be missed by his co-workers at Marty's Auto Repair. She knew which plots to point out (like Jimmy H. Johnston and Larry O), and which to hurry by without comment (like Eddy R. Wilbur).

Marilyn Pringle had even written a small history of the Stanley B. Boroughs Cemetery, which she aptly called A Small History of the Stanley B. Boroughs Cemetery. In her small history, she recounted the lives and accomplishments of all the cemetery's famous people like Thelma R. Randall, Jimmy H. Johnson, Lawrence O. Billings, every single Wilbur except Eddy R, and she most certainly would have devoted an entire chapter to Gretchen Kidder's firefighter father if only he had given his life so heroically before she'd written her book.

Strangely, not a word was written about Stanley B. Boroughs, after whom the cemetery had been named. Also strangely, his grave was nowhere to be found in the cemetery and neither Selma Hartt nor Glen Boson could have told you anything about him. The identity of Stanley B. Boroughs was a mystery as mute as the bodies turning to dust in the ground of his namesake; that is, until Bobby Parker stumbled over his own loose shoe laces and plummeted arms out into Glen Boson's meticulously manicured lawn. Normally, this would have been a fairly safe, injury-free, scramble-up-and-get-back-into-the-tour kind of thing. George Killam, the boys' gym teacher had Bobby and all the other boys in his class fall from a standing position into a push-up position twice a week, and that was on a hardwood gym floor. This was just soft cushiony grass.

On the surface.

Just under the surface it was not so soft and not so cushiony. It was hard as rock. It was rock. Granite to be exact. And there's something about a sudden impact against granite when you're expecting cushiony grass that takes your mind and body by surprise, and that's exactly what it did to Bobby's mind and body, so much so that instead of landing in a push-up position and then bouncing back up, he sprained both his wrists and let out a terrible bellow.

Dozens of grade twelve history students turned to face Bobby, most of them wondering who he was, some of them vaguely recollecting having seen him somewhere, one of them thinking: Oh yeah...that kid. Yeah, I think he was wearing a sweater, or something, all of them, including Marilyn Pringle, wondering what the hell all the noise was about. This was no place to be waking the dead. Bobby Parker sat on his knees staring at his swelling wrists, tears and confusion streaming from his eyes.

It was Billy Morris who noticed the gray granite just barely visible where Bobby's left hand had torn away a clump of grass just before its not-at-all-cushiony hardness sprained both his wrists.

"Miss Pringle!" he called. "I think there's something buried here!"

Marilyn Pringle strutted over, curious about this 'something buried' that she was certain was mentioned nowhere in her little history. Visions of a revised and expanded version crowded her mind as she and dozens of grade twelve history students gathered around the shallow hole in the ground made by Bobby's hand.

"It looks like rock," said Billy Morris.

"Could be," agreed Marilyn Pringle, and she pushed aside bits of dirt and grass with her index finger. "Yes, I think it is." And she pushed a little more vigorously to reveal what looked like part of a plaque buried under the grass. Within minutes, Marilyn Pringle, Billy Morris and several other students had the entire plaque exposed. It was badly worn. The letters and numbers carved into the stone were barely legible, but legible enough. They read:

Stanley Bertram Boroughs
Hanged 1879
Buried in earth, burning in Hell

Hanged? Everyone thought it at the same time. Marilyn Pringle's vision of an updated short history evaporated. Most of the students felt something like a chill rolling over their bodies, standing there in a place of death named after a man who'd been hanged, a man who was buried right in front of them and apparently burning in Hell. Billy Morris beamed. "Wow! A real live hanged man!" he said. "And I found him!"

After a few minutes Marilyn Pringle and her grade twelve history class moved on, abandoning the tour and starting the two block hike back to the school half an hour early, jabbering loudly about their discovery and sneaking up behind each other and yelling: "Yah!"

Bobby Parker walked with them quietly, trying to hide his tears but nobody noticed him and nobody snuck up behind him and yelled: "Yah!" Nobody even noticed that he was missing from class while he was in the school infirmary having his wrists bandaged. Ten minutes after Bobby Parker left the school infirmary, the school nurse was back to reading one of her romance novels and had completely forgotten about Bobby's sprained wrists. But everyone in the school remembered Stanley B. Boroughs, hanged man. And of course, Billy Morris became pretty much the most popular boy at Morton L. Kidder Memorial High School.

***

Bobby Parker took Social Psychology 303 in his sophomore year at college. That year he had a particularly heavy load of courses and everybody knew that Social Psychology 303 was a "bird" course. It was impossible to flunk Social Psychology 303. This was because the head of the Nursing Faculty had made the course a prerequisite for a degree in nursing: if you flunked Social Psychology 303, you didn't get to be a nurse because apparently you didn't know how people acted as individuals in groups. Professor Erik Vonnegut, who taught Social Psychology 303, called this utter nonsense. "After all," he argued, "can anyone point to a thought or an emotion that needed a suture or to have its temperature taken?"

71

But the head of the Nursing Faculty, Dr. Ramona Harvey, was adamant: pass Social Psychology 303 or forget about nursing. So Professor Erik Vonnegut said, "Fine. But don't expect anyone to ever fail this course. Ever!" And he made it virtually impossible for anyone to fail his course. To pass Social Psych 303, you had to write an exam at Christmas. If you had passed any first year sociology or psychology course (which you would have, because at least one first year course in sociology or psychology was a prerequisite for Social Psychology 303), then you didn't even have to study for the exam. It was that easy. And if you passed the exam, all you had to do for the second term was write an essay, a short story, a poem, or a letter to Professor Erik Vonnegut explaining to him why you felt that you should pass his course.

Dear Prof Vonnegut,

I feel that I should pass Social Psych 303 because I went to some of the classes when I didn't really have to. And I passed Psych 100 last year.

Brad Landry

Dear Mr. Landry,

72

You have a direct and uncluttered style
of presenting all that you learned in Social
Psychology 303.

B+

Prof Vonnegut

Sometimes, there were more than four hundred
students in the amphitheatre for the first day of
Social Psych 303. They were there just to make sure
that they would be permitted to pass the course
without having to do any work, and each year,
Professor Erik Vonnegut would assure them: "No
one will fail. There will be regular classes, and I
will try to make them interesting. Your Christmas
exam and your second term project are the only
compulsory elements of this course." After which
the class shrunk to five or six students for the rest of
the year.

So the line-up for Social Psychology 303 was
the longest line at registration. It was a two or three
hour wait, but it was an entire full-credit course for
less time than it took to register. Bobby had been
waiting in line for two hours and fifteen minutes.
There was a woman with long chestnut hair in front
of him. He fell in love with her hair, with the way it
flowed so confidently over her shoulders and the
way it complemented her perfect posture. There was
something about her hair that stirred feelings so
deep in Bobby Parker that even his DNA rippled
with excitement. Strands of his life code threatened
to unravel as they vibrated madly in the presence of

this woman's chestnut hair, so shiny and silky and shimmering and reminiscent of something he couldn't quite put his finger on.

It had exactly the same effect on him in the registration line-up for Social Psych 303 as it had had at the village market in Catal Hoyuk nine thousand years earlier.

That's when he'd first met her.

Her name had been Opa and his name had been Tuk, which in the language of the Neolithic peoples of southern Anatolia circa 7000 BC, meant "he who is easily forgotten and ignored." Opa was Neolithic for "in your dreams." Opa was a potter, a creator of things made of clay. Tuk was a gatherer of clay, a muddy and sodden thing that blended in well with riverbanks and escarpments. Tuk brought clay to Opa and the other creators of things made of clay. If you were to ask any of them where the clay came from, they would answer: "From the river bank." Although, some might say: "No, I think it came from the escarpment." But none of them would remember Tuk, not even Opa, who saw Tuk almost every day when he brought her fresh clay from the riverbank. Opa was one of those who thought the clay came from the escarpment, and she had never been quite clear on how the wet buckets of gray stuff got from the escarpment to the potting hut even though on several occasions, Tuk had handed them to her directly, and she had even thanked him.

Tuk was in love with Opa. He'd always been in love with her, right from the first time he'd seen her walking down the main street of Catal Hoyuk, the largest of the Neolithic settlements with more than two hundred huts, completely naked. She'd been three years old then and he'd been completely naked himself although nobody had noticed. It was just the way children dressed nine thousand years ago. What Tuk had fallen in love with were Opa's huge brown eyes. They were like huge clay saucers full of beef stew. Tuk loved beef stew. And even at the age of three, walking stark naked down the main street of Catal Huyuk, Opa moved with a relaxed gracefulness that threatened to strangle Tuk's heart with joy, and as she grew so did her hair, and Tuk's obsession with her beef stew eyes moved to the chestnut waterfall of her hair, the way it flowed so confidently over her shoulders and the way it complemented her perfect posture.

He left things at the door of her hut, which was on the hut's roof as were most of the doors in Catal Hoyuk. They were things like fish bones he'd found by the riverbank and interesting twigs with shapes that had caught his attention. Opa's parents kicked these gifts off the roof and into the street and complained about the culprits who kept throwing garbage around their door. "It's enough to drive you back to hunting and gathering and forget about all this farming and crafting and being the seat of modern civilization," said Opa's father even though it was too late for him to forget about civilization. He'd become too civilized and his gut was much too big from drinking beer from the clay gourds his daughter sometimes fashioned for him to even think about romping around in the woods and plains looking for berries and prey. Given a bow and arrow, he would almost certainly have shot both his

75

feet off. He was about as likely to return to the hunt as he was to surf in the desert around Catal Hoyuk.

But Tuk never noticed that his gifts had not been accepted. After all, he never approached Opa's hut until after dark, so he thought that she had received every one of them and that she would be wondering through every moment of her days who this wonderful boy was who had given her such wonderful things.

One day he decided it was time to declare his love, to reveal the source of all those magnificent offerings. He wore his best cowhide thong and took a gift he'd been saving for years, a small piece of driftwood with tiny branches broken and twisted in on themselves to form an intricate maze of tube-like patterns. Tuk had rubbed the palm-sized artifact with his thumbs for more than three years so that all its surfaces were smooth and refined just like Opa's hair, he thought. He approached her hut with gift in hand, penis erect under the thong (after all, Opa had developed gifts other than beef stew eyes since her naked walk when she was three) and the gait of a man about to fulfill his destiny. He arrived just in time to see Opa leaving her childhood home hand-in-hand with her new husband, a tall sinewy farm boy with bluish-black hair named Akma.

Tuk stood and watched as Akma helped Opa out through the door in the roof of her parents' hut and then led her to their marriage hut. He watched her chestnut hair flutter in the wind and sparkle in the sun. He watched it flow confidently over her shoulders and felt it wind around his heart and squeeze it to death.

76

Nine thousand years later Tuk, reborn as Bobby Parker, fell in love with that hair again and fell in love with Opa once again. Now she was Karen Tillson and she was standing right in front of Bobby in the line-up for Social Psych 303. They were both registering for the same course; they had something to talk about. Bobby took a deep breath. He steeled himself and lifted his hand to tap her on the shoulder. He didn't know what he was going to say. He didn't even know why he was going to tap the shoulder of this strange woman with the beautiful chestnut hair. He just knew that he couldn't not tap her shoulder, that his hand was drawn up by an unseen force that might have been nine thousand years old, or something like that. At the exact moment that Bobby's hand was about to touch her shoulder, she turned and faced directly at him. There was something about her eyes that reminded Bobby of beef stew. Her eyes broke away from him and she glanced at his hand and stepped around it. She smiled as she walked past Bobby as though he was nothing more than a parking sign and she said: "Akma! Are you signing up for Social Psych 303 too!" Karen giggled and even her hair seemed to giggle with glee as she walked up to a tall sinewy boy with bluish-black hair and put an arm around his neck, the other arm being full of books, binders and purse. Akma smiled broadly and said: "You think maybe psych stuff too hard for farm boy from old country?"

A vague sense of river and mud drifted over Bobby Parker like familiar clothing as he stood invisibly in the lineup for Social Psychology 303, trying not to hear the girl he'd loved for millennia fawning over the boy who'd been a wedge between them for nine thousand years.

***

Four years later, Bobby had a degree in business administration and was one of a handful of students ever to attend every class in Social Psychology 303, although nobody, including Professor Erik Vonnegut, noticed. It was time to get a job and get a job he did.

The first one he applied for.

Here's how it happened...

The interviewer, Mr. Burpee, had the flu. His nose was clogged, his lungs were congested, his arms and legs ached, his eyes watered, his ears buzzed, his teeth hurt, and his mind was slow. Very slow, like phlegm dripping off an ice cube. Normally Mr. Burpee was a good interviewer with that rare aptitude that all first-rate interviewers possess—the ability to make the final assessment of the interviewee thirty seconds into the interview.

Not today.

Today, Mr. Burpee should have stayed home in bed, drinking plenty of fluids, getting lots of rest, and downing chicken noodle soup by the barrelful. But Mr. Burpee had a character flaw, or more like a career flaw. He felt that since he was in the human resources department of Waterside Insurance Inc, and since he was in a position to decide who would be hired and who would not, and since he was in a position to say who would stay and who would not after they were hired, and since he was in a position to determine who would be promoted or not if he let them stay, since he had such a potential impact on the lives of just about everybody who worked at Waterside Financial Inc, he felt it was his duty to set an example. He was never late for work, he never took longer that the allowed fifteen minutes of coffee break in the morning or the forty five minutes of lunch break and he absolutely would not take a single minute of sick leave unless he was completely incapable of standing erect.

Today, he was barely capable of standing erect. And his mind was slow.

Thirty seconds into the interview with Bobby he still hadn't made his mind up one way or the other; in fact, he had to squint his watery eyes at Bobby's resume just to remember his name before saying: "So, Mr...Parker...can you tell me why you want to work for Waterside Financial Inc?" The buzzing in his ears was so loud and the throbbing in his forehead was so intense that he didn't hear a word of Bobby's reply which included a five minute description of what he'd done that summer – mowing the lawn, talking to his dog, staying up till (omigod) 9:30 – in fact, Mr. Burpee had dozed off a few minutes into the reply and waked up just as Bobby finished saying: "...9:30." Mr. Burpee thought that Bobby meant that he had to leave at 9:30 and, checking his watch, noticed that it was exactly 9:30.

"Well, Mr...uh...Parker, thanks for coming in...and we certainly appreciate your interest in working for Waterside Financial Inc."

79

They shook hands and Bobby left. Mr. Burpee looked at his checklist. Nothing was checked. Nearly an hour of interview and not one single checkmark. Nothing like this had ever happened to Mr. Burpee before. Every interview he'd ever conducted had resulted in a meticulously checked checklist with each check supported by notes in the margin, observations and insights scribbled at the top and bottom of each page and on the back. Everything from posture and quality of voice to the color of each interviewee's teeth was documented and signed off at the end of the interview.

Three minutes after Bobby Parker's departure, Mr. Burpee couldn't even remember what he looked like except that his hair was dark brown.

Or was it light brown?

Mr. Burpee opened a file on his desk containing his interview notes on the other six candidates for the job. He blinked and rubbed his eyes as he scanned the sheets of paper and concluded that all of the other candidates had scored low to average, and not one of them had gleaming white teeth. Bobby Parker may have had gleaming white teeth. Who knows? And maybe his hair was dark brown. And the position was only for a junior clerk, a position that would be virtually unnoticed in the sprawling Waterside Financial Inc building. Mr. Burpee did the only thing that seemed right in the situation—he completed the checklist, notes and all, and gave Bobby Parker the highest score of all the candidates. He buzzed his secretary and told her to notify Mr. Parker by phone the following day and send letters to the other candidates.

Then he fell asleep at his desk. When he awoke three hours later, he couldn't remember a thing about Bobby Parker or the interview and, although he would pass Bobby in the halls and see him at company functions until he retired twenty years later, he would never recognize him or recall his name.

***

Thus it was that Bobby Parker's professional career was launched by a man who'd forgotten that he existed within minutes after hiring him, and that pretty much set the tone for the next thirty-five years of Bobby's working life.

It was an entry-level position that Bobby was to hold right up to the day that he retired. And although his salary increased a bit each year, he never went beyond the position, never transferred to another office, never went on a business trip, never attended a convention or trade show, never applied for another position within the company, never did anything except things that involved forms and files and filling in the blanks that others had missed because they didn't think they were important enough to bother with. By the time the forms and the files reached Bobby, they'd already seen their usefulness. They'd already initiated and finalized whatever it was they'd been designed to do. In effect, they were the dead remains of transactions that no longer transacted, making Bobby something like an undertaker or gravedigger for expired documents. He stamped them, filed them, forgot them.

As did everybody else.

His office was gray on gray. One desk. One chair. One stapler. One phone. Six large file cabinets. Everything was distinguishable only by its degree of gray.

And there were four walls.

Gray.

Bobby Parker liked his office. In fact it was mainly this that got him to work on time and kept him at his desk till exactly five o'clock each day, this and the fact that he had nothing better to do. He lived in an apartment, so he had no lawn to mow and his dog, Rex, had long since pooped out. All he had to do, really, was stay up till (omigod) 9:30.

Oh yes, there was one other thing in Bobby's office: a rubber stamp with matching inkpad. Even more than his gray office, Bobby loved his rubber stamp. He used it to stamp all the dead documents that came into his office before he buried them in one of the six large file cabinets. The stamp made it official. The document was dead and Bobby Parker had the last word. It gave him the only sense of authority he was ever to feel in his life. It gave him his only sense of purpose.

Until he met Libby.

***

Her name was Libby Freeman. She was the darling of the Communications and Marketing Group at Waterside Financial Inc. "You little darling," people used to say to her because she was so happy and carefree, and she took an interest in people who weren't popular or intelligent. She couldn't pass an open guitar case, a wooden box or a hat on the sidewalk without dropping a coin. From three blocks, she could make a panhandler's nose twitch. She gave the dumpy pimple-nosed boy who delivered interoffice mail a hug once or twice a week, giving him something to feel good about and something to fantasize when he masturbated right afterward in the staff washroom.

Libby wasn't what you would call beautiful but she was harmoniously attractive in a this-piece-fits-nicely-into-this-piece way. All the parts of her were connected appropriately: her arms, though long, were joined high to her shoulders; her head, though small, grew a natural Afro that completed her head space nicely; her legs, though short, extended from a long butt. There was something cooperative and team-spirited about her body that made people think: "You little darling."

On top of this, Libby Freeman took care of herself. Her teeth gleamed, her skin was clear, and her eyebrows were plucked to perfection. You would never see a run in her stockings, a missing button on her blouse, or a tear in her slacks. She left a hint of soap scent in the air wherever she went, and the sound she made when she blew her nose was like good clean air passing through a field of clover, like a sniffle from fairies hiding under the dandelion leaves, a sound to make even the hardest heart say: "God bless you Libby Freeman, you little darling."

One day Libby sat at her desk pondering two problems. Lying directly in front of her on her desktop was an Equipment Purchase Approval Form A-21-Z (e34). It had been used to purchase a new typewriter for Libby. The typewriter was sitting on her desk, all shiny and new. The problem was: what to do with the Form A-21-Z (e34)? Libby had never purchased anything as expensive as a typewriter with company funds before, so she had never even seen Form A-21-Z (e34) until just a few days ago. Now it was sitting on her desk beside her new typewriter. The form had been used to initiate a transaction and now that transaction was over and the form was a dead document.

Libby called the receptionist.

"What do I do with the EPA Form?"

"Room 95-C."

Libby Freeman stood up and walked to the door with Form A-21-Z (e34) in hand. She was aware of the difference in her motions since yesterday, how she moved with more care, with a new awareness of her body, a body that she now realized could be a damned unforgiving thing. Yesterday her doctor had told her that she was going to be a mother. He had to repeat this message a few minutes later when she regained consciousness, and the message—with all its implications—was still sinking in.

Libby, that little darling, was single and although she knew who the father was, she was certain that the Director of the Communications and Marketing Group at Waterside Financial Inc was not about to leave his wife and three children so that he could marry a woman in his department with

84

whom he'd exchanged no more than a few dozen words before exchanging several million bits of genetic information.

Libby Freeman was now a desperate little darling on her way to Room 95-C with a newly dead Equipment Purchase Approval Form A-21-Z (e34) clutched in her hand.

Sitting at his desk in Room 95-C, Bobby Parker stamped a Preliminary Fiduciary Assessment and Recommendation Form F-44-N (a07) which had initiated and finalized more than twenty million dollars' worth of transactions but was now a dead document, a stationery corpse, stamped and ready for burial in one of the file cabinets lining Bobby's walls. Bobby looked at the black ink left by the stamp. He read the big black letters:

ARCHIVE

Those letters—in that order—had become a sort of motto for Bobby. He carried them around in his mind and thought about them frequently. He noticed that none of the letters in the word repeated themselves. Each letter was used just once, and the first letter in the word was also the first letter in the alphabet. Plus, take out the V and you had the name of Bobby's favorite comic book character. Bobby liked to think about these things because he took his job and the big rubber stamp seriously. After all, he was the last human who would ever see the documents that came through his office. Once they were in the file cabinets, clams would wear hula

85

skirts and do the Dirty Boogie before they would be removed, read or remembered.

As Bobby sat at his desk rereading the stamped letters on Form F-44-N (a07), the farthest thing from his mind was that, in a few moments, his entire life was going to be changed or, at least, modified.

All that Libby Freeman could think of as she walked down the hall to Room 95-C was: I can't tell Richard. He'll want me to get an abortion. This was not an option for Libby, being firmly against abortions and being, of course, a little darling. So her next thought was: I'm going to have the baby. Which naturally led into: I need a father for the baby. And considering the circumstances: Soon. I need to find someone soon. And suddenly, she was standing in the doorway of Room 95-C looking in at a man with a round face in a sort of square way whose hair was…was that light brown or dark brown? But he was dressed appropriately.

He'll do.

Just as Bobby was about stand up to take the officially dead Form F-44-N (a07) to its final resting place he noticed movement in his doorway and looked up. There was a woman standing there looking at him. She had a form in her hand, her teeth gleamed, and she had no missing buttons. Bobby immediately fell in love.

Libby spoke first: "Is this…?"

"Yes," said Bobby.

"So I…?"

"Yes," said Bobby.

"And you…?"

"Yes," said Bobby.

***

Two weeks later:

"I do."

"I do."

That night they had sex, and seven and a half months later they had a baby girl named Roxanne. Bobby never did do the math.

A year after Roxanne's birth, they bought a modest house in the suburbs with yards front and back and a garage-mounted basketball net that nobody ever used. Libby was happy with the house and the baby and rarely thought about Bobby, who was content to mow the lawn twice a week but, because Libby had allergies, was not allowed to have meaningful talks with a pet dog. He could, however, stay up till 9:30 (omigod) whenever he wanted. Libby, being Catholic, refused to allow Bobby to use contraceptive devices which was an excellent excuse for her to not have sex with him until as she put it: "I'm ready to have another baby. Some day." Bobby nodded at this and went outside to mow the lawn. At midnight.

Three years after Roxanne was born, Libby was pregnant again, which meant it was time to have sex with Bobby. Which she did, for the last time ever. Seven and a half months later she gave birth to a baby boy, Leo, who would never know that his real father was the Director of the Communications and Marketing Group at Waterside Financial Inc. Of course, like his sister, he would barely be aware of the man who was purported to be his father. He wouldn't even be able to tell you if his hair was dark brown or light brown.

And that was about as good as it ever got for Bobby Parker: job, wife, house and two children. Mow the lawn. Stay up till (omigod) 9:30. Stamp dead documents and wonder, occasionally, why neither of his children looked even remotely like him.

Until…

***

He knew as soon as he woke up that morning that the day was going to be different than anything in his entire life. Even before his eyes opened—during those seconds when dream disperses into the murky world of reality—he felt a strange tingling in his stomach, a buoyancy in his head, and a quickness in his breathing. Nothing, other than sex, was ever quick in Bobby Parker's life. And when he opened his eyes the ceiling seemed higher, the windows larger, Libby's snoring quieter. Everything seemed to shine with internal light as though basic essences were declaring their purpose in the chain of life and the rendering of reality. Yes, it would be a day of discovery and revelation.

Bobby did something he rarely did: he smiled. It wasn't a big smile, more like a rearrangement of his mouth into a configuration that could not be mistaken for a frown or anything sadness-related. It was something like the expression on a clam when, presto, it was dressed in a hula skirt and doing the Dirty Boogie. That kind of smile.

On the other side of town, Karen Farq awoke feeling like a sponge that had soaked up a river of sadness, as was the norm in her life these days. Karen Farq, widow of Akma Farq, had been mourning the death of her husband for one year, two months, three days, two hours, seventeen minutes, three seconds, four seconds, five, six...

She measured her days by the chokes in her breath and the tightening of her stomach. But just as she was about to feel that familiar catch in her breath, the catch released and elation swept over her skin and into her muscles and deep into her organs, and her breathing became deep and satisfying. Today was going to be different.

Back on the other side of town, Bobby Parker sat alone at the breakfast table munching Cheerios with skim milk. A playful light danced in the corners of his green—or were they blue—eyes. The Cheerios exploded against his palate with an oatiness of almost unbearable intensity. The skim milk flowed over his tongue like a tidal wave of calcium goodness. Today was going to be the most special day of Bobby's life. Something good was going to happen. He knew it with every crunch of milk-sopped Cheerios. Today was that day that he'd been waiting for—whether he knew it or not—for every day of his entire life, and maybe even for millennia.

Karen Farq was doing the same thing in her shower, feeling every square inch of her body surface throw its pores open and sop up the warm suds. The follicles of her shampoo-soaked hair sang songs of waves and silkiness. Karen hummed a tune of balance and smooth sailing, a melody whose joy transcended time. She carried the tune with her from the shower to the bus, and all around her people swayed imperceptibly and Karen's tune quieted their busy lives.

On another bus, Bobby Parker whistled a tune that he hadn't whistled since he was a kid. It might have been a show tune; it might have been a hymn; it might have been a few bars from a song he'd heard on the radio. He didn't know and he didn't care and none of the people around him even noticed that he was whistling. He didn't care about that either. All he cared about was the way his body attached to the floor of the bus: with lightness, as though he floated over the hard rubber surface just far enough to feel the vibration of travel but too far to feel the bumps as he rushed toward whatever wonderful destiny that permeated this day.

As Karen Farq walked along the sidewalk, it seemed that birds sang in unison with the pulse of blood in her fingertips and toes. Her long chestnut hair caressed the wind and guided its path through the crowd, shushing its flight so that it touched the busy flood of bodies with millions of microscopic kisses. She was getting closer to something, she could feel it in her stomach like a balloon about to pop, or spore about to drop from a mushroom. This was a thing of destiny and it was seconds away from manifesting itself.

A block away, and heading directly for Karen, Bobby Parker felt the approach of something special as though it were a mouthful of walnut fudge and every step he took was a chew swallow and bite into the next step toward that walnut fudge special something that sweetened everything around him.

And Karen Farq felt that her heart would burst and her mind would explode any moment, any second, and maybe every cell of her body was already bursting with joy as she stopped at the intersection—just as she was destined, just as it was written in some eternal journal—she stopped and held her breath and looked around...

...while Bobby's heart soared right out of his chest, or so it felt right down to the exquisite pain of flesh splitting like a cocoon releasing the next phase of his life ...

...as Karen's eyes scoured the intersection...

...and Bobby, right across the street from her ...

...just as her eyes panned ten feet within spotting him ...

...and he looked down at the sidewalk in front of him ...

...as her eyes panned five feet within spotting him ...

...and his heart nearly jumped physically out of his body ...

...as she panned two feet within spotting him ...

...and he bent forward to pick up the quarter on the sidewalk ...

...as Karen Farq's eyes panned right over Bobby Parker's stooped body and she saw Louise Fullman, her one and only female love from those first high school forays into sex, and she realized that, yes, she had loved Louise all these years and yearned for her gentle feminine caress. She hurried across the street through honking horns and catcalls.

And Bobby picked up the quarter. A brand new one, so shiny that it must have just come out of the mint, sparkling and bright. It was just as Bobby had known: this was his day. How could things be any better than this? he thought as he stared at the gleaming coin in his palm.

Twenty feet behind him, Karen Farq threw her arms around Louise Fullman, and Louise, who'd recently come out of the closet, planted a hot-tongued wet one right into Karen's mouth. Traffic and passersby be damned.

For the rest of the day Bobby tasted walnut fudge and whistled something that might have been a show tune or a hymn, or maybe just a few bars of from an old radio song. Who knows? It was the best day since those summers of his youth when he had a dog to talk to and staying up till (omigod) 9:30 had that special magic of a summertime thing like beaches and baseball.

We won't get into what Karen Farq tasted for the rest of the day except to mention that it wasn't particularly dependent on any season.

***

So, what did Bobby Parker feel when he looked at his children?

Not a hell of a lot.

Instead of recognition, he felt what might be described as an itch. It was an itch somewhere inside his head where he couldn't scratch it without gouging his eyes out or slicing off the back of his head with a letter opener. They were like strangers, like two people who were suddenly on the doorstep of his life and he let them in without knowing where they'd been or whose germs were on them. He let it go for nearly ten years.

And then he couldn't take it anymore.

He had to do something.

So he took them camping, just him and nine-year-old-Roxanne and six-year-old-Leo...in the woods. It was supposed to be a three-day trip but it didn't get past the first night.

It was a trip that couldn't survive a campfire.

Not that they had a campfire. Bobby had never been camping before. He'd never had to start a campfire before. He'd never had to contend with swarms of bugs (ouch), figure out the directions for assembling a tent that was made in (ouch) Korea, or be in such close continuous contact with other human beings before.

Ouch.

And now he was alone with nine-year-old Roxanne and six-year-old Leo and it was the worst eight hours of their lives. They'd had nothing to say to their father during the hour-long drive to the campsite and he'd had nothing to say to them. Roxanne, the oldest, sat up front beside her father. Leo sat in the back where his father stared at him in the rearview mirror for nearly the entire trip, and it wasn't a warm smiling stare of a loving parent or something like a wink and a nod as though to say: "Lookin' atcha kid!" It was more like a clinical probe, a visual catheter, or rubber-fingered poke up the butt to check for hemorrhoids. It was a stare full of doubts and questions, and the happiest moment of Leo's life was when they reached the gates of Carson W. Higgins Memorial Park where Bobby had to keep his eyes on the narrow wooded road through the campgrounds.

It took Bobby nearly two hours to put up the tent. It was right out of the box new, and the directions for assembly were written in an indecipherable Korean-English dialect based on the philosophy that random words arranged on a page might eventually bear meaning. Or maybe not.

Bobby had the 'or maybe not' arrangement.

Ouch.

The whole time he was putting up the tent he thought: This is not as easy as stamping dead documents. And by the time he was finished, his face, neck and arms were swollen with mosquito bites.

While he was putting up the tent and feeding the mosquitoes, Roxanne and Leo huddled off to the recreation center where they played ping-pong. They didn't talk much, except to say things like "Nuts." and "Why do we have to do this?" but after a few minutes at the ping-pong table, they were oblivious of anything but the small white ball bouncing back and forth. Back and forth. For two hours. Without a word. Back and forth. Ping. Pong. Ping. Pong.

If they didn't have Bobby's genes, they certainly had his ability to obscure time with simplicity.

When they went back to the campsite, a big green tent with yellow trim towered over them. It was pushed right up against a stand of spruce and alders; in fact, the back end of the tent had about a foot of alder bushes under the floor. This caused the guy lines for the rain fly to be misaligned giving the tent a tilted and skewed look. Bobby was bent over an orange rusted fire grill blowing into a white plume of wood smoke that diminished with each blow.

"Do either of you know how to start a campfire?" he asked.

Roxanne and Leo shook their heads 'no' simultaneously.

They ate peanut butter and jam sandwiches for supper. Then Bobby went to the park store and bought a fire-starter brick. The brick burned well, but it didn't do anything to the logs other than blacken them, and while the brick blackened the logs, Bobby, Roxanne and Leo sat around the grill, the kids gazing into the burning brick and Bobby gazing into Roxanne's and then Leo's eyes. The deeper he looked, the more intense was the itch at the back of his mind. He gazed deep into Roxanne's eyes, looking for the tiniest resemblance to himself. There was nothing he could latch on to, nothing to make him think by bringing this child into the world, I reveal myself. There was just nothing of himself to see.

The same was true when he looked into Leo's eyes. Everything bounced back like a telephone ringing in the desert. After a while, the kids started to glance back at Bobby, at first irritably, and then angrily. It was Roxanne who settled it:

"I want to go home. Now."

Half an hour later, half disassembled tent stuffed in the trunk beside loose sleeping bags, and a brick still charring the surface of logs in the grill, Bobby, Roxanne and Leo were pulling away from the campsite, on their way home, away from a thicket of questions so thick you couldn't set it on fire with a burning brick.

Not a word was spoken on the trip back. Not a glance was exchanged after Bobby flipped up the rearview mirror. Not a suspicion was felt as they pulled into the driveway and the Director of the Communications and Marketing Group at Waterside Financial Inc climbed out the back window.

***

And then one day, Bobby Parker stopped using the stamp. He wasn't sure exactly how it happened. He'd heard rumors of a thing called the paperless office and around the same time, large plastic objects with screens and clickity-clackity keyboards began to appear on everybody's desk except his, but he noticed that, although his desk seemed to have less paper, the stacks of papers on everybody else's desks seemed to grow rather than diminish. He overheard some people at the cooler one day saying that these new things were called computers and many of the employees at Waterside Financial Inc were afraid that one day they would replace humans. They weren't sure when this would happen, but guesses ranged from a few months to a few years.

It took exactly one month for them to replace Bobby Parker.

Sort of.

Three months to the day that the first computer appeared, dead documents stopped flowing into Bobby's office. Now, the forms were all completed on the new computers and then stored on them when they were no longer needed. A file named C://ARCHIVE.DAT replaced all the file cabinets and the stamp with the big black

ARCHIVE

There was no reason for Bobby to come into work but since nobody knew that he was there anymore—now that they weren't bringing dead documents to Room 95-C, and not that they knew he was there even when they did bring the documents—he kept coming in. He sat at his desk each day and waited for dead documents. He waited for seven years. He went to the cooler for water twice a day but nobody noticed him, nobody spoke to him. He bought coffee and a donut when the coffee cart came around but nobody ever saw him, not even the succession of coffee cart attendants who would have been hard-pressed to remember anybody in a building where the men looked like penguins and the women dressed in mostly gray, let alone remember somebody whose hair might have been light brown. Or maybe dark brown.

He waited for seven years and every day he thought about that brand new quarter he'd found on the sidewalk and he remembered how special that day had felt, and during that time nobody was replaced by the computers. In fact, new people were hired to fix the computers and put new programs on them and connect them and upgrade them and administer the computer network, and the only things that seemed to be replaced were the typewriters, including Libby's brand new typewriter, which she had only used for a few weeks before marrying Bobby and leaving her job to raise her boss's family.

***

One day Bobby came into work and there was a letter on his desk. He opened it and read:

Dear Mr. Parker:

The management and employees of Waterside Financial Inc congratulate you for thirty five (35) years of dedicated service and wish you all the best in your retirement. Our new ABR System will process your retirement benefit and begin direct deposits effective immediately.

Once again, many thanks.

Please note: Remove all personal belongings from your office as it will be renovated beginning next week. Thank you.

Yours,

Edward Cuttman
Director, Employee Benefits and Insurance Plans

So that was it.

No more waiting for dead documents. No more coffee and donuts from the cart. No more being invisible at the water cooler. No more Room 95-C. No more Waterside Financial Inc. No more bus rides to work in the morning. No more bus rides home at the end of the day. No more bagged lunches. No more 9 to 5.

Bobby Parker thought that he would miss all of these things, especially the rubber stamp, but he didn't. He quickly settled into days of soap operas and walks in the park. In the summer, he mowed the lawn almost every day. In the winter, he shoveled snow into one pile and then shoveled the pile into another pile. In the fall, he raked leaves. In the spring, he planted things and fertilized the grass. He read a lot of books but he wouldn't have been able to tell you what they were about a day after reading them. He wouldn't remember the name of the lead character or the protagonist.

His children had grown up and left school for college. He couldn't remember anything about them except that, now, it was easier to get into the washroom in the morning. Occasionally he met his wife, Libby, in the hallways or in the kitchen. She always seemed to be on her way somewhere as though she had a job or some very demanding volunteer work. What she really had was a series of torrid affairs that had started with the Director of the Communications and Marketing Group at Waterside Financial Inc and moved up the ladder into the offices of executive directors and vice presidents. It was almost like she still worked at Waterside Financial Inc, only now she rarely worked sitting down. A few years after Bobby retired, the affairs dwindled away as her face wrinkled and her figure became…less appropriately connected and team-spirited. But they still referred to her as "that little darling." When she was within hearing distance.

She left the world of obsessive romance and entered the obsessive world of bridge. It was her former high school buddy, Laura Jenkins, who introduced her to the game.

"They meet three or four nights a week," she told Bobby, hoping that he wouldn't ask if he could come as well.

"Didn't Laura Jenkins have a father who died in a car accident?" said Bobby.

"Yes, she did," said Libby, glad to change the topic.

And that was it. It was the last time they spoke to each other for the rest of their lives. They lived in the same house but their hours were different and, since Bobby's presence on earth was so much like a pebble that disintegrated right down to the atomic level when it hit the surface of the water that it left no ripple, Libby was barely aware of his presence. Her new lover was bridge and she dove into her new lover like a fifteen-year-old on a hormone high.

Which, for Bobby, left only one more thing to look forward to besides bursitis and incontinence.

***

Death.

***

But let's back up a bit first, back to that Sunday afternoon when Bobby Parker was walking along the sidewalk thinking: Oh, this and that, and for no reason other than to change the rhythm of his movement, he began to skip, somewhat slower than normally.

Somewhat slower than normally.

And why would somebody like Bobby Parker, even as a child, do anything slower, faster, and in any way different than normally?

Well, in Bobby Parker's case, it was because Death was momentarily distracted. You see, Death was watching Bobby that day, drooling and rubbing his hands together and goading Bobby on, putting silly thoughts into his head like: Oh, this and that, and causing him to whistle something that might have been a show tune or a hymn, or maybe a few bars from some old radio song, anything that would take Bobby's mind off the world around him. Death was nudging Bobby toward the intersection with the faulty light, the light that would be green all around when he reached it. Green for Bobby, and green for a certain pick-up truck.

And then Death saw Ted Jenkins.

He saw him drive just over the right shoulder and then veer toward the center line, but before reaching the line, for three entire seconds that could have been three centuries in Death's waiting room, for three splendid seconds, Ted Jenkins' car was aligned perfectly in the center of his lane and Death let out a whoop and a cheer, and then frowned when the car broke from the alignment and crossed the center line. But then, Ted Jenkins nudged the wheel and his car was once again, for three eternal seconds, aligned perfectly in the center of his lane and Death was ecstatic.

Death was so wrapped up in each of Ted Jenkins' three seconds of perfection that he completely forgot about Bobby Parker. He stopped nudging him forward so that Bobby slowed down and skipped somewhat slower than normally, and when he reached the intersection, Death was cheering Ted Jenkins' perfect alignment just as Ted saw Bobby on the sidewalk and nodded to him. And, of course, as Ted's eyes turned in Bobby's direction, so did his car, out of its perfect alignment in the center of the lane and over the center line and right into the pick-up truck that was supposed to kill Bobby Parker.

Death was pissed.

This hadn't been the plan. Now there would reports to write. Interviews. Interrogations. Excuses to make. Cross-examinations. Hearings. Forms to complete. The plan had been changed, and now there would be change management on a cosmic level. Bobby Parker was still on earth. Ted Jenkins wasn't. Fortunately, he was only supposed to have one child, Laura Jenkins, who would one day be Libby's best friend, except that, now, Libby's last name would not be Perkins and the humor of matching up Jenkins and Perkins for Bridge Night would never happen. The driver of the pick-up would have survived in either case. And since Bobby would never have children genetically related to himself in either case, things were not as bad as they could have been.

After the reports were written, the interviews and interrogations and cross-examinations conducted, the excuses made, the forms completed and change management implemented on a cosmic scale, Death forgot all about Bobby Parker, as did most of the world around Bobby (after all, if even Death isn't interested in you…) until Bobby had lived his average allowable age for a married white male in his particular milieu—when nobody would notice—and then Death came to Bobby Parker as he mowed the lawn.

"Time to chalk it in, Bobby," said Death.

Bobby just kept mowing the lawn.

"It's time, Bobby," repeated Death.

Bobby just kept mowing the lawn.

"It won't be painful or gross," said Death. "By the time the worms come, you'll be somewhere else."

Bobby ignored Death and mowed his lawn in perfectly straight rows that would have made Ted Jenkins proud of him.

"It's inevitable," said Death. "You will come because you have to come."

Bobby mowed and mowed the lawn, row after perfect row, from one end of the yard to the other.

"There's nothing for you to hang on to here, Bobby."

Suddenly, the lawn was completely mowed.

Bobby Parker smiled and died.

***

When they found his body in the back yard, collapsed beside the lawn mower, there was nothing much in Bobby Parker's face except Oh, a little of this and a little of that. His mouth was slightly puckered as though he might have been whistling, and he looked completely satisfied with the way things had turned out.

Still Life with Muse and Rain

Jo sat alone at a small round table with two steaming coffee cups and a tiny ceramic ashtray. So very Bohemian cool. She was my cigar-smoking muse, my twist-this-stick-up-your-ass literary kick-start. She'd just swallowed me into the deep green depths of her eyes and spit me out her ears onto the walls saying, "That's how I inspired Pollock."

I really hated it when she got into these trips, but I never doubted that I needed this.

She puffed on her cigar and crossed her leg in a long arc that started in a bowl of poi somewhere in Maui and settled gently over a perfectly sculpted knee right before my Jackson Pollock eyes.

Today was going to be especially painful.

She wore the TBD—the Tiny Black Dress. It squeezed out the essence of thighs and breasts and permeated the air around her with enough visual pheromone to drive every man within ten feet crazy beyond words. I was already crazy beyond words, but that didn't make me any less immune. She was wearing pink...

"Do you want to rip my pink panties off with your Jackson Pollock teeth?" she said.

"I...uh..." said I from this part of the wall and that part of the wall.

"Answer me, pointillist punctuator."

"I was thinking..."

"That's your problem."

She raised an eyebrow over the color green and sucked me off the walls, right into the emerald pits

105

of her eyes and spit me back into my chair through one very erect nipple. She loved tormenting me.

"Tormented writer suits you better than tormented art," she said as she flipped a few threads of TBD over a perfect nipple.

"There's a difference?" I asked.

"Now you're beginning to learn, pretentious noun nudger," she scoffed. "What have you learned?"

"Art hurts?" I chanced.

"You're guessing."

I drew back fearfully. Muses are not beings to displease.

"I was creating an answer," I said.

We sat downstairs, by the door, in the darkness of two very large picture windows. I'd long stopped wondering about these things.

"Create when you're alone," she said. "You're with me now, verb vermin. Talk."

"About what?" I asked.

"About the tit I shot you out of. Did you enjoy it?"

Ha. I wasn't going to fall into this trap. "I've been hearing conversations in my kitchen."

"You mean, you've been having conversations in your kitchen."

"No. Hearing them."

"And who's talking?"

"Cutlery."

"You mean knives and forks and spoons?"

I nodded yes. "And spatulas."

106

She puffed on her cigar and blew out the story of my life. It evaporated into the air before I had a chance to read the first word.

"What do they talk about?" she said.

"They talk about life, about how they've been deprived of it."

"Your cutlery is becoming like you. Now, how about that tit, period pusher?"

"How is my cutlery becoming like me?" I said.

"They're trying to not be cutlery," she said. "Which do you fear more, me or my nipple?"

Why does she do this to me? I wasn't falling for it. I said, "I'm writing again."

"Oh, that," she said. "About time."

"I'm writing more than ever. A whole page a day."

"Short days?" she said.

"Long days," I said. "Painful days. The words keep coming, but they don't make any sense. I don't understand anything I write."

"I inspired a story," she said, "about a man who was happy all his life and then one day he asked what the purpose of his life was."

"And?"

"Nobody gave him an answer that made him happy."

"And?"

"He realized that just being happy was purpose enough and stopped asking stupid questions."

This thought traveled through the picture windows and caught the attention of three raindrops just two seconds away from becoming wet ground. They stopped in mid-fall and shivered around it.

Several thousand raindrops falling behind them decided this was very unraindropish of them and pummeled them so hard they splattered onto the ground without any true appreciation of that first instant of becoming mud.

"The greatest temptation is to look for things until we lose them," she said. "You look sad and confused, noun hound. Do you need help?"

"I had help," I said. "It didn't help." I felt a pang of cliché and changed the subject. "There's no music in Molly's today."

We listened to the silence for a moment. A long moment. I thought how nice it would be to become a TBD if I ever grew up and spend my days wrapped around a muse. We were the only ones in the place. There had been others, but as their relevance had diminished, they'd left. I looked into Jo's eyes. Thousands of eyes peered back at me through the green, all of them screaming ecstasy.

"Have you had any interesting waking experiences lately?" she said.

"I don't think I've been awake in a long time," I said. "Everything seems like a dream to me. Yesterday—at least, I think it was yesterday—I cut my finger while I was slicing cat food. It felt like being awake, but I have too little to compare to be really sure."

"So, you have a cat," she said.

"No, I was just slicing cat food," I said.

"When you cut your finger," she said, "did you think of me?"

Damn. Another trick question. But I was on to her. I had an answer. I slurped down my coffee and ate the cup. Her eyes narrowed. I ate the ashtray. Her brows furrowed. I ate my spoon. She leaned slowly forward like a fountain of liquid alabaster wrapped in black with oceans of green eyes. She blew a tsunami of cigar smoke into my face and all the citadels of my life evaporated. "Wrong answer, paragraph parser."

Oh shit.

She absorbed me into her eyes and I was a fresco on the surface of her retina. "I can see you better now," said the green of her iris.

I said, "I think of you when I run screaming and scratching the flesh off my bones in the void." This was a total lie, but I knew it was what she wanted to hear. I hoped.

She thought about this for a moment. Being inside her head, I could feel the thought. It was doubtful at first, but gave into a seed of initial plausibility. She shot me out one very elegant nostril off one very firm breast and back into my seat. She leaned forward. I visualized car jacks under my eyes to lift my gaze above those very firm breasts and into the sprawling green pastures of her eyes. "Don't eat anything else on the table," she said. "It annoys me when you do that. It also annoys me when you visualize car jacks under your eyes."

I blushed.

"You're blushing."

Blushing deeper, I changed the subject. I was running out of strategies. "I don't know what's happening to me. I've been tripping over metaphors, drowning in symbols, sinking in structure, shipwrecking in un-modulated literary constructions." I had no idea what I was talking about.

"And it really annoys me," she said, "listening to you spout off at the mouth when you have no idea what you're talking about."

Time to shut up and listen.

"That's right, clause crawler. Now listen." She leaned forward spilling infinite cleavage across the expanse of my vision. "The story is in the telling."

She paused.

For about a minute.

A minute with a silent muse is like a lifetime in a country song. "Are you equating my cleavage with the telling?" she said.

Reams of cleavage stories rushed past my eyes. I snapped them upwards into the green fields of my torment—whatever the hell that was supposed to mean. "But…where's the art in that?" I said.

Wrong question. I was on the wall again. Point of entry: left ear. Point of exit: the other nipple.

"You're missing the point, meta-moron. The telling is the art." She flicked ashes onto the tabletop as she regarded me with a look that carved the word distain into my psyche, a look that scoured about twenty-five square feet of wall space. "Troubadours mesmerized their audiences, but they didn't concern themselves with art. They focused on one thing…a compelling story. The story doesn't come out of the art; the art comes out of the story."

I thought about this for a moment—not an easy task when your brain is interspersed with body parts dripping over twenty-five square feet of wall. I'd never heard her go into this much detail before, explaining things to me instead of just tormenting me, torment after torment, on a painful ladder to self-realization. Maybe I'd be off the hook today.

"Now, tell me what that means, ellipse licker."

Shit.

"Um...jimmy jumbo jack-a-doo."

Jo's eyes lit up like green fire. She smiled as she sucked me through a deep drag on her cigar and threw me back into my chair with a wink of her left eye. "Now, you're getting it, quote mote."

I pushed the table aside and stood up, staring into Jo's eyes, bathing myself in the green fire of her irises. "Jack-a-doo kalamazoo!" I said.

Jo stood up, long legs rising forever, hips pressing the meaning of hips against the TBD, and said, "Kalam-a-lani combo too."

We were dancing in the absence of light from the two giant picture windows. "Toobity roobity flippity boo!"

"Boobilly woobilly flippitty poo!"

Arms flailing, heads rolling, fingers snapping out the tune, we danced like monkeys on amphetamine highs.

"Poola-monga, poola-monga poola-monga, bop!"

"Bop biddily be-bop-a-loo!"

From around the corner leading to the kitchen, Molly stuck her head out and said, "You two sit down and stop the racket. And you..." Pointing at me. "...stop eating the cups and utensils."

Let me tell you something about Molly: Even muses don't mess with her. We sat in our chairs

111

facing each other, the table still to the side. Nothing between us.

"The river that argues with itself becomes a bog," said Jo.

Something about this made sense to me. Don't ask me what, but I felt that it summed up my life.

"Just flow," she said.

The space between us was just a few feet. Jo looked like she could burst out of the TBD in an explosion of musaphor that was making my body vibrate to rhythmic variations that resonated somewhere in the back of my head under a thin shred of right-side thinking.

"Just flow," she said.

The space between us was just a few inches. Under those deep olive eyes Jo's lips parted and the rhythms flooded my head, breaking past barriers of judgment and smashing through roadblocks of editorializing self-expectations. I wasn't sure I knew what this meant, but I wanted more of it. Much more.

"Just flow," she said.

And, just as my lips were about to touch hers, she disappeared.

A Touch of Time

She was much prettier than he'd imagined. Dusty brown bangs floated around her forehead with long waves splashing against the air around her neck. Her lips were two waves of flesh on the crest of a kiss. Her figure fit everyman's calendar dream—not overly undersized, not overly muscular or plump or buxom or plank-like. He could have sworn that her eyes glowed blue. She was just right. As he knew she would be.

So much for the warnings about Internet dating. He'd just hit the World Wide Jackpot and he wasn't about to wonder how he'd become this lucky.

Her name was Persephone. He didn't find it strange at all. His own name was Mordecai. Mordecai Morris. And he hadn't spoken to his parents in a long time. He couldn't remember Persephone mentioning her parents in any of their chats. He wondered if they were scholars or teachers or just well-read average Joes who thought they might wrest a name out of time and bounce it off the walls of the modern world. But he liked it. It suited her. She seemed to know a lot about history and the classics, and had described some of her favorite historical events in minute detail, as if she'd been on a movie set, designing the costumes and directing the course of action, much like a technical consultant drawing from personal memory.

He thought it was pretty damn cool that she looked as good as she did. This was just about the best thing that had ever happened to him, or likely ever would.

"You're Persephone?" he asked, smiling a little mischievously, knowing the answer.

"I don't think so," she said with a devilish smile. "What makes you think so?"

God, she was just like in her chats.

"Oh, the fact you're wearing a black turtleneck, red tartan skirt, black leggings, and you're sitting at the table I reserved for us."

"Nice guessing, Morry." It was what she called him. He loved it. It sounded even better than it read. "Hope you can read Manchurian," she said.

"This is a Manchurian restaurant?"

"You made the reservations."

"Oh, yeah." He pulled his chin lightly between two fingers. "I guess that would explain the name: The Frozen Horde. I thought it had something to do with iced desserts and lots and lots of blueberries or something."

"Blueberries!" she squealed and grabbed his hand.

They were sitting in a café outdoors, in what looked to be a medieval French city overlooking a cobblestone street busy with men in tight knickers and long white wigs, and women with gowns flowing into the horizon. He thought he'd seen this place in very old prints and paintings. After a bowl of Bluet en Glace, they were sitting in The Frozen Horde relieved the menu had pictures of the meals.

Strange, though, he wasn't hungry anymore.

***

114

She was drop dead gorgeous with the kind of lips a man could sink a kiss into and smother in lipstick with the tip of her tongue running along the edge of his soul. Big blue eyes peered through chocolate bangs, and her body could have been whittled from a stone of pure desire. She wore a skintight red gown plunging between spectacular mounds of white flesh. His eyes sizzled, his groin smoldered, his brain nearly snapped in half. She knew how to make an impression on a second date. Or was it their third? Who cared? She was drop dead gorgeous and he was the luckiest man on earth.

"Been waiting long?" he asked.

"And who might you be?" she replied.

He loved this game. "I'm the one who made the reservations for the table you're sitting at."

"Oh, him … the one who can't read Manchurian."

"We weren't hungry anyway."

"Speak for yourself," she said. "Iced blueberries do not a meal make." Blueberries. Ice. Something rattled at the back of his head, but evaporated into the Lost Regions of his gray matter at the sound of her voice. "So, do you speak Italian?" she asked.

"Everybody speaks Italian," he said, picking up the menu. "Spaghetti. Lasagna. Linguini …"

She cut him off with the most amazing laugh ever to tickle his eardrums and her voice slid over the table like a spilled bowl of honey stew. "How did you know I love Italian food?"

"Everybody loves Italian food," he said, and quickly regretted his words. "I mean, not that you have common tastes or anything . . . I mean . . ."

His ears buzzed with joy at the sound of her laugh. "It's OK. You're right. Everybody loves Italian, but I especially like it . . . I guess, for its historical content."

"Historical content?" he asked. "That's a strange reason to love food, but, if you say so . . ."

She reached across the table and took his hand and they were sitting across the table from Galileo Galilei as he tore off a chunk of Cabot while just around the corner in the kitchen Miro Sorvino sliced a wedge of Brushchetta and Luigi Pirandello twisted his fork into a mound of Spaghetti alla Bologna and Michelangelo Buonarroti gazed up from his wooden table as he chewed a mouthful of Tortellini di zucca and Frank Zamboni brushed ice from his jacket as his mouth watered thinking of Pizzette e Salatin and Federico Fellini scooped a steaming portion of Cannelloni al Ragu . . . and he still wasn't getting it as he dipped a garlic stick into a pool of spaghetti sauce and wondered about the wooden bowl just as it turned to porcelain and Persephone smiled at him and asked if they should order another bottle of wine.

Another bottle? How many had they had? He tried to focus his thoughts but he was caught in the glow from her eyes and that was all that mattered and he said yes, another bottle of wine. Something red and Italian.

***

116

She was amazing. Life danced in her eyes. She was as fresh as the first time he'd met her and fallen in love on the spot, or had he already been in love after their weeks of sending and receiving over the Internet? He didn't care. She was timeless and he told her so, "You're timeless."

She smiled bouquets and heartbreak and took his hand. "Something like that," she said as they strolled past a heavily armored Samurai warrior outside a Japanese palace stretching into an ancient Far East sunset.

"But why me?" he asked.

"Why not?" she replied.

"There's nothing special about me," he said.

"Need there be?" she asked.

"But you're so … perfect," he said. "So out of my league. Why me?"

"I have a different perspective."

He decided to leave it alone as their walk took them along a pedestrian bridge made of a single giant piece of plastic spanning two magnificent skyscrapers surrounded by flying cars and people streaking through the air in jetpacks.

Their walk finished in front of the coffee shop around the corner from where he lived. He asked if she'd like to go in for a coffee. They walked through the door and he noticed immediately that she was much prettier than he'd imagined with her dusty brown bangs floating around her face, her hair splashing against the air around her neck.

He suddenly had a craving for frozen blueberries.

***

His hand was wrinkled and liver-spotted, his nails cracked and dried. His eyes beamed youthfully, but the pinched gray skin around red-veined whites looked like something from the Bin of Ages. His legs wobbled whether he was standing still or walking. His head shook when he talked as though trying to shake the words out of his mouth.

She sat across from him, young and beautiful as her eyes enveloped him with their blue glow. His voice cracked as he spoke. "We've had a wonderful life together."

She smiled and nodded and said, "Yes, we have."

"I've loved you from the beginning," he said.

"I know," she said. "And right to the end." She took his hand and they were standing in total darkness until, an instant later, the darkness exploded with color and fire rushing light years in every direction, populating the emptiness with stars.

And he was in the Frozen Horde, sitting across from the most beautiful woman he'd ever seen. He looked at his watch and smiled. He wasn't surprised. Not a bit. Just happy for the fraction of a second she'd spent with him.

He looked one last time into the blue glow of her eyes and winked happily as he turned to dust.

118

Food for Words

I once applied for a hamburger. I didn't expect to get it, especially after getting the go-ahead on a feed of tacos and Mexican beer earlier that year. But the week after I wrote for it, I checked my email and there it was: a coupon for a fully dressed king-size hamburger with fries and soft drink of my choice, although the fries were synthetic, as were the hamburger patty, the bun, the pickle, lettuce and ketchup. But the mustard and pop were real.

This was back before the fourth blight, when people were only mildly starving, when there were two billion fewer people scratching the planet's surface for crumbs of anything that would keep them alive for another day. Another hour. But it was after we stopped burying our dead and started recycling them like in the movie Soylent Green, which was made so long ago I don't think most people had ever seen it. But we heard about it when they first started talking about recycling the dead. Lots of people were against the idea, but everybody was starving and it was getting hard to find places to bury the bodies. Plus, there was already mandatory organ donations (wherever those went), so we were already sort of into the recycling thing.

But let me tell you, that hamburger was delicious. I don't think I've ever tasted anything as good as that burger, real or unreal. And the fries! I don't know what real fries taste like—I don't think they grow potatoes anymore since the farmers committed their mass suicide to protest what was happening to them and their way of life—but those fries had a taste that filled my mouth and nostrils at the same time. It was a solid taste, like you would associate with real food. The root beer wasn't so bad either, being real and all.

And then it was back to starving. Things have gotten worse since then and I've given up on ever getting another hamburger or anything like that. I've scaled my expectations down to more realistic things like powdered milk, pollock, noodles...stuff like that. Most of it's probably recycled people, but you never know because they don't put that kind of information on the food labels. *May contain human parts*. Ignorance makes for blissful eating. I tried telling my friends and family to keep it simple and humble, but they kept writing essays about the big stuff: steaks, turkey, spaghetti with meat sauce and garlic bread. They're all dead now—starved to death. Into the mixer.

I keep my essays limited to the possible things. Last night I wrote an essay about how eating a bowl of beef-flavored texturized vegetable protein soup would improve my attitude toward work. I work for a small company that advises people. We cover just about everything. When somebody wants good advice, they come to us and if we don't have the advice on hand, we find it for them, or we just use our imaginations. We've never once failed to advise a client. Sometimes they take our advice, sometimes they don't. But they pay for it and there's no refunds because once advice is out there, hell, there's no getting it back.

Tonight I'm writing about macaroni and cheese. The cheese may be a little extravagant but sometimes you have to push things a little into the "I'm way out of control" zone. But not too often and not too much. You could starve to death. My theme is Macaroni and Cheese: A Meal for the Masses. Which it was in the long ago when there were farmers and cows around to make milk and use it to make real cheese. Damn farmers took the cows and pigs and chickens with them and started the first wave of blights that threw the world's biggest cities into war zones with everybody killing off everybody—trying to steal their food—and breaking into stores and food banks and the government food distribution centers, even after the centers ran out of food to distribute and the stores were full of empty shelves and the food banks were bankrupt.

But that's ancient history. We have better ways of feeding the populace now. And better ways to determine who should survive. These days, we weed out the stupid and the arrogant. Literacy rates are higher than they've been in all of human history—mostly because the illiterate were the first to starve off under the new system, but also because a lot of people became literate really fast. Of course the really stupid ones wouldn't know how to turn on a computer and send an email. I mean, how were they supposed to submit their essays? As for the arrogant, well, did I mention what happened to my family and friends who wouldn't take my advice and tone it down?

Now, something like macaroni and cheese creates a nice balance with your basic pasta on one hand and synthesized cheese (probably cheese-flavored human extract) on the other. One for nutrition and one for taste. Plus, it's easy to prepare: boil pasta, add cheese, stir, eat. If ever a food was made for the masses! And there's something humble and unassuming about macaroni and cheese, something to tame the tethered masses, remind them of how lucky they are to not be arrogant or stupid.

These are things I'm putting in my essay. I can almost taste that macaroni and cheese now. I don't want to get too cocky, but I've learned a lot about what works and what doesn't in an essay. Certain things seem to be "right." For instance, mentioning things like humble and unassuming seem to work. Mentioning things like bold and strong can get you starved. Mentioning balance is another good thing. Talking about how much you need what you're writing for is almost certain to fail. What you need is good writing skills and a realistic approach to composition. It also helps to know your place.

I have a nice writing desk and a nice room. I have a view of the river. Last week, I saw a man fall into the river—though it almost looked like he jumped—he disappeared under the gray water and didn't come back up. I didn't report this. You have to be careful about whose attention you draw. And besides, I doubt if that man would have been recyclable after being in that water.

If water doesn't come in a bottle, you don't drink it. You don't use it to cook food and you don't use it to wash either yourself or your clothes. Tap water is still good for washing floors and other stuff, and if you have real grass in your lawn, it might be safe for watering. That river water though…just as bad as lake water. Good thing there's lots of bottled water. Farmers didn't have any say in that.

I share a bathroom with about twenty other people who have exactly the same kind of room as me. And like me, they all live alone because, like me, they don't have Relationship Permits and they haven't had their parts re-connected so that they can have babies. I think everyone's in agreement that we don't need a lot of new babies. But that doesn't stop people from writing essays about why they'd like to have a baby. Not me, though. I stick to food. I've heard about people being allowed to have a baby but they spent so much time taking care of the baby that it cut into their food essay writing time and they and their babies starved to death. You have to be careful about what you commit to.

But I like it here. It's quiet. Nobody intrudes on my personal space. Hell, I don't even know the names of anybody in this building and they don't know my name. It's safe that way. And you don't have so-called friendly neighbors yakking in the hallways at all hours of the day and night and distracting you from writing essays. Loud neighbors can get you starved. But we're always sure to smile and nod to each other in the halls and coming in and out of the washroom. When you don't smile and nod, you're thought to be out of balance and being out of balance can draw attention.

I'd like some macaroni and cheese, please.

I think I'll end my essay with that. I don't think it's too presumptuous, and it might even give the editor a smile. I've heard that people with really good writing style and things like a subtle sense of humor and wit get offers for work that pays in money and food coupons, both. I'm hoping that I'm that good in another year or two. I'm getting better every day. And I've gone from 80 pounds three months ago to 83 pounds yesterday, so my writing must be getting better.

At first the whole essay thing didn't go over well. There were a lot of stupid people on the planet whose grammar was so bad you could barely make out what they were trying to say, let alone what they were trying to write. Some people say a lot of it came from the way people were writing online, especially in the comments sections on news sites. Plus, they had a lot of stupid opinions. And there were a lot of arrogant people who could write well, but they also had a lot of stupid opinions. Their downfall was that they were too arrogant to admit their opinions were stupid, and that attitude showed in their essays. Into the mixer.

They say almost three quarters of the world's population died off when the food all but disappeared. Most of them died in food wars where one nation invaded another for its food, and there were food civil wars where people from different religions and political persuasion in the same country slaughtered each other for their food. But apparently, that kind of thing had been going on for a long time. This time, though, it was pretty much final. Neither side had food. But that didn't stop the slaughter.

Nobody knows who came up with the idea to make people write essays for their meals and babies, but there's lots of rumors. Some say it was a group of disgruntled grammar teachers who were also gentleman farmers. Others say it was an international conspiracy pulled off by newsroom copywriters who gained control of the internet and everybody's bank accounts. Some said it just made sense, so shut up and don't ask questions—just write.

The people who just wrote are still mostly around—except for the stupid ones, and the arrogant ones. I'm not sure if it's a better world or not since the blights, but I guess there's a lot less stupidity and arrogance. I guess we can be thankful for that. And that's a lot to be thankful for. In fact, that's just what I said to one of my clients when she wanted advice on things to be thankful for. We never got to collect the final payment from her because she died before it was due. I think I heard it was suicide. If only she had come to see me for more advice.

Anyways, I've finished my essay and now I just have a little polishing up to do before I send it in.

Macaroni and Cheese: A Meal for the Masses

A long time ago, the Farmers all killed themselves because they didn't know their place and once you don't know your plac e, things get out of balance and bad things start to happen, like mass suicide in which all the cows die as well, and real cheese becomes a thing of the past because there's no more milk

But we still are lucky enough to still have macaroni and cheese because we have awesome sophisticated machines that "recycle" human things we don't need any more and turn them into food (which we do need), such as cheese.

Macaroni and cheese creates a nice balance because you have your basic pasta on the one hand and delicious cheese on the other. That's one for nutrition and one for taste. Plus, macaroni and cheese is so easy to prepare: boil pasta, add cheese, stir, and eat. Food for the masses!

Macaroni and cheese is also humble and unassuming. It knows its place, as do people who ~~crave~~ eat it. I've even heard that every bite of macaroni and cheese reminds one of how lucky one is to not be stupid or arrogant. So, no! I do not want ~~savoury~~ steaks, ~~mouth-watering~~ pork chops or ~~scrumptious~~ chicken.

I'd like some macaroni and cheese, please.

And I still have time for a good start on tomorrow's essay, before they turn the electricity off.

Rabbits In Her Eyes

She had rabbits in her eyes. I swear it. I saw them hiding behind irises and lenses, sliding across the rainbow surfaces of her retinas, swarming and spilling out of her eyes, and I knew I'd never be the same.

***

I met her the night I tried to kill myself. I'd pretty much had it with life and decided that I'd given it my best shot and now was a good time to shoot myself, a good time to end the bad taste that filled my mouth with the thought of living another pointless day. But I didn't have a gun and would likely botch the effort and end up trapped in a vegetative mind for the rest of my useless days.

Fortunately, I lived close to a very high bridge.

***

I'm not sure what my thoughts were as I passed street lights crazy with buzzing insects on my way to the bridge. What was this going to be like…jumping off a bridge, tumbling through the air, splashing into water? I'd heard it would feel like slamming into a brick wall but I was sure it would be fast, just a second or two of pain before oblivion. Maybe I thought those things, maybe I didn't, but suddenly I was in the center of the bridge and it was late, dark and quiet. Perfect!

Except for one thing.

A woman stood in the spot where I had my heart set on jumping. Her white gown flapped in the wind like a half-wrapped flag and her long blond hair fluttered ghostly under the incandescent bridge light. She was beautiful, like cold white marble carved to perfection, timeless, beyond the moment. But that didn't give her the right to stand in the very spot I'd chosen to make my last stand...or jump. I felt like yelling, "Hey you! If you're going to jump, then jump. You're holding up the line."

Instead, I halted a few feet from her and stood with one hand on the railing trying to figure out what the hell was going on here...and what was this thing I felt like a field of leaves rustling inside my chest? This was something new, something I hadn't felt in all the mileage of that pot-holed path I called my life.

I was in love.

I let that thought squirm around in my head for a moment or two. I was in love and the thought raged between the dendrites and axons in my brain. I was in love and something powerful and unsettling expanded like a great bubble in my chest and stomach, taking my breath away.

I wasn't sure how to open a conversation with her. I wasn't even sure if she knew that I was there, so I dove right in. "Uh...hello."

Brilliant.

Serenity simmered quietly over the surface of her marble-like body; it suffused her billowing hair and her intricately sculpted face. But there was something in her eyes, a dark and fearful presence.

She turned her head in my direction and stared right through me. She turned her head back to the darkness of the water and I wondered for a second if I was just a figment of her imagination that she no longer wanted to acknowledge. I tried again.

"Um…hello…I hope I'm not intruding, but I think you're beautiful and I just fell in love with you." She turned her head towards me again. She'd heard me. She was looking at me, not through me, looking right into my eyes.

"Do you think we could talk about this?" I said.

Framed in wood railing and steel girders, she looked otherworldly in her white gown against the dark sky and the cold steel. I noticed something strange about her eyes. They appeared to be moving…not the kind of movement that comes with rolling your eyes or blinking, something else, something I had a hard time getting my head around. These thoughts ended abruptly when she spit on me.

I didn't think I deserved that. I was new to this jumping off the bridge thing. I didn't know the rules and protocols. You never read about that in the media. It's always so and so jumped off the so and so bridge last night and ended up wrapped in a fishing net. They mention the jump and the body recovery but they never mention the rules they followed for the jump. This suddenly concerned me. I wanted to get this right. I mean, you only get to do this once. And to make everything still more complicated, I was suddenly in love with a woman I'd known for just a few minutes and who was already spitting on me. Her eyes shot back to the

129

dark water a few hundred feet below. She showed no emotion in her eyes nor in her body. She seemed relaxed and resigned, waiting for the moment. I followed her gaze into the darkness.

"Sure is a long way down, isn't it?" I glanced at her briefly and then back at the water. "A long, long way down." I leaned against a girder. "So, what made you choose this bridge?"

She swung her eyes at me like slapping me in the face with a chilling glare. And that's when I saw them. The movement in her eyes caught me and swallowed me and I was in a place of half-light with my body massaged in a hundred places by a squirming mass that felt like thousands of throbbing muscles sliding over my body. As my senses adjusted, my vision filled with rabbits, a solid reality of rabbits, each one a feeling or memory, a laugh or a tear. I instinctively understood that these were the rabbits of her life, a tide of muscle and fur pushing and pulling her to the bridge.

I snapped out of it.

"Is there anything I can do to help you?" I said, realizing as the words left my lips how ridiculous the offer was. We were here to kill ourselves. The only help for either of us was to just accept the plunge into the end of pain. "Or maybe we can just hang out for a while. Seems like a nice evening." It was actually cold and dark and the thick scent of rain was in the air. Her blank stare was relentless. Again, I felt myself succumbing to her eyes.

"You have interesting eyes." She stared at me without blinking. I stepped closer and stretched out my arm and touched her eyebrow. She didn't flinch or back away, just gazed into my eyes as I gazed into hers until I was inside again.

I was walking around with my hands in my pockets and trying not to touch or bump into anything that might break. I didn't want to leave any internal scars on the woman I loved. I looked around. There was a farmhouse ahead of me, pastures to the right and a field of corn to my left. The sky was cloudless blue and the air was crisp with the sweetness of life. Was this a happy place, her happy place? Was she sharing it or revealing it? Was there something here that she wanted me to see, something that would make me understand why she wanted to die? I walked toward the farmhouse. As I drew closer I noticed something hanging over it. It was a dark shape, a rain cloud not more than a few dozen feet across and equally as high. I saw a drop of rain dislodge from the bottom and plummet down onto the roof of the house. Instead of splashing over the shingles, it spread over the roof like a liquid black carpet and melted into the house. Suddenly, a thundering scream so solid in fear that it blocked the sun blasted out of the house and everything plunged into a darkness so thick I could feel it flowing over my skin. I couldn't see the house through the pitch blackness but I could feel it, like the house and I were connected by the dark. I heard panicked breathing, short bursts of breath, fast and shallow. I sensed small hands stroking frantically over a sniffling patch of fur with whiskers and long ears. Small eyes peered through the darkness at a place where the darkness wavered with movement. Small arms pulled the fur closer to a body shaking and cold until the patch of fur shimmied over a young girl's body and disappeared into her eyes where it merged into a sea of pulsating fur. Rabbits filled every horizon of her being.

I panicked and pulled away, back to the bridge.

"What was that?" The words shook themselves out of my mouth. "That scream? That house? Those rabbits? What?"

I saw the desperation well up in her eyes. Her chest heaved and she took a deep breath. Rabbits started pouring out of her eyes and over the railing. Splash upon splash echoed in the darkness below the bridge. I panicked. I tried to say something to her but I couldn't move, I couldn't talk, and the rabbits kept streaming out of her eyes. For a moment I thought about jumping into the water to save the rabbits. I thought about covering her eyes with my palms. A blade of cold shot through my body when I noticed that she was smiling as the rabbits jumped out of her eyes.

I reached out and grabbed one of her shoulders. It felt like touching a sheet of paper. There was no substance. No weight. No solidity. The rabbits kept pouring out of her eyes. She turned her head toward me and I was suddenly covered with rabbits. They jumped off my head into the water. They jumped off my chest and arms into the water. I felt their sharp paws clamp into my skin as they sprung into the air. I couldn't see her face, only the rabbits, one after the other in a never-ending crazy fountain of rabbits. I lost my balance and fell against the railing. I lost my grip on her shoulder. She turned her head back to water. Within a few seconds the stream of rabbits slowed until just one last rabbit squeezed out of her right eye and into the blackness.

She turned her head to me and her eyes were white with emptiness. She smiled and disappeared.

I stared into the empty blackness. Not even a ripple in the water. Nothing to indicate that anything had happened. The rain arrived, pounding in with a torrential downfall that soaked me through in a matter of seconds but I barely noticed. I couldn't tear my eyes away from the water. I sensed that something had been torn out of me at a very basic level of being. I felt as empty as the dark, but with feelings of lightness or release…an absence…and at the same time, I felt an odd sense of loss. Could I really have been in love with her? Did she really exist, even in death? Was I in love with a hallucination? I was unbalanced to begin with…here to kill myself. But now the rain-pummeled water looked darker and colder than my life. Puddles swelled up on the walkway, reflecting wavering light from the bridge lamps. I began to shiver involuntarily as I stepped into the puddles of a still uncertain future but having loved something in the night.

Cloud Walker

Joey Kovacs was tired of being dead. He wasn't sure how long he'd been dead, but he knew it was long enough and he'd had enough of it. The guy with the long hair, beard and robes had been friendly enough and had welcomed him warmly, but he'd been short on details. "Welcome," he'd said, all smiles and ethereal glow. Then, he'd just walked away and disappeared as Joey looked around and checked out the surroundings.

There wasn't much to check out...clouds, sky, more clouds. He was standing on a cloud, which seemed weird at first. Clouds are vapor. When you stand on vapor, you fall. But there Joey was, standing on vapor and not falling. He thought for a while that maybe the bearded guy had fallen into a cloud somewhere. He was sure he would have heard a scream though. He couldn't see the ground or where the sky ended so he assumed it would have been a long fall. A long scream.

After he'd grown used to the idea that he wasn't going to fall, he started to walk around on the cloud. Not far at first...he wasn't sure if he should wander far because the bearded guy might come back and he wanted to be there when he did. After a while though, he started to wander farther. The cloud seemed to go on forever, like walking a treadmill at a brisk pace and watching the scenery stay the same.

At first, he thought a lot about his previous life: his friends, his wife, his kids, his co-workers. He wondered how they were doing, how they were taking his death. He tried to remember what had happened, but nothing came to mind. It was like, "Hey, look, you're alive! Hey, look, you're dead!" And here he was, dead. Walking on a cloud.

This wasn't what he'd expected.

In fact, he wasn't entirely certain about what he'd expected. Big party with all the people he'd ever known suddenly whooping it up in a cosmic festival with no end. Or maybe he'd sink into some kind of universal awareness and become one with the stars. He hadn't given it a lot of thought, but there seemed to be a lot of possibilities, all of them more interesting than this. He looked around. Clouds. Sky. More clouds.

He didn't leave footprints when he walked the cloud. Wisps of vapor floated around his feet with each step and there didn't seem to be any change in the density of the vapor around or under his feet.

He lost track of time. Nothing changed. There were no variations that would allow him to say, "OK, this ends here and that begins there...so...we have this and that." There was no this and that. Only this. Clouds and sky. This cloud he'd been trekking for who knows how long. This endless sky. He couldn't remember sleeping since he'd died. He just kept walking and walking. He hadn't eaten since he'd died. This made sense to him in a weird way. *You eat to stay alive. I'm dead. I don't need to eat.* The good thing about this, though, was that he never had to shit. Not that he hadn't enjoyed a good crap when he was alive, but it would have been unseemly here, with all the clear blue sky, the white fluffy clouds, the absence of toilet paper.

He tried to remember what his life had been like, who he was, what he'd done, where he'd lived, who he'd known. There were flashes, a face here, a building there, a stream of blurred actions that seemed familiar but didn't form a complete picture that he could identify with any kind of certainty. He couldn't remember the last time he'd had one of those flashes and, in all honesty, he didn't care anymore. He didn't want to think about who he'd been and what he'd done. That had nothing to do with anything anymore. If he'd been a bad person and there had been a hell, he'd be there right now. So it didn't matter if he'd been good or bad.

It had occurred to him once that he might be in hell, a hell where you didn't roast your ass off for all time, but suffered from loneliness or boredom. But he wasn't lonely and he wasn't exactly bored. A little variation would have been nice, but its absence didn't bother him. He just kept walking. There was no day-after-day or night-after-night. There was just an eternal sky and clouds. He could see well enough but he had no idea where the light came from. There was texture to the sky and he could discern the folds and crevices of the clouds, but there were no shades or shadows that would indicate the direction of the light that made them.

No…he wasn't in hell. He wasn't in pain. He wasn't feeling that he was being punished for anything. He was just…dead. And he was here. Walking on a cloud surrounded by infinite blue sky.

But he was tired. He'd been walking a long time. He had no idea how long, but it felt like a long time…not in the sense of one day flowing into the next, but more like a sense of fatigue that etched itself into his awareness a little deeper as he walked. It wasn't something he could measure. It was just there, somewhere in the fabric of his walking.

He supposed that was another thing he'd had wrong. Who would have thought that you could get tired when you were dead? He'd always thought of it as the ultimate state of relaxation unless, of course, you went to hell. He didn't think that hell would be relaxing.

But this wasn't all *that* relaxing. He was just walking all the time. Walking on clouds. His feet weren't sore. His legs were fine. He hadn't eaten in ages but he wasn't hungry. But he was tired. He wasn't sure how he would explain the tired he felt if he had someone to explain it to. So he decided to explain it to himself.

"Well, Joey, it's like this…you're not physically tired."

"Then how do you know you're tired?"

He walked for a while, thinking about this. There were only the clouds, the sky and himself…no one else. He wasn't sure how long he walked and thought but, eventually, he said, "I'm having an internal monologue and I would really appreciate it if you wouldn't interrupt."

"Oh, I see…talking to yourself, are you?"

"That's right. I'm talking to myself and I'd appreciate it if you wouldn't interrupt."

"OK, then…I'll just…listen. That OK?"

"I suppose so. Just don't talk."

"Got it."

"OK, now where was I?"

"You're not physically tired."

"You're talking again."

"But you asked a question. I answered."

"It was rhetorical. I wasn't asking you. I was asking me. And just who the hell are you anyway?"

There was a moment's silence.

"Could you ask another question?"

"What do you mean another question? Who are you?"

More silence.

"Haven't got a clue."

Joey looked around. Nothing but clouds and sky. He looked behind. Same thing. He turned around. Just as he was about to take a step: "I wouldn't do that."

"Do what?"

"Go back."

"And why not? I don't seem to be getting anywhere going forward."

"I don't think it's allowed."

"That's crazy. I'm going back."

He lifted his foot and stomped down hard. And fell right into the cloud.

"Told you not to do that."

***

He wasn't sure how long he'd been falling. He couldn't see the sky anymore. He couldn't see the clouds because he was presumably inside it…falling. Whatever the other voice was, he hadn't heard from it for a while. In a way, he regretted that. As irritating as it was, it was something more than just clouds, sky and an eternal walking. And now he was falling endlessly. He thought it was strange that he wasn't getting wet from the vapor. And he wondered why he still felt fatigued. Falling didn't take any effort. He didn't have to move his legs. He didn't have to swing his arms or remain erect. All he had to do was just…fall. He thought that it might be resistance to the air and the vapor as he fell, but he didn't feel any resistance. He didn't feel anything. He thought for a moment that he should feel cold. He checked to see if he was wearing an overcoat, but the vapor obscured his sight, it was that thick. Cloud thick.

He suddenly realized that he had no idea what he was wearing. Dead all this time, and he had no idea. He figured that, if he couldn't see what he was wearing, he would feel what he was wearing. He put his hands on his chest and ran them down over his stomach, genitals and legs.

Genitals.

He was naked.

Shouldn't he have a robe like the bearded guy?

He was sure he was wearing something when he died, but when he died was a faraway memory that was getting increasing faraway with every second he fell.

Oh well, I'm in a cloud. Who's going to notice?

It was exactly at that moment that Joey fell out of the bottom of the cloud and into the clear blue sky, which didn't seem to have any sort of horizon in any direction.

Figures.

He looked down and confirmed that he was naked. He was sure he'd looked down before now, at some point when he was walking on the cloud. He wondered how he'd missed this important piece of information. But then, did he really need clothing when he was dead? It wasn't like he was going to any parties or business meetings.

Except the business meeting he just fell into. There was a long business table with chairs around it, all of them occupied by people with clothing. He stood behind his chair, naked. No one seemed to notice. He talked about charts, graphics and numbers as they flashed by on a PowerPoint at the far end of the table. Men and women guzzled coffee and devoured donuts as they looked, wide-eyed at the PowerPoint and nodded agreement with unworldly enthusiasm. Joey had no idea what he was talking about. The material in the PowerPoint made no sense to him. It could have been hieroglyphics. And his explanations made no sense even though the words seemed to hold a kernel of truth: "Correlations to the frontier. Horizons of jettisoned burlap." No one even looked at him. They stared at the screen as they downed the donuts and coffee and nodded agreement.

Joey kept looking down to see if he was still naked. He was. He wondered how long it would take before the people sitting around the table would notice. And how long before they noticed that he didn't have a clue what he was talking about.

He wasn't sure how long the PowerPoint had gone on, but it seemed like a long time. He had no idea who the people around the table were or what they were doing here listening to him babbling about nonsense on the screen, but they sure could throw back the coffee and donuts. It was almost like they absorbed them.

He tried a few things that he thought might shake things up. At one point, he said: Yep. I'm naked. Just standing here without any clothes on. Naked."

This created a stir, like a ripple of dominos around the table, but none of them looked at him. They looked at a meaningless chart on the screen, tapping each other on the shoulders, pointing at the chart, nodding agreement, shoving donuts into their mouths and washing them down with coffee.

"Would anyone like to take a closer look at my cock? It's right here. Out in the open. For everyone to see."

No takers.

Joey was beginning to feel that he would rather be walking on clouds than giving a PowerPoint presentation in the nude. Especially when he didn't know what the presentation was about and he didn't feel like coffee and donuts.

Suddenly…

he was back on the cloud…walking. Still naked. He wondered if he would ever have a robe like the bearded guy. That robe had been white. He wondered if they had other colors. Like maybe a blue robe. Joey thought he would look good in a blue robe. Something to match his eyes. The instant

141

he had this thought, he had another thought: *What color are my eyes?* He was kind of sure they were blue, but he wasn't a hundred percent sure. He seemed to remember his eyes going with a brown suit and then blending in with green grass.

Maybe he would stick with the white robe.

The cloud hadn't changed. The sky was the same. He was still walking. He didn't wonder about things as much. He didn't wonder about the people he'd left behind. He'd long since forgotten who they were or what they looked like. He didn't wonder about anything he'd done when he was alive. Maybe he'd been a great tennis player or a musician or a successful businessman. It didn't matter anymore. He was here, walking on a cloud surrounded by clear blue sky. It didn't bother him that he was naked. Who was going to see him? The path he followed wasn't even a real path. It was just the way forward, a path marked only by his forward motion It wasn't like a path in the park where you might pass people walking their dogs, or mothers pushing strollers full of babies. This was a path of forward motion delineated by the coordinates of his body following his feet.

It was a path that left no prints, no trace of its past and no return.

It was a path forward.

But forward to what?

He wondered about that for a while. Given that he'd forgotten everything else, there wasn't much else to wonder about. Where was he going? What was in store for him? Would he spend infinity walking on this cloud? He seemed to recall sinking into it at one point, but the details were fuzzy. There was a feeling of air rushing past his ears, and then…nothing. But there was something just before that. He was sure of it. What was that?

"Thinking about me?"

Joey looked around. Cloud. Sky. Naked body. Nascent path.

"Hey, Joey…you do remember me, don't you?"

"You made me fall into the cloud."

"I think you might have that wrong. If you'd listened to me, you wouldn't have fallen into the cloud."

"So…what are you? Some kind of spiritual guide? An advisor?"

"Hey Joey…if you're looking for guidance or advice here…forget it Telling you not to walk back was the extent of it."

"You mean I'm on my own."

"That's about the size of it."

"But why even tell me not to walk back?"

"Something you already knew, Joey. Something you already knew."

"So who are you? What are you?"

"I guess I'm something that won't go away."

Joey thought about this. He wasn't sure how long he thought about it. He thought about it as he stepped forward on his path, step-by-step, along the misty firmament of the cloud through the clear blue sky. He thought about it until…

"Why won't you go away?"

"Well, Joey, I guess that's up to you."

"What do you mean…up to me? Why is it up to me?"

"The way things are."

"You know..." He searched inward for the rest of what he wanted to say. Most likely because he wasn't sure what he wanted to say. He thought deep into this as he followed the path that his steps defined, and it finally came to him: "You're really irritating."

"No argument from me."

"I'm not arguing. I'm stating a fact. You're irritating."

"Maybe that's what I'm supposed to be."

"Great. So why don't you go and irritate someone else."

"You know I can't do that."

Joey felt the fatigue bearing down on his being like a blanket soaked in the concept of weight itself. He felt heavy and he knew that, if he stopped walking, he would fall into the cloud and fall forever. He didn't want to fall forever, so he focused on walking even though lifting his feet became increasingly difficult, like they were encased in iron. His arms sagged like waterlogged seaweed. His neck barely supported his head. He looked around at the cloud and sky and said: "Hey, voice! You still there?"

"As long as you are, Joey."

"Why am I so tired?"

He wasn't sure how long he walked before he received a reply, but it seemed like a long time. It seemed like clouds rolling over clouds in slow motion for a long, long time.

"Maybe you're not tired."

"No...believe me. I'm tired. I can feel it. In fact, that's all I can feel...tired. I'm tired."

"Maybe yes, maybe no. Maybe what you think is tired is something else."

"And what else would that be?"

"Maybe you're just heavy."

"Going to offer me diet advice now?"

"I don't mean heavy with pounds of fat and gristle."

"So what do you mean?"

"Let me see if I can explain...you're dead, right?"

"Apparently, yes."

"So...your body is back where you left it and what you have now is not really your body." The voice paused. "Because you left it behind when you died."

"OK then. So how do you explain that I can see my arms and legs? I can see my lower body. I'm using my legs to walk on a cloud."

"Here's a clue...ever hear of a thing called persistence of vision?"

"Yes. Of course. It's when..."

He thought about this. Persistence of vision. Bit by bit, it began to make sense. He wondered how he could have missed something so obvious. How could he have been so stubborn? It started to make sense. The voice had a good point and the more he thought about what the voice had said, though he wasn't really sure anymore what that had been, the lighter he felt, the less tired. He forgot about is body. He forgot about the path. He forgot about his

thoughts as he walked straight into the infinite
comfort of the clear blue sky.

We Need to Talk

"We need to talk."

Sure, dead three years and now she wants to talk.

"I mean it, Charley. We need to talk. We have unsettled issues. We need to settle them."

"I'm not having this conversation with you, Susan. You're dead."

"You'll be dead someday too. You'll be here, where I am, Charley, and you won't be able to get away from it. We need to talk now. Get this over with."

"Why now? Why not when I'm dead?"

This was so much like her—bringing shit up right out of the blue, always taking me by surprise. But God, she's still so beautiful, even in death, floating a few inches above the living room floor, long white gown billowing from some unseen breeze, long ink-like streams of...

"I'm doing this for you, Charley."

"Sure you are Susan. Gimme a break. You never did anything for me. You were always about you. I can't believe you want to do rat shit for me now. Why would I?"

"Because I'm dead. It gives you a new perspective." She has that same old peeved look in her eyes, as though everything somehow pissed her off, as though the universe was constantly failing her. "Besides, that's not entirely true. I did lots of things for you."

"Name one."

147

"I faked orgasms. A lot of them. Pretty much *all* of them. You're not that great in the sack, Charley."

"You can take off now, Susan. Go back to wherever and whoever you're making miserable now. I'm over it. Over you."

"No you're not."

"It's been three years, Susan. I'm over you."

"You're still single. Haven't dated in three years. You still love me. You always will."

"You've been stalking me! You're dead and you're stalking me!"

"Charley, the dead don't stalk. We haunt."

I throw my arms into the air. "I'm not doing this, Susan. You're dead. Gone. And I don't still love you. I didn't love you when you were alive and I sure as hell don't love you when you're dead. So stop haunting me."

God, she has this…what? Sensual translucence in death. Or is this just the same lack of substance she…

"Go ahead, Charley, live the rest of your life in denial. But if you want me to stop haunting you, there's a few things we have to work out."

"When I'm dead. We'll work them out when I'm dead."

"Could you be more specific?

"What d'you mean…'specific'?"

There she goes with the head-cocked-to-the-side-because-you're-an-idiot look. "Dates, times?"

"You mean, when I'm going to die?"

"Duh."

You'd think that three years of death would give a person some insights on the errors of their former lives, like the inherent evil of being a controlling, manipulative...

"Well?"

"I'm not going to answer that."

Ignoring me, she looks around the room and her eyes stop on the couch I bought just hours ago. "Where's the red couch?"

"I sold it."

"I loved that couch."

"I hated it."

"You owe me an apology."

"A what?"

"You forgot my birthday."

"What the hell are you..."

"You forgot my twenty-second birthday, Charley. Didn't even buy me a card. No gift."

"Susan, that was ten years ago!"

"No cake."

"I'd just gotten back from a business trip. I was exhaust..."

"No flowers."

Again, right out of the blue. I can't believe this. "You didn't say anything at the time. Why now, ten years later?" I throw my arms up. "And why now, when you're dead?"

"I was afraid I might mention..." She puts fingers to her lips. She always did that when she pretended she'd let something out accidentally, but all she really wanted to do was tell me something she knew was going to piss me off. And I always fell for it.

"Mention what?" Still falling for it.

"You'll just get mad."

"Mention what?" Hook, line and…

"It was your fault. If you'd just remembered."

"What, Susan?"

She floats over to the new couch. A dark brown couch. Second hand. Comfortable. Exactly the couch she would have treated like a flea-bitten dog and never allowed past the door. She sits and crosses her long, long...

"You went straight to bed. I went out, met Jerry, went to his place…and had sex with him."

"You…?"

"Charley, drop the wounded face. It was only the third time."

"You had sex with other men three times?"

"No…sex with Charley three times. Don't even get me going on the others."

"You cheated on me!"

"You didn't give me flowers on my birthday." And now she leans forward, deliberately letting the top of her gown fall enough to show those beautiful breasts that I used to spend so much time... "Besides, it was only sex. You had my heart."

"You never had a heart."

"Look who's talking, birthday-forgetter."

"You cheated on me."

"Charley, we just covered that. Get over it."

She's winding my head up again, screwing my brain with her twisted logic, just like she did when she was alive. But, oh, those legs, those…what the hell am I thinking? She's dead. "You have to leave, Susan. Get back to being dead."

150

"Not until we're finished, Charley. And we're not finished."

"We were finished when you died. When you…"

"You told me once that you would follow me anywhere. You swore you would, Charley. You said, no matter where, no matter what, you would follow me to the end of time. You broke your word, Charley."

"Susan, you died."

"So? Has time ended?"

"*Your* time did."

"You didn't specify what time; you said, 'the end of time'. That's all time, Charley, *all* time."

"You expected me to die…just because you died? That's crazy!"

"No, Charley. That's love. That's commitment. That's keeping your promise. You didn't follow me."

"You were cheating on me."

"You didn't know that."

"But…"

"I told you, Charley, we already covered that. Get over it. You always get stuck on all the wrong details. A hug would have been nice. Flowers would have been better."

"If I buy you flowers, will you go away?"

"It's too late for flowers. I'm dead. Now, I have to settle for tormenting you eternally."

"You're going to torment me eternally because I forgot your birthday…just once…ten years ago?"

"You only turn twenty-two once, Charley. Just once. You never get to turn twenty-two again. You

151

missed something that was going to happen just once in my life and for all eternity, and now I get to torment you…forever."

"That's just plain vindictive, Susan."

"You only get one shot at twenty-two, Charley."

"And besides, all you said was that we need to take care of some unsettled issues. You said we were going to talk, get this all over with. And now you're talking about eternal torment."

She thinks about this a moment. "I changed my mind."

"You…"

"The dead's prerogative, Charley." She stands up suddenly. I step back. "You're not afraid of me are you?"

"No. You just took me by surprise."

She puts her hands on her hips. "Look, Charley, things didn't turn out the way I expected."

"I know. You died young."

She squints her eyes. "You didn't have anything to do with that did you?"

"Giving you a stroke? I don't think so."

She nods agreement. "What I meant is that things didn't turn out the way I expected here…in death."

"How so?"

"I expected clouds, halos, harps…flowers. But it's not like that."

"And just how is it?"

"It's work, Charley, work. We have to take care of things like balances in the universe, making sure that the properties of the universe are all in working

152

order. I saw a place about a thousand light years from here where they let gravity slip for just a few minutes. For a while, we were almost the only intelligent life in the universe, but we fixed it. These things take a lot of math. You know how much I hate math."

"That sounds really tough, Susan. But it sounds like you get to travel a lot. You used to love traveling."

"Do you have any idea how cold space is, Charley?"

"But you're dead."

"The view between galaxies is cold. It's dark. Empty. Cold." She runs her fingers from her cheek, down her neck to her chest as she says this with a faraway look. And suddenly snaps out of it. "But I'm doing something new now." She looks relieved, almost happy. "They're trying a new program, running a pilot project. And I'm in it."

"Well that sounds good, Susan. I'm happy for you. What is this pilot project?"

"Well…you're not going to believe this. I mean, when I heard, well, it just blew me away. The coincidence."

"Coincidence?"

"Yes! Of all the people in the world, I got you."

"Me?"

"You!"

"For what?"

"I get to be your guide when you die."

"My guide?"

"That's the pilot project! And I know, it's an old idea, this whole thing about the long dead guiding the newly dead, but it's never actually been done before."

"And you're going to be *my* guide?

"Isn't that wild?

"But you just said that you're going to torment me for eternity."

She thinks for a moment. "I changed my mind. Now, we have to talk."

"You can't just keep changing your mind…"

"We already covered that, Charley. Get over it. Like it or not, I'm going to be your guide in the afterlife and before that happens, we have to settle a few things."

"But there's nothing more to…"

"Look, Charley, I didn't ask for this. Luck of the draw. But it sure beats the math."

I shrug my shoulders in frustration. "So what else?"

"Watch the tone, Charley. I'm going to be your guide."

"OK. What…other things do we have to settle?"

"You didn't tell me I was beautiful before we left the apartment for the one time you ever took me to a play."

"But…"

"I bought a new evening gown just for that. I spent hours on makeup and had my hair done."

"I never took you to a play, Susan. You're getting me mixed up with someone else…someone you met before me."

"Maybe I should just go back to eternal torment."

"I said you were beautiful when you met me for lunch that time in the bookstore."

She thinks for a moment. "Hmm. OK, I'll let you off with the play incident. That might have been someone else."

"Before or after we met?" I say this sarcastically. Susan frowns.

"I'm not sure, Charley. Do you really want to know?"

"Is there anything else we have to talk about?"

"Lots of things. And we have to settle them quickly. After I guide you..." She puts a finger to her lips and looks at me as though she's just let something slip out. Once again I fall for it.

"Yes? After you guide me...?"

"Well, I suppose I can tell you since we already covered that...and you've gotten over it. After I guide you, I'm going to be guiding Jerry."

"Jerry? You're going to guide Jerry?"

"Charley, I only slept with him three times. Get over it."

"But Jerry's in the hospital with cancer. He only has a few days to live!"

"All the more reason to get things settled quickly, Charley."

"Susan! If he only has a few days to live and he's going to outlive me, then I only have a few days to live!"

"There you go again, Charley. Jumping to conclusions and focusing on all the wrong things. You always did that."

For a moment, I think I see a bright spot. "So...you mean that Jerry's going to live longer?

155

The cancer's going to go away? He's going to live a long life?"

"Probably not. The cancer's really advanced. I'd be surprised if he lasts more than a day or two. His own fault though. I told him to quit…"

"So when am I going to die?"

She looks thoughtful. "I don't know. Soon, I suppose. I just know that I'm supposed to guide Jerry after I guide you. So, how do you feel? Any pains, dizziness, rumblings? Anything that might be fatal?"

"I was feeling fine until you showed up."

"Headaches? Nausea? Bowels OK?"

"Susan!" She looks at me almost startled. Good. "When are you supposed to guide Jerry?"

"That's confidential information. Besides, I just know that I'm supposed to guide him after I guide you. They didn't give me any dates. Do you have any premonitions? Some people just know when it's their time."

"No! No premonitions. And I'm pretty damn sure it's not my time." A hopeful thought comes into my head. "How long does it take to guide me?" I'm thinking that, if it takes a long time, then Jerry's on his way to…maybe some kind of miraculous recovery.

"Not long."

Damn.

"Just a few basics: the math of maintaining creation, time management—eternity's a long time, you know—some yoga. The basics."

"So…exactly how long does it take. I mean, you're the guide."

156

"It's hard to say, Charley. Time is different when you're dead. You suddenly have lots of it. And there's no real day or night, no seasons. Besides, Jerry's a goner…soon. And you're a goner before him. Live with it."

"Susan, I'm not ready to die. I have things to do, places to go."

"Like, what and where?"

"Well…you know…things…places. All that stuff you do before you die."

"You're never going to do any of it, Charley. You never do anything. You work, you watch TV, you sleep. If your life were a restaurant, the menu would fit on a thumb tack."

"But I have…"

"I just remembered…there's a flower shop right by where you work. You could have stopped in for a few minutes. You could have bought me flowers."

"Susan! I'm going to die! Soon! And you're still going on about the flowers?"

"Look at the bright side…you won't be dying alone. I'll be here with you. How about numbness? Blurred vision?"

"Come to think of it, my throat feels a bit tight."

"Now we're talking. Difficulty breathing?"

"No! My breathing's fine. You almost sound like you want me to die."

"Charley, I'd like to start my new job sometime this century. You can be really inconsiderate, you know. Feeling any hot flashes, or anything?"

"Sorry to disappoint you, Susan, but no…"

157

"What?"

"My chest."

"Your chest?"

"It feels weird. Like it used to when I was a kid."

"You mean when you used to get allergic reactions?"

"Yeah, but I haven't had one of those in years." I start coughing. My throat feels like a vice is clamping in on it.

"Charley, when did you buy the new couch?"

"Today. Why?"

"Charley, did you get a second hand couch?"

"What does that have to do with…"

"You bought a second hand couch."

"I got a good deal." I'm coughing non-stop now and wheezing.

"It's probably full of fleas."

"Fleas?"

"You told me you almost died as a kid from an allergic reaction to fleas."

Suddenly, I can't breathe. I start gagging. Susan claps her hands together and smiles.

"Susan, do something!"

"I am."

"What?"

"Waiting to start my new job."

Some more gagging, some reddening of the face, and it's over. I look at Susan and she's beaming. "Now, that wasn't so bad, was it?"

I look at my body lying on the floor, spittle dripping from my mouth. I look irritated. "That's me."

"That *was* you." She extends her hand to me. "You said you had things to do, places to go. Well, you were right."

"But I meant…"

She wraps her fingers around my hand and tugs lightly. "Time to go, Charley. But, before we begin the, let's say…orientation…we need to talk."

After the Flood

"That was you." She extended her hand to me.
You said you were going to go. Well,
now we're on the

The city was muffled still, like sobs and
caresses after a lovers' quarrel, the quiet of
expended emotions and relaxing muscles. It had
been a time of war, war between the land and the
water, the invading brown boil spilling over the
boundaries of its geological cut through the land,
but now the water was receding. It was ending. The
quarrel. The war. An end to long days of detours
and traffic jams, the slow car-by-car crawl through
city streets throughout the days and evenings, the
quietly amazed witnesses with their cameras and
cell phones pointed at flooded street corners. Their
hushed remarks, slightly guilty, to be here reveling
in disaster.

There'd been nothing serene about the days of
rising waters. The panic, the closures, the empty
shelves in stores. These had been the days of late
arrivals, cancelled appointments, the bravery and
freedom of valid excuses for absence.

Karen looked down at tiny twigs and pockets of
river flux the water had left on the pavement as it
began receding into those dimensions called "river."
She pushed her foot forward and nudged a piece of
smooth bark-stripped wood back into the water with
the tip of her brown leather boot. She stood at the
edge of the retreating water where just two days
before, tall as she was, she would have been up to
her knees in the swirling deluge and she would have
been in imminent danger of having her legs crushed
by a dead log inches under the surface of the water.

160

But the flood season was over for now, for this year. It was mid-June and the water levels were lowering everywhere. The sun was out more often; the clouds seemed to have given up in exhaustion. Trees were budding. Plants were greening. The smell of dog and cat shit melting with stubborn snow banks inundated the city with the aroma of Spring.

In spite of the trying weeks behind her, Karen felt a sense of optimism and new beginnings. Possibly a time to rebuild?

Pumps hummed and sputtered like background music threading through the city.

By the side of the road, or what could be seen of the general pattern of the road under the shallowing water, was a sunken park used for concerts and markets in the summer. A statue of a large wide man with a serious expression rose out of the water like a copper giant re-born out of primordial water. Down the street, a group of children with three women ogled the flooded park, their eyes wide and their lips sealed by disbelief. Was that really the corner where they'd had a picnic lunch last summer? *Is that where we played tag?*

That's where we sat for the concert that Tuesday evening under a warm blanket of early summer air and stars. She caught herself. She wasn't one for dwelling on the past, she saw it as disposable. Hang onto this, toss that. *Focus on what feeds you and carries you into the next day.*

She'd made him happy. *His eyes laughed. His eyes glowed with pleasure, the pleasure I gave him.* She smiled at the thought of him enjoying her.

That's all she'd asked; that he would enjoy her as much as she enjoyed him.

But that was almost a year ago. *Almost a year*.

Down the street, one of the children, a girl about ten, took off a shoe and dipped her toes in the water. Even from her distance, Karen could see the initial shock in the child's eyes before she laughed and yelled, "It's cold."

Karen smiled. She unzipped her boots and took them off. Holding them in her hands, she thought, *Yes, time to get these feet wet*, as she stepped cautiously, but freely, into the water.

Coffee

She was more than deadly beautiful…she was coffee.

Steaming hot dark roast coffee.

I should have known better. I should have stayed away from her but here I was standing inches away with a gun pointed at her stomach. My mouth salivated at the thought of coffee wearing skin tight blue jeans. Her bright green eyes simmered like pools of quiet rage. She was calm, deadly. I wanted to run. I wanted to turn away and toss the gun, run like hell to the nearest bar and drink Scotch until my mind crumbled and I crashed onto the floor.

She smiled.

Oh shit.

She moved. The movement always followed the smile. I suddenly felt myself crashed on the floor. Without the Scotch.

"So, you thought you could kill me?" Her voice was cold and riveted, implacably tight. "You should know better by now."

I should have pulled the trigger sooner. Why didn't I? Why did I hesitate? What was this spell she held over me? So many questions and the answer standing right above me holding her hand out to help me up. She had my gun in her other hand, where it would be safe from my fears and anxieties.

We stood in the middle of a field in the middle of nowhere somewhere in the middle of something still in the making, like the beginning of a journey with no end in sight and I'd just had my boarding pass collected. It was too late now. She tossed the gun into the air where it turned into a cloud and rained down onto the ground causing green sprouts to wiggle and struggle out of nowhere, suddenly and surprisingly there.

I struggled for words, thoughts, an image of some sort to give form and meaning to my response. "I didn't expect you so soon." There. There it was. My excuse.

"Sounds like just another excuse to me," she said as she pulled me up almost to eye level, always just below her eyes. "You didn't really think you could get away from me, did you?"

Of course not. How could I? What was I thinking? "I don't think I'm ready. I don't think I can do this. Why are you here so soon?"

Infinite laughter tumbled out of her mouth like a swarm of bees pollinating the ground around us. Half drawn flowers popped up and half swayed in the full breeze of her breath. "Not ready is not an option," she said. "I'm here and I'm not going away until we've finished."

She was right. I was trapped. There was no escape. It was always the same. "I wasn't really going to pull the trigger. I mean, that would have been like pointing the gun at my own head and shooting. It wouldn't have worked out well for me."

"Now you're making sense. You're seeing things more clearly." Rainbow hair tumbled over her shoulders. Its shine warmed the ground under us. The flowers bulged with color. "It's always difficult to wake up after a comfortable dream."

I knew she was right. I just didn't want her to be right, but there was something reassuring in her words, something compelling and hopeful. I looked up at the cloudless sky. There was a hint of blue in the void but when I tried to focus on it, it seemed to slide off somewhere into the perimeters of my vision.

"So, what would you like to talk about today?" she said. "What does the world suggest?"

I suddenly felt as though I were standing before the maw of a bottomless cavern, standing in a puddle of slippery mud, afraid to look forward and too late to look back. "I think this conversation is over," I said. "I need to vacuum my carpets and stare at news reports. I have other things that need to be done."

"But you can't." She smiled. "You're here now, engaged with me." She raised her right arm and snapped her thumb and finger in front of my face. "Awake." The sound of the snap curled into the air like a sparkling blue diva and danced into the sky where it spread from horizon to horizon over the pure whiteness of the land. Grass grew under our feet.

The feeling of grass under my feet felt familiar and reassuring, like angst dissipating in the face of an unknown possibility. "Will you stay with me?" But I already knew the answer. It was the same as always.

Laughter, as she evaporated into the vistas of a blazing hot sun in a brilliant blue sky emerging over a forested landscape creating itself all around me.

100 People, 10 Bats and 1 Cat Blowing Up

The Office

It started as a vague awareness of something drifting in the air, a connection floating between the dust motes, barely perceptible by a sixth sense or whatever psychic warning that causes the herd instinct to stop and listen. Shiela Montgomery stopped chewing her mid-morning Coffee Crisp. Her eyes narrowed as her mind tried to tune into whatever it was that had just locked the room into an instant in time. Danny Yates' fingers halted their crazy keyboard dervish as his wrists pressed down against the cushioned tray, his fingers raised over the keys like vipers set to strike. Chloe Sanders cocked her head to the right and looked at the pipes and electronic circuitry in the ceiling as she thought, *Is this place going to blow up?* There had never been any doubt in her mind that someday the place was going to blow up. She'd always hoped it would happen on her day off or when she was on lunch hour. But no, here she was, sitting at her desk at the tail end of a monumental quality request form and the damn place was going to blow up. All those pipes and circuitry.

It was like a moment echoing between two solid walls of time so fast that its movement merged with time into motionlessness. So fast, it went nowhere.

Oh shit, thought Chloe Sanders.

The moment collapsed on itself with a furious shake.

Oh shit, thought Shiela Montgomery.

A distant rumble. And then the release.

Oh shit, thought Danny Yates, a split second before his skin peeled away from his bones and his bones disintegrated as the wave of nuclear hellfire tore through the office, the building and the city.

"That was intense," said Chloe Sanders.

"I guess I never really expected it to be that fast," said Danny Yates. "I didn't even have time to think about it. Did anyone else feel that rumble?"

"It seemed like it was a thousand miles away...and then...woop," said Arthur Williams, who'd been in the office all along, watching Chloe eating her Coffee Crisp and wishing that he'd had a chocolate bar as well.

"And I always thought it would be the pipes and circuitry that would blow us up," said Chloe, shaking her head in disappointment. How could she have been so certain and so wrong?

"Well," said Shiela Montgomery, "we finally got rid of that ugly ceiling. It made me feel like I was working in an oil refinery."

"Or deep down inside the city's sewage systems," said Olivia Portman, who had blue Wiccan symbols tattooed on both her arms. "Right down under the city with the stench and the salamanders." She'd been fantasizing having oral sex with Arthur as he watched Chloe eat her chocolate bar just before they all blew up.

Their location and surroundings were uncertain. They were aware of themselves and of each other and they were vaguely aware of the absence of things, like the ceiling. Their desks were gone along with their computers and swivel chairs. There were no walls, no windows, no floor. It was certainly a much different environment than it had been a few minutes before. Chloe's Coffee Crisp bar was gone before she'd had a chance to finish it and she felt a little ripped off by the timing of things. *The nerve: blowing a city up before people have a chance to finish their chocolate bars.*

"So...how do we enter this into our timesheets?" asked Jamey Dunlop, who was always asking stupid questions instead of trying to figure things out on his own. People tried to avoid him because he always had a question, even when he didn't. He just saw you and he'd ask a question.

"I don't think you'll have to worry about your timesheet anymore, Jamey," said Olivia, who was wondering if it would still be possible to have oral six with Arthur.

"I don't care if I ever have to fill out another timesheet for as long as I live," yelled Janet Campbell from over in PR. She hated numbers, and timesheets were all about numbers. "Timesheets suck!"

There followed an undercurrent of mirth, like dozens of people smiling together as though they'd just shared a large pizza with the works and a case of cold beer.

"But you can fill yours out if you want to, Jamey," said Danny Yates, smirking. He didn't like

Jamey, who annoyed him with stupid questions even when it was obvious that he was deep into coding and didn't want to be interrupted.

"OK," said Jamey. "How do I get to my timesheet from here?"

"Jamey!" said Alice Turnbill, a systems analyst who was in town once a month for team meetings and who felt a little picked on that the city would be blown up on the one day of the month that she was in town. "Just find 'here' first and take it from there. Easy-peasy."

Another undercurrent of mirth ensued. Some people were beginning to think that maybe being blown up wasn't such a bad thing. It sure beat that ugly ceiling. All those pipes and wires.

"OK," said Jamey. "How do you get to here?"

Stifled laughter. You could feel it holding its breath, beating hard against the urge to let loose.

"Why don't you try looking under the third brick to the left, Jamie," said Alex Gray, a consultant who'd been with the company for nearly three years and nobody actually knew what he did as he sat at his desk by the window with a beautiful view of the city. Andrea Carr from accounting suggested one day (by the water cooler, of course) that downloading porno was a fast rising corporate concern. She looked at Alex as she said this. Now, as far as the rest of the office was concerned, Alex Gray spent his days by the window with the great view of the city downloading porn. Nobody even suspected that he spent his days making entries into an online religious journal, a sort of diary in which he spent his days writing about his love for God and all of God's creations. For one week of each year, he wrote and published the company's annual glossy, full-color, twenty page letter to the shareholders about how well the company was doing and how safe the shareholders' money was with the company. Alex's job was to gather the photo images, write the text, put it all together in a publishing program, send it to the printers, hand the printed copies over to the chairman of the board who would then pass them on to the shareholders. It took Alex a week to do all this. He made $85,000 a year. But the shareholders loved their annual twenty page letter. Alex's words to Jamey were the first words many in the office had ever heard him say.

"OK," said Jamey. He was quiet for a moment. And then, "Does anybody know where the third brick from the left is?"

It was around this time that Danielle McLeod, a Level 1 Policy Analyst from the Compliance Division, realized that one of her arms was protruding from her chest. She noticed that the nail polish on the thumb was scorched. *Damn*, she thought.

Arnold Hicks from the mail room, who'd been in the office delivering mail when he was blown up, and who weighed close to three hundred pounds, saw his feet for the first time ever, sprouting from either of his shoulders. *So, what's holding me up?* he thought.

"OK," said Jamey. "I'm serious now. Does anyone know where that brick is?"

"Up your ass!"

170

A silence followed. No one knew where that voice had come from. No one knew whose voice that was. But there was a very distinct undercurrent of mirth to be felt. The voice came from Jasper Goudy, a sidewalk skeptic who spent his retirement days sitting on a bench outside the building passing judgement on passersby. He generally kept his opinions and judgements to himself, thinking them so loudly that he was certain the air in front of his forehead heated up with the energy of his thoughts. When he was blown up, he bounced off the top of a bus and bounded into the air, through a window and into Carla Fitch's top right desk drawer, where he became a vocal part of a desk. He wasn't sure where the rest of his body was, but he was certain that his head was in the desk. Carla, who was in charge of the company's eLearning program, was on vacation in Paris, which was being blown up at the same time as her desk was being blown up with Jasper's head in it. Coincidence?

"Yeah, Jamey," said Jennifer Likely, Director of Compliance Training. "Up your ass!" Jennifer had always wanted to say something like this to Jamey Dunlop. She hated his continual whining and questioning. But more than just saying "up your ass," she would have loved to strangle him to death or pour starter fluid over him and set him on fire. These were things she fantasized as she sat at her desk and watched Jamey asking other people how to do this and how to do that, or listened to him whining about some piece of software not working because he was too lazy to read the specs and there was nobody around him who'd used the software so

171

he had nobody to ask. On one occasion, she was stapling papers together when she heard Jamey whining about something and she thought how nice it would be to put staples in his forehead and eyes. She smiled as she stapled and fantasized. "Up your ass you fucker," she yelled. It felt good. "Fuck you, Jamey Dunlop, fuck you…fuck you. Ha ha ha ha ha!" Jennifer, though dead from being blown up, was having a wonderful time telling Jamey to fuck off. In fact, she couldn't remember ever having this much fun when she was alive. She was, after all, in compliance. What kind of life was that? She liked being dead. She got to tell Jamey Dunlop to fuck off. She got to say, "Up your ass, Jamey Dunlop." She smiled as the explosion did crazy things to her anatomy.

Garth Peterson wasn't as happy as Jennifer. He was in charge of enforcing workplace inclusion policies and he believed that people like Jamey, as irritating as they were, should be embraced by the corporate community and his annoying behaviors accepted by his co-workers. Garth was also a very sensitive man and felt a deep sense of hurt at the use of Jennifer's language, which, he felt was entirely inappropriate given her role in compliance. Garth's role was already tough given that all the people he worked with were white, straight, middleclass atheists. And none of them were handicapped. *Well, maybe now that they were being blown up.* Garth spent most of his workdays taking professional development courses on inclusion in the workplace. So far he'd taken one hundred and twenty-three courses on company time and company expense. He was an expert on inclusion and he'd hoped that someday the company would hire someone in a wheelchair or from a foreign country who didn't look like everybody else so that he could practice those one hundred and twenty-three courses on that person. He felt a bit piqued as he realized that his great hope had just been blown away.

Jason Hart was pissed. *This shouldn't be happening to me*, he thought. Jason was a branding evangelist. His job was to visit potential clients and lie religiously about the benefits of dealing with his company, and he was good at it. They paid him over half a million dollars a year to lie. Religiously. (Alex Gray was jealous of Jason Hart. He figured that, if he could work for a company for as long as he had with no one knowing what he did, then he could lie better than Jason and he should be the one making over half a million dollars a year. Plus, it would give him something to do.) Jason was pissed because he was supposed to meet with a potential client later in the afternoon and he'd been preparing his lies for weeks. They were beautiful lies about deliverables that wouldn't be anywhere near the quality of what he would promise, lies about timelines that no one in their right mind would believe...until they were steeply engulfed by Jason's lies. He'd even put together a PowerPoint presentation to visually enhance his lies. He had charts and graphs and anecdotes and statistics and meaningful graphics and photo images and quotes and excerpts and interviews and testimonials and recommendations and imaginary sources that he would mention in passing as he clicked quickly to

173

the next screen before the potential client had a chance to actually see the sources let alone ask about them. Jason was gifted at leading his victims down a cherry-walled path and into the trap. But today, he'd been blown up before the meeting and he was pissed.

Donna Hartley was a project manager who hated Jason Hart even though their names were sort of similar. Time after time, Jason had made promises to clients that she and her team had struggled to fulfill, usually unsuccessfully. And when that happened, she'd usually been left holding the shitty end of the stick while Jason went off to lie to another sucker and get her and the other project managers into more shit. She'd made complaints to senior management about Jason, but his lies were bringing in money and feeding their Christmas bonuses, so nothing was ever done about him. Not even a scolding finger. Donna wasn't too happy about being blown up, but she was happy in the knowledge that Jason was being blown up as well. If she'd had a mouth left, she would have smiled.

Carla Mason, a junior corporate intelligence analyst, had waked up that morning knowing that this was the day that she would be blown up. She'd been tempted to inform her boss, Jane Powel, about her findings, all of them pointing toward the city being blown up along with a large part of the rest of the world, but she'd finally thought, *No, let them read the newspapers and news sites themselves.* Besides, ever since the Christmas party when, in a drunken stupor, she'd told everyone about being attacked and raped by Egyptian hieroglyphics when she was a child, most people didn't take her seriously. But she was good at running errands and was willing to work evenings and weekends on meaningless projects, so she got to keep her job. As she was being blown up, she kind of liked the idea that she wouldn't have to work late.

Darren Leckie was an intermediate advertising copy writer who, like Alex Gray, had nothing to do. All the work he was supposed to do was farmed out to companies in India and Indonesia where they did the work of a team of Darrens for a fraction of one Darren's salary. His appearance in the company was symbolic. He represented everything the company stood for in its hiring policies to create local jobs. Basically, Darren was an imaginary persona for an imaginary policy creating imaginary jobs for imaginary people. He was almost relieved to be blown up and he hoped those assholes overseas were being blown up as well.

Cora Albright was probably the only person in the company who actually acknowledged Darren's existence. Cora was a Tier 4 Policy Implementation Specialist and the person responsible for hiring Darren so that if someone called the company about the advertising copy, they could speak to someone who spoke English. No one ever called, which pretty much made Cora's life even more meaningless than Darren's. Three days earlier, her doctor had told her that she had to give up drinking because her liver was on its deathbed and was going to take her with it in less than a year if she didn't quit drinking. But booze was all that kept Cora from exiting the building through the window instead of the elevator at the end of each day. She was feeling kind of groovy about not having to take that thirty storey ride down to another evening of vodka and orange. She was about to do the most significant thing she'd ever done in her years with the company, which was to join the chorus and yell, "Fuck you, Jamey Dunlop!" But her mouth was suddenly two blocks away from the thought.

Jenny's Got a Bat

Jenny Steward was eight years old. She smiled as she stood beside her mother in the lineup at the bank. Today was going to be the most special day of her life. She was going to take ten dollars out of her bank account, money she'd been saving for over a year, money she'd made from birthdays and from selling orange juice from her stand at the end of the driveway for 50 cents a glass. She had more than ten dollars, but ten was all she needed for now. She was going to buy a baseball bat and a ball. When she'd told her mother, her mother had smiled and said, "You're such a tomboy." She'd smiled so lovingly into her mother's eyes. Her father had said, "Just like Daddy's girl. I'll teach you how to use that bat." Another loving smile. Her brother had laughed and said, "Girls don't know anything about baseball, especially you." She hated her brother. He was mean and he pushed her around and bullied her. She stood beside her mother and smiled as she imagined getting home with the bat and the ball. She didn't need the ball, but it was necessary to get it so that no one would guess. It was going to be a huge surprise when she held the bat in her hands and used it to beat her brother to death. Outside, in the distance, she thought she heard a rumble. She ignored it. She was finally going to get rid of her brother.

Lisa Calloway hated banks. She hated walking into banks and standing in lineups while listening to the scribble of checks and forms becoming financial realities. She swore she could hear the ink flowing onto the paper and see in her mind's eye the greed glimmering in the bankers' eyes as a signature here and initials there shackled another human into a lifetime of debt slavery. She hated the subservient hush of the lines of sheep. She reached into her purse and ran her index finger along the cool metal barrel of the .38 calibre pistol she'd been practicing with at the range for the last two months. Her eyes burned with hatred.

"Everyone! Get down! On the floor! Now!"

Chad Everett watched himself as though he'd stepped out of his body and become an observer of his own actions. He yelled again, "Down! Right now! Everybody! Or I'll blow everyone up!"

People in the lineups, tellers behind counters, bankers and customers at desks and the two guards by the door stared in horror at the explosives wrapped around Chad's upper body. He stretched his right arm into the air where everyone could see his hand clenched around the detonator. "Everyone stay calm! Do as you're told and you'll all be OK. Get down now!"

177

He walked in a circle as he talked to give everyone a view of the explosives. Around him, people practically fell to the floor, some crying and whimpering, some annoyed that this bullshit was cutting into their lunch hour. *I'm in control,* he thought. *For the first time in my life, I'm in control.* It was an intoxicating thought for a man who'd been a victim all his life, a piece of human debris washed about wherever the tides of life and circumstance had taken him and never once in control of even a small piece of ripple in all those tides.

Lisa Calloway thought, *What the fuck?* As she lay on the floor, she debated whether or not to sneak the gun out of her purse and shoot this idiot with the bomb tied around him, but then she'd likely be blowing herself up. That wasn't in the plan. A part of her mind kicked up an alarm flag as it sensed a rumble in the distance.

"Everyone stay calm! This will be over soon!" Chad was impressed with himself. He sounded just like those guys in the movies when they robbed a bank…stay calm…this will be over soon. He fancied himself a natural pro at this. It was just as he was relishing this thought that the floor began to vibrate and there was a very distinct rumble in the distance that was suddenly a rumble just down the street and then it was washing the walls away and sheering the flesh off Chad and the others right where they stood and lay.

Just before his brain turned to steam, Chad thought, *Fuck, they told me it was a fake…*

Jenny Steward was disappointed that she wouldn't get a chance to beat her brother to death with a baseball bat. Gail Baker, one of the tellers waiting to be robbed by the guy with the bomb, managed a half smile as she thought, *Looks like getting off early to…* Daniel Turner's last thought gave him a warm feeling inside, *No more mortgage payments, I get to keep my money and…* And then the hot storm incinerated him where he stood. Charlie Beach felt the rumble, the vibration, the shake, and he felt regret as he thought, *Just when I was going to make the last car payment.* Judy Gumble, Tania Corbet and Sonya Turbin all thought the same thing as they lay on the floor, their plans to rob the bank together thwarted by some idiot wrapped in a bomb and then being blown up after cooperating with the asshole. What they thought was: *Shit. Damn.* And *Fuck.*

One way or another, it was a bad day for the bank.

And for everyone else.

To Be Eaten by Dragons?

Louise Harmon was obsessed with being blown up. As long as she could remember, she'd had fantasies about being blown up. Her favorite dreams were the ones in which parts of her body were flying all over the landscape. She read stories about people being blown up in Afghanistan and India and she was jealous. She couldn't understand why she'd been born into a small town a million miles away from where everyone was being blown up.

179

Louise, of course, had few friends. In fact, she had just one friend, Kyle Saunders. Kyle wanted to be eaten alive by dragons. Louise felt that she could respect Kyle's desire, even though she felt that her death wish was a little more realistic. And he didn't talk much about it. He just stated clearly and concisely, "I want to be eaten alive by dragons." And left it at that, which was fine with Louise because it meant that she could spend all their mutual time talking about being blown up.

"I mean, don't you think it would be cool to feel every cell in your body separating from every other cell in your body?" said Louise as she and Kyle sat on lawn chairs in his back yard. Kyle always nodded agreement, even though he thought it would be much better to have all your cells digested together inside a dragon's stomach.

"Can you imagine that feeling just before you feel the full force of the explosion?" she said dreamily. "I mean, that split second right before. What would that be like? Would it be heat? Numbness? A full-body itch? A tingle? I somethings think that it would be like picking the scab off a sore…like ripping up the top layer and then the next layer and the next." Kyle nodded agreement, noting mentally that his friend was missing the joy of feeling razor sharp teeth dicing her body into succulent portions ready to be swallowed.

"And just imagine…being completely evaporated. Can you imagine?" Louise's eyes were beginning to bulge a little with excitement. "Evaporated! I mean, turned into mist, gas, vapor.

Wouldn't that just be the coolest thing you could imagine?" Kyle nodded, but he really couldn't understand how Louise could miss the exquisite splendor of having her body torn to shreds by giant reptilian claws and tossed into a maw smelling of brimstone. What was wrong with her?

"I mean, nothing left of you but a giant hole in the ground where you were standing." She was beginning to froth at the mouth. "Your vapor mixing with the smoke and fire." Kyle nodded cautiously. It looked like Louise was about to explode just from wanting to be blown up. He imagined her head expanding so that all the parts of it separated into blood soaked projectiles and he had to admit...it seemed like a pretty cool idea. But it lacked the dignity of a mythic creature, something feared and revered through the ages. Something so fearsome you could stand proud and say, "I was eaten by a dragon."

Louise suddenly went silent. Her eyes sunk back into their sockets. She wiped the froth from her lips. "I don't know, Kyle," she said wistfully. "Is it too much to hope for? I mean, I could die tomorrow from a car swerving off the road and onto the sidewalk. Where's the beauty in that? Run down by a frickin' car."

"So ordinary," said Kyle, nodding agreement. "Everybody gets run down by cars."

"Exactly," said Louise. "I mean, why couldn't I have been born some place where people are being blown up more than they're being run over by cars. It's just not fair!"

Kyle forced a smile and said, "Don't worry, Louise. Some day you're going to be blown up. I just know it. You are."

"Really, Kyle?" she said. "You really believe that?"

"I sure do," he said. A smile curled across the lower half of his face. "I have an idea. Let's try something."

"Does it have something to do with being blown up?"

"Yep."

"Not being eaten by dragons? Blown up."

"Blown up."

"OK, what is it?"

"Let's both close our eyes and visualize being blown up."

Louise rolled her eyes. "Kyle...I do that all the time."

"But this time we'll be doing it together. A group effort. We both merge our energies and lift ourselves to another plane of being where you get blown up."

Louise laughed. "Kyle! That's crazy!" She punched him lightly on the shoulder. "But...OK. Let's do it. It might be fun."

"OK. But first we have to touch foreheads."

Louise looked at him suspiciously. "Kyle, if you try to kiss me..."

"I'm not trying to kiss you! Eeuw." He made a face convincing enough that Louise that he didn't ever under any circumstances want to kiss her.

She wasn't sure how she felt about that, but this game was starting to excite her. "OK," she said as she leaned her head forward.

Kyle did the same and they were touching foreheads. "Now," said Kyle, "put all your thoughts and energy into being blown up."

They both squinted their eyes as they concentrated. And concentrated.

After a few moments, Louise said, "You're not thinking about being eaten by dragons, are you, Kyle?"

"No. I'm thinking about your head disintegrating and spraying all over the walls and ceiling."

"OK. Good, keep focusing on that."

They squinted their eyes and...

"Did you feel that?" said Louise.

"I'm not sure. You mean the rumble?"

"Yeah. The..."

And in that instant, Kyle knew that he was never going to be eaten by dragons as he and Louise evaporated together.

A Bomb in the Bug

"OK," said Toby, "If they press Shift + Enter, the program displays Error Message 489.489.89."

"Brilliant!" said Alec and Gerald, as the gawked at the flow chart on the giant white board, thick with lines and geometrical shapes in red, green, blue and black.

Emory studied the chart. He didn't get it, but he was new in the swamp (the programmers' work area) and he didn't want to start off looking stupid by asking stupid questions. But the more he thought about it, the less it seemed like he would be asking a stupid question. *How could they miss something as basic as that?* he thought. He figured he must have heard wrong. "So," he said, tentatively, humbly. "They press Shift + Enter…and then what? Before they get the error message?"

The other three looked at him as though his head had just fallen off and none of them wanted to be the one to clean up the blood. "Emory, my lad," said Toby. "What company did you say you worked at before here?"

The question caught him off guard. *Why is he asking me that?* "Um…well…I wasn't really working for any one company. I did remote contract work for a few companies…until I could get in full-time some place…and…"

"Emory," said Toby. "You're not doing the piecemeal thing anymore. This is the big leagues. When you fuck up on a contract job, you don't get paid. When you fuck up here, you get more work."

Alec and Gerald grinned and nodded. Toby smiled sagely. Emory thought about this. It didn't make any sense to him. He finally gave in. "I don't get it."

The other three chuckled. Alec reached out and patted Emory on the back. "It's all about supply and demand," he said. "And demand is always more important than supply. Would you agree?"

"I…guess," said Emory. "But I don't see how that applies here."

"It's simple," said Gerald. "Once we supply the client with the product, that's it."

"Project finished," said Toby.

"Game over," said Alec, "and no more invoices. No more checks. No more pay for the company. No more raises…for us."

"But what does that have to do with giving and error message when the user presses Shift + Enter?" said Emory. "That's a standard combination for functions. They'll get an error message before they even press a function key."

"Exactly!" said Toby.

"He gets it!" said Alec.

"But I don't get it!" said Emory.

"We build demand into all of our products," said Gerald.

"They have problems with the software and we do patch work," said Toby. "It's written into the contract. And if they say it's our fault, we blame it on their operating system or browser…or any one of ten thousand other things they'll never understand."

"Mostly," said Alec, "they just say fuck it and sign off on the patches. They just want to get things working because they're losing money if they aren't working."

"People don't expect better from software these days," said Toby. "And they don't want to do anything about it themselves so they get somebody else to do it."

"And that would be us," said Gerald.

"But what if we gave them software that worked," said Emory, "and the client was happy and recommended us to other clients and…"

"Tried that with other companies," said Alec. "All of them out of business now."

"You find out where the money is and you squeeze it dry," said Toby. "Only thing that works. Only thing that keeps you in business. The never-ending patches. And sometimes they'll even go for upgrades and add-ons if you keep them on the line long enough."

"It's the way things work, Emory," said Gerald. "And it's not going to change anytime soon."

"But what if we can change…" Emory shut his mouth in the face of three incredulous faces.

"That…" said Toby, "would be the day the world blows up."

"Even you just saying that…" said Toby, who suddenly perked his head as though trying to hear something. "Did anybody here that?"

"Hear what.."

And that was the day their world blew up. Thanks a lot, Emory.

Slurping Coffee

Bonita Valdez loved slurping her coffee, as in…she never sipped. No, that would be a waste of good coffee according to Bonita. "You have to slurp it to get the full taste. It has to be noisy to be tasty." Some people swore that she inhaled her coffee with the gusto and volume of a steroid-pumped-up metal band from hell to the extent that you could feel her drinking coffee from two blocks away. Dianne Swazey watched in horror as Bonita lifted the cup to her mouth. Dianne hated Bonita. They both arrived at the Bayside Coffee Shop at the same time every morning. They worked in different buildings, but they went to the same place for coffee. Dianne had no choice. It was the closest coffee shop to her work, the only one close enough that she would have time for a coffee and there was no way she was taking it back to the office and get stuck working on something on her coffee break. She was trapped. She had to listen to that "fat horse bad-hair-day-everyday loud insufferable bitch" drink coffee like a pig at the trough. Dianne wanted to look into Bonita's eyes as she strangled her to death and say things into her dying eyes like, "Didn't expect this on your coffee break today did you, Bonita?" "I hate you. I hate you. I hate you."

Things like that. But there she was, the cup inches away from her mouth, her lips parting slightly to breath in the coffee, getting ready to announce to the entire coffee shop that she had coffee. Dianne's finger tips tingled. She wanted to feel them on Bonita's throat. The cup was just about to touch Bonita's lips. Dianne cringed. The lip of the cup touched the lower lip of the pig monstrosity and Dianne closed her eyes wishing that she could cover her ears, but that would probably make Bonita slurp louder, make the others in the coffee shop point at her and giggle. Just as Bonita was about to slurp, the wall behind her disintegrated and all the disintegrated parts of it streaked right through

187

Bonita, disintegrated her before she could slurp. *Oh thank God*, thought Dianne just before she disintegrated along with Bonita.

Oh thank God, thought Doris Hanover, who was sitting two tables away from Bonita and had been fantasizing strangling her to death for almost two years.

Oh thank God, thought Barb Watters, who wanted to run across the room, grab Bonita by the hair and pound her face into the table over and over as she shouted, "I hate you! I hate you! I hate you!"

Oh thank God, thought Damien White who'd been secretly in love with Dianne for over a year but was too shy to approach her. Instead, five days a week, he watched the woman he loved suffer from the sounds of the "the large one's" inexcusable bad manners. The metal knife he was holding as he thought about walking up to Bonita's table and slashing her throat turned to liquid in his hand as his hand turned to ash and roared away with the coffee shop.

Shit, thought Bonita as her lips flew away from the cup's rim, denying her the pleasure of sharing her coffee with the rest of the customers.

Sweet Dreams, Sweet Chelsea

Chelsea Landing stared in the direction of the city. The early evening light was disrupted by a blinding flash. She felt a little woozy. The sleeping pills were starting to kick in. Soon it would all be over. The pain would be gone. She wouldn't have to wake up to another hateful day in the hateful trap she called her life. She wouldn't have to go work and sit on the outer peripheries of an office full of faceless people. She wouldn't have to come home to an empty apartment with a sink full of dirty dishes and curtains that had kept light out of her living room for months. She wouldn't have to stare at a television screen as meaningless events and characters swept by her attention while her mind focused on trying to focus on anything outside her mind. She'd almost felt a sense of joy, certainly of release, as she swallowed one pill after another, one by one, swallow by swallow, until the bottle was empty. The wooziness felt good.

*Oh well, may as well or may as well not...sleep it away or blow it away hahaha ha...*thought Chelsea as she joined the startled gasp of an entire neighborhood escaping the traps of their lives.

You Are Not Connected

Shawna Gorman was the ultimate phonie. She lived *for* her cell phone, she lived *by* her cell phone and she lived *in* her cell phone. She was the fish and her cell was the ocean, and trips to the surface were suffocating excursions into a world that had ceased long ago to be real for her. If it wasn't contained in a text or Facebook message, it wasn't real. If it didn't appear in a tweet or Instagram image, it never happened. She knew she could make calls on her cell and actually talk to other people, but why would she do that? What would she say?

Today, she was having some afternoon sex with her boyfriend, Mark, who she'd met on a dating site. He could text faster than anyone she'd ever met and it excited her to see how soon he could get a message back to her after she texted him. It was like he was responding as she was texting. She was texting him now, telling him what a great a fuck he was as he was text-fucking her. It was so much more exciting this way. And she would have the messages stored in her account, almost like a scrapbook of their sexual encounters. And some of the selfies were just plain delicious. She had a whole library of selfies of herself coming with Mark and sometimes she posted them publicly with the message: *Real or posed? You guess.*

Everyone pretty much guessed right.

She was just about to take another selfie of herself coming with Mark when suddenly…her connection broke, not with Mark (she could easily deal with that) but with her phone (which was not so easily dealt with). She pushed Mark's body off her and sat straight up, gazing in horror at the message on her screen: *You are not connected.* Mark, still in heat and wondering why his penis was suddenly getting cold, checked his phone to see if he was still with Shauna. The message on his phone didn't make any sense. *Not connected?*

Mark looked at Shauna. Actually looked.

Shauna looked at Mark. Yes, *looked*.

They both looked confused as first their ears, and then their noses and lips tore off their faces and rushed off to their final connection.

190

One for the Road, Roy

Everyone in the Cliff Edge bar was quiet. There was something in the air. No one could put their finger on it. It wasn't like anything any of them had ever experienced before. Christine felt it as a faraway tingle somewhere in her body. She didn't really have enough time to pay much attention to it, being on a monumental self-pity trip and all. She was on her third White Russian and if she'd had enough time to think it, she might think, *what's that?* But at times like this, timing is everything.

Four stools to her left, Jake was busy drenching his soul in cheap Bourbon. He felt the tingle as well but didn't have time to switch from feeling sorry for himself for being laid off from his third job in as many months because you could dress Jake up in an expensive three piece suit (as he was now) but you couldn't take him to work. Strike three! Yer out! And he was. His parents took his key to the house. They stopped him right at the front door, pushed three suit cases at him and took his keys to the house. Now Jake was faced with the terrifying prospect that he might actually have to find a job…and keep it.

Roy felt it. In fact, he was the first. As the bartender, it was his job to instinctively and immediately sense anything out of the ordinary in the bar…and this sure as hell wasn't ordinary. He felt it all over his body, like a buzz under the skin. It interrupted his train of thought as he looked at his tip jar: "Cheap…"

Fatima was about as close to a living ornament as any bar could have. No one could recall her not sitting at the end of the bar. No one could recall her ever ordering a drink, though there it was, right inside her cupped hands…a half-finished Manhattan. Even Roy sometimes wondered where those Manhattans came from. It seemed that her eyes never moved and it was never apparent where, exactly, she was looking. Fatima never thought about anything. She never spoke (except, theoretically, to order another Manhattan) and she never moved. She was the perfect ornament. At this particular moment however, she sensed a fluttering rushing through all the nerve endings of her body, but she was too much the ornament to acknowledge it.

Sitting at a table behind Jake, Rhonda, who'd just been fired from her middle management job for having sex with one of the mail clerks, eyed Jake closely. She'd seen him come in and immediately calculated his net worth as an extrapolation of his expensive suit. She concluded that he could afford her and all she had to do was come up with a good pick up line. She considered spilling her drink on him, but the suit was expensive. She considered spilling her drink on herself, but that would seem too clumsy. She was just about to come up with the perfect approach when she felt a strange tingling.

Chet was drunker than he was ten minutes ago, which was drunker than the previous ten minutes but not as drunk as he was going to be ten minutes from now which was about as drunk as he was yesterday at this time and the day before at this time. Chet measured the minutes and hours of his life by the sip. Ten sips, ten minutes. Sixty sips, one hour. It was all he was aware of, all he ever thought about. Sips. He didn't even feel it…like the others. He was too focused on sips.

They dressed in similar blue plaid shirts and navy blue corduroy pants with matching blue suede shoes. Dale had short blond hair and Ronny had short black hair. No…they weren't twins. They were both in love with the same woman, a woman with a penchant for plaid, corduroy and suede in her men. Until a few hours ago, Dale and Ronny were both living with the woman they mutually loved who, the previous day, had met a man with a ten gallon hat, a red checked shirt and dirty blue jeans. She told them that her taste in fashion and men had changed and that living with two men was confusing. She told them to pack their things and leave because her ten gallon new boyfriend was moving in that afternoon. Dale and Ronny were confused and wondering what had just happened. They barely noticed their mutually dressed bodies beginning to hum somewhere deep at the cellular level.

Everyone in the bar saw the flash and the rush as everything swept away, giving them just enough time to re-live their entire lives and gather whatever wisdom they could glean. Or, in lieu of wisdom…they might have one last thought.

Christine: "What's…"

Jake: "Shit."

Roy: "…bastards."

Fatima: "…"

193

Rhonda: "Hey you…"
Chet: "Eight."
Dale: "?"
Ronny: "?"

A Cut Above

Kelsey Marie stared angrily into her eyes as she thrust her face closer to the mirror. "I'm sick of the hypocrisy!" She lifted her right arm with her fist balled around a red paring knife and stabbed her reflection in the mirror. The knife snapped in half. But that was OK…she had a 'selection of various colored paring knives on the counter. She opened her hand and let the red handle drop into the sink and picked up a blue knife. It was short, with a viciously serrated cutting edge. She looked into her eyes…wide, dark and teary. *Life*, she thought. *Why does it have to be so messy and cluttered?* She cocked her head to the right as her expression changed from outrage to sympathy. "You poor thing," she mumbled. "You're such the poor little victim of the assholes who run it all." Sudden anger exploded in her eyes and she straightened her head. "And you let them do this to you!" she screamed. "You let them do this to you!" She stabbed her reflection again. The blade snapped off the handle and sliced into the palm of her hand. Blood flowed down her arm to her elbow. It dripped off the end of her elbow into the sink. She seemed confused, not quite comprehending what she was seeing. "Look," she said, nodding to her reflection as though the reflection shared her amazement and would look into the sink on its own. "Look what they've done to you." She opened her hand and the blue handle dropped into the sink beside the red handle. She snatched a yellow knife, gripping it tightly and forcing blood to surge around the blade in her palm and spill down her arm. She stared into her eyes. "You promised yourself you wouldn't let them do this to you again. You promised. But you did, didn't you." She thrust the knife slowly toward her reflection without hitting the mirror several times before lifting it over her head and bringing it down fast across the right side of her face. A thin red line appeared from the top of her eye, across her cheek and down to her chin. Tiny bulbs of blood spurted from the line and ran down her face, flowing into each other to form large drops of blood at the tip of her chin. The drops splashed into the sink. "Now look what they've done to you," she said with a quiet, shaky voice. "Look what they've done to your face. You're not pretty anymore. They've taken your prettiness." The shake dropped from her voice, replaced by an ominous resolve. "But you know how to stop them, don't you? You know how to make them fuck off, don't you?" She stabbed her reflection again. Blood streaked over the mirror and her reflected face. The knife twisted in her hand and the serrated edge slid across her fingers, cutting into them at crazy angles. She opened her hand and stared in horror at her bleeding fingers. "They just won't stop! They won't stop!" Holding the tip of the knife with her left hand, she gripped the handle, lifted her arm over her head and brought the knife down across the left side of her face. She smiled at her reflection in the mirror as she watched the blood streaming from the left side of her face merge with the blood from the right and alternately pour and drip into the sink. "There," she said authoritatively. "They won't fuck with you again. Ever!" She turned to the right, dropping the knife into the sink and reaching her arm out to grab a towel from the wall just as the wall smashed into her face and her body burst into flames for an instant before all the rage that she was flashed into the charging fireball.

And they wouldn't fuck with her anymore.

High School Confidential

Jason was in love with Hannah. She sat in the row to his right, three chairs forward. He loved the way her long blonde hair flowed over her shoulders and showered down the back of her blue dress. The back was cut low and islands of flesh peeked through the shower of blonde. For Jason, natural science class was a forty-five minute erection that lasted after class, all the way home and into his bedroom where he filled his hand with thoughts of Hannah.

Clark was also in love with Hannah. He sat in the row to the right of her, five chairs behind her and two behind Jason, where he could keep an eye on his unlikely rival. Clark had an advantage over Jason. He was popular, Jason was obscure. *Who the hell do you think you are, staring at my girl, you fucking loser*, thought Clark as he watched Jason watching Hannah.

Hannah wasn't technically Clark's girl yet. He was going to ask her out after school today. She would, of course, say yes. After all, look who was asking her out. A group of the school's most popular students would be watching. Hannah would see them. She would be flattered. Honored. She would blush and say, "Yes. Of course, Clark...I'll go anywhere with you." Yep, Clack had things pretty much sown up with Hannah. She was his girl.

He pulled on the paper clip attached to the elastic held between his thumb and forefinger and let the paperclip loose. It shot across the aisle and straight into Jason's neck.

Jason's entire body started at the sting. He slapped his right hand to the spot where the paperclip had hit. He turned and saw Clark smiling cruelly and giving him the finger. His erection quickly sagged into self-remorse. But that wasn't going to stop him from asking Hannah if she'd like to do something after school. He didn't know what, but he'd think of something. Or maybe he'd just go home and jerk off.

Hannah's nipples were erect again, and they would be erect for the rest of the class and all way home and into her bedroom. She was in love with Rachel, who sat in the row to her left and one seat ahead of her. She loved the way Rachel's long chestnut hair cascaded over her shoulders and fanned out across the back of her dark brown blouse. She looked down at Rachel's long legs stretching out from her olive green mini dress and

197

fantasized kissing those legs from the knees, up to her inner thighs and burying her head in paradise.

Today's the day, she thought. Today, she was going to ask Rachel if she'd like to hang out after school, maybe go for a coffee and maybe go back to her place and listen to music or watch a movie or get naked. Well, naked would come later. Hannah's parents were gone for three days and she and Rachel had all the time they needed.

Rachel loved natural history class. It brought her and Jason into the same room for forty-five minutes. She fantasized feeling his eyes on her hair as it splashed over her shoulders and across her back. She could almost feel his eyes on her. She imagined him leaning on one arm so that he could peer around the students in front of him to get a glimpse of her. She knew he was interested. He smiled at her in the lunchroom yesterday. She knew that she was a few pegs above him in the social scheme of things, but he was cute and brainy and he had a nice ass. What more could a girl want? He could help her with her homework. And he'd be so grateful to have her as his girl that he wouldn't ever think about being with anyone else.

Rachel decided that it was time to make Jason a happy boy. *After school today. Right after school.*

Janet Granger, aka Miss Granger, hated teaching. She hated her students. They spent most of their time staring down at their cell phones. She could see the light from the cells shining up into their faces. *Fuck them*, she thought. *I'll flunk every god damn one of them.*

Except Clark.

Janet Granger, aka Miss Granger, was in lust with Clark. There was something in his bearing that suggested a man inside, a man who could satisfy her throughout the night. Plus, he was devastatingly handsome. And he was popular with the students. He was the kind of man Janet always wanted in high school but, even though she was exceptionally good looking, she was quiet and shied away from relationships. The popular kids had always regarded her with suspicion.

But not anymore. She was a woman now. University had stripped her of her timid virginity and she really couldn't see anything wrong with getting it on with a man seven years her junior. What was seven years in the grand scheme of lust? When they were in her bed naked together, they would be a man and a woman…in bed…naked…together.

Janet made up her mind that today was the day to make those first advances. She would hint that something might be possible. Maybe some quiet flirting. Didn't every boy want to have sex with his natural science teacher? She had just the plan to get things started.

The bell rang. School was about to end for the day.

"Clark," said Miss Granger. "Could I see you for a moment before you leave?"

Tiny spikes of panic filled Clark's stomach. He had to get to Hannah before she left. "But Miss Granger…"

"It'll only take a moment."

Clark plopped back down into his chair, his head filled with thoughts of strangling his natural science teacher to death. Miss Granger, sitting at her desk, surreptitiously undid the top two buttons of her blouse, revealing some very acceptable cleavage.

In the hall, Hannah went straight to her locker, which was two lockers to the right of Rachel's locker. She was a ball of excitement ready to bounce with the woman she wanted more than anything in the world. She stared into her locker, waiting for Rachel. How would she start? Maybe something like, "Say, Rachel, would you like to go for a coffee? We've been in the same class for three months now and I hardly know you." She felt a finger touching her shoulder and felt a thrill rush through her body. *It's Rachel.* She turned her head. It wasn't Rachel. It was that pesky Jason kid who was always eye-balling her. Just as she was about to tell him to fuck off, Rachel came up one side of him and put her hand on his arm. Jason turned to face her.

"Hey, Jason," said Rachel, all beautiful smiles and legs. "Would you like to go for a coffee? I mean, we've been in the same natural history class all term and I hardly know you."

Jason's mind went numb. Rachel was just as beautiful as Hannah, but Hannah, though he loved her dearly till the end of time, was an unknown. Would she go out with him or would she tell him to fuck off? Rachel, who was just as beautiful as Hannah, was a sure thing. It was too much for him to comprehend. His brain froze.

Rachel's mind was in full gear with the pedal to the floor. "Why, hi Rachel," she said coyly. "Jason and I were just going for a coffee. Would you like to join us?"

Rachel wasn't sure what to think, but here was a chance to get to know Jason better. And maybe the three of them could become friends, though she would be much friendlier with Jason. "Sure, I'd love to go for a coffee."

Just as Jason's mind was beginning to thaw from shock enough to say something, a pallor fell over the hall. The lights flickered and the earth rumbled in some faraway region that seemed to have no direction but have every direction. In an instant, his brain went from frozen to fried, from confused to resolved.

Hannah, still smiling coyly, was suddenly one with Rachel as their bodies slammed together and fused into one thing before being swept into the hallway walls.

It's uncertain what happened in the classroom.

Pushing It

"Damien, please don't do that." Judy's voice was calm as she reached down and picked up the magazine her son had just deliberately pushed onto the floor. The table beside him had a stack of them and this was the second one he'd pushed over the side. Judy put the magazine on top of the stack and looked at her son with a mixture of exasperation and understanding. "You mustn't do that. Now, please, don't do that again."

The waiting room for Dr. Benjamin Canney was small and hot with merciless metallic chairs and fluorescent lighting from the fire pits of hell. There were no pictures on the pale green walls.

Across from Judy and Damien, Ward Andrews shifted uncomfortably on his metal chair. After his last bowel movement, about an inch of his hemorrhoids were still protruding from his sphincter. He was in pain. The bowel movement had been small and he was bloated with constipation. He was tired and cranky and all he wanted at the moment was to slap the little bastard who deliberately pushed the magazine onto the floor. He'd watched as the little bastard pushed it slowly over the top of the stack, eyes on his hand, as his mother said, "No, Damien, don't do that."

Pushing it slowly.

"Damien, I said don't do that."

Over the top of the stack.

"No, Damien. Stop that right now."

Off the stack.

"Damien. Don't."

Onto the floor.

"Damien, I told you not to do that."

He'd watched as the woman bent over and picked up the magazine and he'd thought, *Lady, smack the little fucker in the head with the magazine.*

Two excruciating chairs to Ward's left, Laura Richter barely kept her eyes open. She'd been five days without sleep and even if she did close her

202

eyes she'd still be wide awake. Sleep had deserted her. She was barely aware of anything happening around her. Everything seemed like a long boring dream. Only one thing broke through her wall of dream. A woman's voice. A name. Damien. The woman's voice saying the same stupid things over and over and over. Laura wanted to smash the voice. She wanted to walk across the small room, grab the woman's tongue and rip it out of her head.

The magazine was back on the top of the stack. The boy moved his hand over the table and placed it on top of the stack. He glanced briefly at his mother and moved the magazine slowly, inch by inch.

"No, Damien."

Dennis Lockhart sat in the chair next to Ward. If you were to look very close at his hands, you would see the tremor. Dennis' whole body was tense and shaky. His mind was a puddle of worry. There was something in his left lung. A nodule. It was in the x-ray. A nodule…and they weren't sure what it was.

"It could most likely be just some scarring," Dr. Canney had said. "But, we'll get a CAT scan just to be on the safe side."

The safe side? Today, Dennis was going to find out just how safe that side was. The uncertainty of the situation had done some strange things to him. He'd been spending money a little more freely, perhaps too freely. *But what the hell…it's only money.* And he was talking to God a little more. Making up to him. Paying more attention to the spiritual side. If Dennis were a gambler, he'd be known for always hedging his bets. For the last

203

week, whenever he'd heard someone sneeze, he'd mentally said, "Bless you."

At this moment in his life, he was in a forgiving mood. God was forgiving and so Dennis would be.

"Damien, please don't do that," said Judy as she watched her son slowly push the magazine across the stack.

Lord, please forgive that young boy for being a nuisance and a burden on his mother, thought Dennis.

"No, Damien, stop it," said Judy.

Lord, please forgive that woman for not knowing the first thing about how to raise a kid.

The magazine slipped off the top of the stack.

"Damien, how many times do I have to tell you not to do that?"

Lord, I know there must be some good in that child, somewhere, hidden deep inside that child somewhere, and I pray that you allow that goodness to flow up into that child and make him a good little boy, even though his mother may not be deserving of a good little boy.

The magazine slid slowly across the table, over the side and onto the floor.

"I told you not to do that, Damien. Now, stop it," said Judy as she bent over to pick up the magazine.

Lord, failing goodness in this child, is it possible that there might only be evil and now would be a good time to strike him down? Just wondering. Amen.

Lady, thought Ward, *make that little fucker stop it or I will. Stupid little brat.*

204

What is wrong with that woman? thought Laura. *What is wrong with you? Why don't you do something instead of just saying the same thing over and over? I want to kill you.*

The magazine was back on top of the stack. Damien moved his hand slowly toward the stack. This time, he looked square into this mother's eyes. His face was blank. He just stared into her eyes as he placed his hand on the magazine.

His mother stared back. "Don't, Damien. I told you not to do that."

Judy's face flinched as she bent toward Damien to warn him again. She put her hand over her stomach, where the bandage was, covering the cut from the knife, where her son had stabbed her that morning. It wasn't deep. It wasn't serious. No need for the emergency room when Dr. Canney could fit her in. And she was sure that it was just an accident. She was afraid her son would hurt himself playing with the knife. Maybe she shouldn't have tried to take it from him so quickly, but she was worried that he would cut himself. Surely to God it was an accident.

The magazine slid across the top of the stack

"I'm telling you, Damien."

Stop telling him and start slapping him, thought Ward.

Lord, please smite him, thought Dennis

I want to stick my fingers into both your eyes, thought Laura.

The magazine slipped off the stack and slowly slid across the table.

"Stop that right now."

205

Take the fucking magazine and spank the shit out of him with it, bitch.

Lord, please make him go away.

How can you be so stupid? How can you be so stupid?

The magazine slipped over the side of the table and onto the floor.

"Damien!"

And, simultaneously...

"Lady, will you do something about that fucking kid!" yelled Ward.

"He's not listening to you. You have to *do* something," said Dennis.

"Where do you get off calling yourself a mother!" yelled Laura.

Judy and Damien stared at the three with wide unbelieving eyes.

Very subtlety, a smile began to appear on Damien's mouth. It stretched wider as he looked first at Dennis, then at Ward and finally at Laura. The three saw the smile and wanted nothing more than to do terrible things to him. He reached down and picked up the magazine. He put it on top of the pile, looking into the eyes staring at him, smiling at them. Just as he was about to start pushing it, the magazine burst into flames along with his hand and his smile.

Howard and Darlene

"That's right...run off to the washroom and feel sorry for yourself again," said Darlene. At just five

206

feet nothing, the depth and power of her voice was astounding. It cut through the walls, the ceiling and the floor and permeated the lives of the apartment dwellers surrounding her and her husband, Howard. Everyone in the building hated her, but the power of her voice towered so far above her that no one messed with her self-proclaimed right to make her husband's life a daily torment.

Howard was six feet seven inches tall and weighed two hundred and sixty-five pounds. He was often referred to as "the gentle giant." More often he was referred to as "that poor man." He crossed the livingroom and disappeared into the hall. Darlene waited for the washroom door's lock mechanism to click before throwing another fusillade of insults at him. "Every time! Every time I try to get through to you! You run to the washroom! And you call yourself a man!"

Howard pulled down his pants and sat on the toilet. He propped his elbows on his knees and rested his face between his hands. He blanked out his wife's voice and let his mind drift into happier times, years before when he first met Darlene Hubbard in college, when she was young and beautiful and encouraged him to be his absolute best. He recalled phrases like "you were meant for this," "you can do this," "I have faith in you."

She'd been the most loving and supportive person he'd ever met.

Until they married.

It was like someone had waved a wand over them and said, "Act II, Tragedy."

Suddenly, Howard wasn't meant for anything, he couldn't do anything and Darlene didn't have an iota of belief in him. He guessed that she'd expected a big house, new car, new furniture and whatever else the day after the marriage and when that didn't happen, she simply gave up on him and made every day of his life a clear reminder that she'd given up on him.

"Bartender!" she yelled. "I married a damn bartender!"

Howard thought about how they'd met when he was working at the Ranch Grill bar just outside the campus. Love at first sight.

"And that's all you'll ever be!"

She'd worn a black knee high skirt with a red blouse and her eyes were wide and focused right into his soul. He was pouring a beer, most of it onto his hand, until the customer whose beer he was pouring (mostly not into the glass) noticed where he was looking and said, "Her name's Darlene. She's single. And there's a reason for that."

But Howard was too stricken to hear what the customer said other than "Darlene" and "single."

"I could have married Noah Winters," she yelled. "He has his own business. You hear that, Howard? His own business. He sells hats. Baseball hats. He's making a fortune."

She'd sat at the bar all evening and waited for him to cash out. They'd gone straight to her place and stayed there the rest of the weekend. She was his first.

"You'll never own your own business," she yelled. "No, not you. Always happy to work for other people, live on measly tips. Never get anywhere."

She'd always, right from the start, been a bit on the bossy side, but Howard didn't mind that. It took the burden of decision-making off his shoulders and made life much simpler for him.

"We'll spend the rest of our lives in this dump!"

It was so much nicer then. Before they were married.

"That's right! Hide in the bathroom! Hide away from the complete failure you've become! Hide away from ruining my life! Hide away from this dump we live in! Hide away from..."

He felt the distant rumble and the blazing fast approach of the death tide.

He smiled.

The Lonely Dead

Judy Baker knew the truth. She'd known it for years. It was something she lived with each day, day after day, year after year. She knew it when she looked into a mirror and stared into the abyss of her eyes. She knew it when she floated through the bustle of hundreds of people on busy downtown sidewalks. She acknowledged its crystal truth when she sat at her desk at work and nobody, absolutely nobody in the office, suspected a thing. But Judy knew.

Judy Baker knew the truth.

She was dead.

She'd been dead for years but for some reason she was still hanging in there with the living, occupying space, sharing the air. She was still getting paychecks. She was still eating and drinking and taking showers. But there was no doubt in her mind that she was dead.

It started one morning when she woke up feeling...different. Everything around her seemed foreign and dreamlike. She felt no sense of ownership over the bedroom or anything in it, including her husband, still asleep and snoring. She walked out of the bedroom and down someone else's hall and into a bathroom that looked familiar but wasn't hers. At least, not anymore. It was all one big existential puzzle until she looked in the mirror and confirmed her worst fears. She was dead.

But somehow the glue that held her spirit in her body wasn't ungluing. She was stuck in it and she was stuck in a world she didn't belong anymore.

It took about a month for her husband to finally ask for a divorce.

"But you don't have to divorce me," she pleaded. "I'm dead. You don't have to divorce dead people."

He looked at her in a strange way. When she reached her hand out to touch his arm, he jumped away. Something like fear crept into his eyes. "You're not dead, Judy," he said. "You're crazy."

What did he know? What did any of the living know about the dead or what it was like to be dead?

She didn't tell anyone at work about her death and though she was tempted, she didn't see anyone in HR to find out if she might be entitled to any benefits. All in all, she thought it was best that her coworkers not be aware that they were working with a dead person, especially the Walking Dead fans. She was certain some of them would try putting bullets or nails into her head. Just because she was dead didn't mean they had the right to mess up a perfectly good hairdo.

But all that was going to change today. Judy was sick and tired of pretending to be alive. She was dead and she could live with that. But she wanted the rest of the world to know. Sure, like her Mr. Critic husband, some might think she was crazy, but she was going crazy holding it in. She wanted people to know what she knew and she was sure that if enough people knew, if they really listened to her, then they would accept the truth and she wouldn't feel so alone. It would be like she had friends on the other side.

She looked around. The coffee cart had just made its round and everyone had their morning coffee. She knew the score. You didn't tell people you were dead before they'd had their morning coffee. She had an ex-husband to prove that. She still wasn't sure how to start or what, exactly, to say. She'd gone over dozens of scenarios, but none of them seemed right now that she was standing up and looking around at an office full of people slurping caffeine. She decided to wing it, just stand on top of her desk and blurt it out. She thought that had a ring of spontaneous honesty to it.

She climbed up on her chair, praying that it wouldn't tilt and send her flying into the floor. But what the hell...she was dead. She stepped up carefully onto her desk. She knew people would be dropping whatever they were doing and looking at her, so best to get it over with quickly. She cleared her throat and looked around.

No one was looking at her. They were looking out the window. She turned her head in the direction they were looking and saw the light and she knew in the exact instant the fireball swallowed her that she would no longer be alone.

Bright Lights, Big Salon

Elsie Warren was the first to feel it. It seemed as though it flowed through the cord of her hair dryer as she dried Andrea Smith's hair. It wasn't a jolt or a surge or anything that would cause her to say, "Did you feel that?" It was more like an infinitesimal displacement of atoms similar to the burp of a ladybug, as noticeable as anonymous music playing on the radio in the background. Not worth mentioning because…what would you mention? "Did you hear that ladybug burp?" And there was no way she was going to ask Andrea Smith a question like that. Andrea would be on social media right after the session spreading the word, "Guess who's losing it?" And then she'd be calling people because her mouth never shut. Elsie hated Andrea. Often, as she was doing Andrea's hair, she would fantasize rinsing with Andrea's head submerged in the sink until her body sagged lifeless over the counter. Sometimes she'd smile and chuckle quietly when she visualized Andrea's

212

dead body drooping with its mouth shut forever. A few times Andrea had stopped dead in whatever monologue she was droning about how her friends weren't up to par in supporting her, and she asked, "What is it? Why are you chuckling?"

"Oh nothing, Andrea. Just thought about something my nephew said this weekend. But you're right, you know, they just don't understand your needs." And it would go on and on until the session was over and Andrea would leave an insulting tip.

There it was again. This time a little stronger, like a June bug belching. Elsie stopped thinking about murdering Andrea while something in the back of her mind said, "Something's happening. Don't know what yet. But it ain't gonna be anything good." It was at that moment that she noticed her coworkers and their customers by the windows stop what they were doing and walk slowly to the large slatted windows and stare out. Suddenly, they were bathed in light, the kind of light you see at the end of the day or the early morning, only brighter, much brighter.

Elsie knew at that moment that it was time to cut Andrea's throat with her scissors and she would have if Andrea hadn't leaned forward and grabbed the scissors from the counter. She yelled something about hating Elsie's attitude. Just as the scissors were about to plunge into Elsie's stomach they became ashes together and were swept into the torrential wind.

Bats

"I'm going to eat the biggest, fattest, juiciest June bug I can find. Gonna eat its head and all," said Jurgen.

"I could go for a dozen or so fireflies. Maybe a load of mosquitos on the side," said Dwight.

Jurgen flapped his wings and made chirping sounds that sounded more like clicks than chirps. "And after I eat that monstrous big June bug," he said, flapping his wings excitedly, "I'm going to find a lone female out for a night time stroll and fly right into her hair!"

Dwight chirped frantically, though it sounded more like bad Morse code, and made a rasping sound. "Yeah! Let's both fly into her hair. Like, roll around, get tangled, make her scream a bit."

"Scream a bit! Scream a bit!" screamed Jurgen, wings flapping wildly.

"Don't ya just love this life?" said Dwight. "Get to fly, eat bugs and scare people. Gotta love it!"

"Remember that red head the other night?" said Jurgen. They clicked their chirps and flapped their wings crazily.

"Ran right into a tree!" yelled Dwight.

"Knocked herself clean out!" yelled Jurgen.

"Scared the shit out of that family walking by!"

"Made the kids cry!"

"And then the whole family ran! Even the father!"

"Let's all of us fly into her hair!" yelled Dwight.

"Yay!" yelled Barton

"All of us!" yelled Harry.

"Right into her hair!" yelled Arnold.

"Flock attack!" yelled Charles.

"Make her scream!" yelled Michael.

"Flap and roll!" yelled Carson.

"No mercy!" yelled Ebeneezer.

"Follicle frenzy!" yelled Chester.

The other bats looked at Chester quizzically, as was the attic norm whenever he spoke.

"Let's go for it!" yelled Jurgen.

Together as a bat horde they let loose from their perches and clicked and chirped and flapped out the ventilation window, straight into the firestorm.

(With thanks to The Queen of the Bats for this one.)

On the Bus

Mandy's eyes assumed the shapes of those mini saucers that come with mini espresso coffee cups. He was staring straight into her eyes! *The bastard!* There was no pretense now. There was no hiding his warped intentions. He wasn't just casually glancing around. His eyes bored into hers with ulterior of intent. He was declaring himself. This was the last straw. Mandy Williams wasn't taking this any longer. It was time to act. It was time to slap someone. She stood up, glaring into his eyes.

What the fuck now? Bitch standing up, giving me the evil eye? Darren decided that he'd had enough of this no-chest, scraggly-haired woman. He stood up.

Mandy watched in horror as the man in the ball cap suddenly shot up out of his seat. *He's going to attack me. He's going to actually physically rape me in front of all these people, right here on the bus!* She looked around. There were about two dozen other people on the bus, heads buried in newspapers and phones, all of them oblivious of the drama playing out right in front of them. She wondered if any of them would even lift a finger to help her. Or would they just ignore the fact that a woman was being raped on their bus. Or, worse, would they just record it on their phones and post her raping on social media.

She sat down.

What the fuck? What's she doing now? Why's she sitting? What the fuck? Slowly, Darren sat down, staring directly into Mandy's eyes.

He's crazy! That man is crazy...and no one on this bus is going to help me. She glanced quickly around. Everyone was absorbed in everything but her impending rape. What's wrong with these people? She looked back at the man in the ball cap. A chill rushed through her body. It seemed to her that his eyes were filled with hatred as he stared directly into her eyes. In spite of the crowded bus she'd never felt so alone and vulnerable in her life. She might as well have been in a desert surrounded by rapists in ball caps for all the people on this bus cared. Suddenly, she hated everyone on the bus. She thought about the people she worked with realized that every one of them were exactly like the people

216

on this bus…uncaring, self-absorbed, completely unaware of her danger. She expanded this thought to include every human being on earth and wished that the entire human species would just blow up.

Oops.

She saw the hot light reflected in the ball cap man's eyes as he stared toward its source.

Rude Awakening

James Bellows wasn't sure what had happened. He only knew that it wasn't anything good. He had no idea where he was. The park behind him, the stone buildings in front of him, the statue of some dignitary to his right…none of it was familiar. He'd never been in this part of the city before. He was sure of that. It wasn't amnesia. He knew who he was and he knew where he'd been yesterday, but just to be on the safe side, he pulled out his wallet and checked his ID. James Bellows. Yesterday he'd slept in and spent the rest of the day vegging out in front of the television and then gone to bed.

And now he was here, standing on a sidewalk in a part of the city he didn't even know existed. Judging by the sun (straight overhead) it was around noon. There was no one else on the street to his right or left. He turned around and looked into the park. Nobody. There was no traffic on the roads. He held his breath for a few seconds and listened. No sounds. Not even birds or distant traffic. It was hot but he didn't hear any of the air conditioners in the windows across the street humming or whirring or making any air conditioning sounds.

The air around him was windless; the leaves in the trees, still. His nostrils should have been overwhelmed by the thick aroma of summer but the air was scentless. The only sensation he had was the heat. It was ungodly hot.

Why aren't those air conditioners screaming to hell? he thought.

He started to walk toward the park, but his legs wouldn't move. He tried to force them but it was like they were glued to the sidewalk.

What the hell.

He reached down with his right hand and tried to push his right leg forward. It was like pushing against a brick wall. He pushed both legs with both hands. Not a budge. A thought crossed his mind. He turned to face the street. It worked. He could turn. He started to walk toward the street. His legs wouldn't move. With his right foot, he tried to step to the side. It wouldn't move. He turned back toward the park.

The heat was becoming unbearable. He looked down the street to his left. For about a quarter mile there wasn't a car, truck or bus in sight. Not even parked along the street. The street to his right was a just as barren.

Where are all the cars?¹ Where are all the people?

He suddenly felt alone, like he was the only person left in the world. He felt like every person in the world had just disappeared. Poof. He was all alone in a part of the city he'd never seen before.

How did I get here?

He thought that he should feel a sense of panic, but he didn't. He felt alone and he felt like it was getting too damn hot. He felt like the heat was searing into his flesh but when he looked down, he was OK except for one thing. He was naked.

What the hell!

He watched as his body burst into flames, too far into the dream and everything happening too fast for him to wake up to feel his naked body evaporating into the inferno of his bedroom.

The Last Word

Anne-Marie and Judy Svenson were sisters. Anne-Marie was forty-one years old and Judy was thirty-nine. Both were single and neither had ever married. They shared a small apartment in a small building in a small neighborhood on the outskirts of a small town in the middle of nowhere. This was a good place for them to live. In a larger burg, with the less accommodating neighbors you generally find in larger burgs, they would both most certainly have had their heads hacked off long ago by those less accommodating neighbors.

They were friendly enough, and they tipped cab drivers and bartenders generously. They paid their rent on time and they rarely complained about the weather. Anne-Marie baked the best bread anywhere bread was baked. Its fragrance drifted out the windows into the streets and into the nostrils of passersby who drooled and suddenly wanted to eat bread. Judy was the go-to person if you had a stain on your clothing. She could remove blood and red wine from white velvet blouses and was the perfect addition to a wedding party, especially if there would be lots of white velvet and red wine. And maybe the occasional fist fight.

For sisters, they didn't look at all alike. Anne-Marie was tall and wide with dark stringy hair and course features while Judy was short and skinny with delicate blonde hair and features that seemed chiseled like the images on a coin. Some people questioned their sisterliness. But nobody listened to those nay-sister-sayers. Nobody had a chance to listen to them. Anne-Marie and Judy made listening to anyone other than themselves impossible.

The truth was: they never shut up. If one wasn't talking, the other was, and when the other shut up, the other would start up. It was rumored that they talked in their sleep. Anne-Marie talked while she cooked bread. Judy talked while she removed wine stains from white velvet blouses. They never watched television: they talked. Imagine a steady stream of words that never stopped flowing, one word after another, one sentence after another...endlessly. Think: river of nouns and verbs and split infinitives crashing into each other in a crazy stampede to the ocean.

It drove people nuts. It was a continuous irritation to their neighbors who, living in a burg in the middle of nowhere and therefore being somewhat accommodating, never hacked the sisters' heads off no matter how much they wanted to and no matter how many times they happily imagined it. This was a very likely the reason why people never came to visit them and they were never invited anywhere unless there was a way to keep them separate, which generally happened after weddings. Weddings involving red wine or fist fights.

But they couldn't help themselves. They'd been doing it since they were very kids. They couldn't remember which one had started it, but one of them had made up her mind that she was going to get the last word in an argument the two had gotten into for some long-forgotten reason. And the other wasn't going to allow that.

Since then, every conversation they had, every verbal observation or thought and every quip, gripe or comment was an extension of that argument and neither of them was going to let the other have the last word. It went something like this:

"Well, that's my final thought on that," said Anne-Marie.

"But what about the coffee on the counter?" said Judy.

"What coffee on the counter?" said Anne-Marie.

"I don't know," said Judy. "Shouldn't there be coffee on the counter?"

"But I wasn't talking about a counter," said Anne-Marie, "let alone coffee."

"So…you're really not sure if that was your last thought," said Judy, "having left out the counter. And the coffee."

"I know what you're doing, Judy…and it's not going to work," said Anne-Marie.

"I'm just making sure that was your last thought," said Judy. "It was ambiguous."

"No it wasn't."

"Yes it was."

"No it wasn't."

"You're not getting the last word."

"Wanna bet?"

"How much?"

Did I mention that it drove people nuts? Did I mention that it was never-ending?

I'm sure I didn't mention that one of them was planning on murdering the other. Just to get in the last word. Judy (The younger one, of course. Wasn't it always the younger one?), had had enough. She'd decided to finally get in the last word, even if she had to murder her sister, and murdering her seemed to be the only way.

Once she decided it was time to murder Anne-Marie, it was just a matter of deciding how she would meet her untimely end. She thought about blowing her up, but she figured that might be a little too obvious. Shooting, stabbing, hanging and strangulation all seemed a bit dicey. They left too many clues. Electrocution was too technical; drowning, too complicated (River? Lake? Stream? Bathtub? Reservoir?) She thought about pushing her sister off a high cliff, but there were no cliffs in the area let alone high cliffs, and the top of a building posed the threat of witnesses…being outdoors and in a populated area. Bashing her head in with a hammer was too messy. Pushing her into traffic posed the same threat as pushing her off the top of a building: witnesses. Leaving her stranded in the middle of a desert would have been nice...if there were a desert nearby. Poisoning seemed like an interesting possibility but, as she thought about it, something occurred to her.

Whatever method she used to murder Anne-Marie, it had to allow Judy to get in the last word and Anne-Marie had to know that she'd gotten in the last word and not be able to do anything about it. She had to be able to hear, but unable to talk.

It was all about the timing.

Anne-Marie had to die the instant after she heard Judy get in the last word. She thought that maybe she could gag her sister, but she would still be able to get in a gagged last word. They would both know that she had said something and that would count as a last word. After several weeks pondering her sister's murder, Judy turned to the well-spring of all questionable knowledge: the internet. She entered various combinations of stopping someone from speaking, talking, enunciating, getting in the last word, dying with something to say but not being able to say it...stuff like that. It took a few hours but she finally came up with the perfect way to kill Anne-Marie and get in the last word: a magical spell.

It was a secret magical spell, so the details can just be summed up by saying it had something to do with a rooster, a lock of Anne-Marie's hair, a crossroad and a sock. And terrible dark things that are too terrible and dark to relate here.

But it worked.

There was Anne-Marie, sitting in her arm chair across the room from Judy, staring wide-eyed and unbelieving. Her lips were turning white from being squeezed together. She mumbled garble through her nose and, as far as they were both concerned, that garble counted as words no matter how indistinguishable they were.

Judy smiled a nasty, humorless smile. "I'm going to get in the last word, Anne-Marie."

Anne-Marie grunted and shook her head NO. And it counted. But it didn't matter. A magic spell had been set in motion and in just a moment, Judy would say the magic word to complete the spell and her sister would die, unable to get in just one last grunted word.

"Grunt all you want, Anne-Marie," she said with an evil sneer. "In just a moment, I'm going to throw this sock of yours on the floor and say the magic word and you're not going to be able to talk, grunt, think, sneeze, burp or anything but die. You're just going to die and I'm finally going to get in the last word." Judy's smile could have tripped an elephant.

Anne-Marie shook her head NO and grunted. Judy smiled wide enough to ensnare a herd of elephants. She lifted Anne-Marie's yellow sock, one half of her sister's favorite pair of socks. She held her arm out as Anne-Marie stared saucer-eyed, grunting crazily. Judy opened her hand and the sock fell through the air and crashed noiselessly into the floor and Judy grunt-screamed through the magical spell that bound her lips together. And that muffled scream counted as the walls, pictures, light fixtures, tables, chairs, rugs, doilies, Anne-Marie and Judy evaporated instantly.

Giving Anne-Marie the last word.

That Lucky Guy

It was always a sunny day for Phillip Caine. No matter how bleak the horizon looked, he would coast into a sliver of sunlight in the Yin and Yang of life. He was impervious to the floods of doubt, and the misfortune and miscalculations that saturated everyday life for the rest of the world. If he'd been on the Titanic, he would have escaped drowning and still have had his luggage with him.

People said of him, "That man's the luckiest human being I've ever met." And it was true. Fortune didn't just smile on that human being, Fortune drooled on Phillip Caine, massaged his back, pedicured his toes and clipped his nose hairs. And it showed. He was like a beacon of smooth light, unwavering, always smiling, never in disagreement with anything or anyone around him. He stood out in busy crowds as a feather that everything else seemed to flow around without touching. You could feel his calm in the crowd.

But he never pushed his luck, he just let it happen. He never bought lotto tickets or bet on horses. He'd never been to Los Vegas and he'd never been to a Saturday night card game with his friends. At least, what friends he had, which wasn't many.

You see, most people have, for the most part, shitty luck. They have bills that keep mounting, kids that keep asking for more, jobs that keep demanding more and paying less and dreams that keep moving further and further away from anything that can come true in ten lifetimes. Most people spend much of their time bitching about their shitty luck and saying things like, "Why can't I win the lotto." or "If I could just catch up on the bills…if I just had a little breathing room." When these people caught on that Phillip wasn't bitching, and then learned that he didn't have anything to bitch about, it was like social ebola. Who wants to bitch to someone who keeps seeing the bright side of things because he's never had anything to bitch about?"

"Every payday I fall just a little bit further behind."

"But you still have a job. A lot of people don't."

"Try as much as I can, but I just can't keep up."

"But you still have your health."

See what I mean? Who needs an attitude like that when you're whining about your whole world falling down around you? Who needs to be reminded that life can be good when you're in a rut as deep as the Saint Andreas Fault?

Some people hated him. In fact, a lot of people hated Phillip. They watched him come into work each morning smiling all over the place and sit comfortably at his desk as though there were no metaphorical chains holding him there, no steel bars around his desk. They watched as he talked to clients on his phone, smiling enough to fill an entire phone grid with happy thoughts. It was maddening. It was infuriating. Something had to be done. A price for all this cheer had to be paid. There was need of a reckoning. Misery needed compliance.

So they plotted. A price would be exacted. There would be a reckoning. Misery would rule.

"I hate that bastard," said Carl Banyon.

"Always smiling. Always in a good mood," said Joan Cummings.

"Guy could win the lottery, but he never plays," said Bill Paulson. "He could make us all rich, but he doesn't play. Bastard."

"He never looks at my cleavage," said Jennifer Hayter. "No matter how low I wear my blouses."

The others looked at her strangely, wondering if she were really into making life miserable for Phillip Caine.

"Not that I really give a damn," she added quickly. "I hate that man. I hate him."

The others nodded. Jennifer was in.

"But how do we get him?" said Joan. "We'll all be out on our asses for harassment with all these new policies. I mean, they're really taking all this political correctness bullshit seriously."

"We'll have to be really discreet," said Bill.

"You mean sneaky?" said Carl.

"Yeah…sneaky" said Bill.

"I like sneaky," said Jennifer. "It's how men usually look at my cleavage."

The others looked at her strangely. *Would she be the weak link in this conspiracy?*

"Not that I care," said Jennifer. "Chauvinist bastards."

"I have an idea," said Joan. The others looked at her. "We drive him crazy." The others waited for an explanation.

After a minute or so, Carl said, "And how do we drive him crazy?"

Joan looked puzzled. She thought a moment. "I don't know."

"Then why did you say we should drive him crazy," said Jennifer.

Anger flared in Joan's eyes. She snapped at Jennifer. "I was just an idea, Jenn, a basic idea. All we have to do now is work out the details. Do you have a better basic idea?"

And now the fire was in Jennifer's eyes. "Well, it seems to me that if you're going to have an idea, then you should have an idea…not just a half idea."

Joan's face turned red. Her fiery eyes began to bulge. "I didn't hear anything coming out of you, Jennifer. But then, you never have any ideas about anything. You just ride the coat tails of…"

"Hey ladies," said Bill, maybe a little too loud. "Let's try working together for once instead of getting into another meaningless squabble."

"And just what the hell is that supposed to mean?" said Jennifer. "For once? What the fuck to you mean by 'for once?'"

"I just meant…" Bill tried to say.

"And what's this about another meaningless squabble, Bill," said Carl. "Sounded like kind of a nasty generalization."

"Fuck you, Carl," said Bill. "Don't try that bullshit about twisting the meaning of everything I say into something else. You…"

"Yeah,' said Joan. "Why do you do that? You do it all the time. It really pisses me off."

"Oh," said Jennifer, "and, like, you don't do the same thing, Joan? Like at the prep meeting yesterday…"

Joan's eyes were bulging now. "Why you little bitch," said Joan loud enough to draw stares from around the office.

"OK," said Bill. "That's enough of this bullshit. We can't even work together for something as simple as…"

"Bullshit?" said Joan. "You're bullshit, Carl…with all your sucking up to Munroe and…"

"And your nose has no shit on it?" said Bill, rolling his eyes.

"Fuck you, Bill," said Joan.

"Fuck both of you," said Jennifer.

"Morning everybody!" said Phillip Caine as he rounded the corner into the office space. "Everyone having a little pre-work chitchat?"

Being a block away from the center of impact, there was no warning rumble.

All four of the plotters' eyes were on Phillip on the one day of his life when he was in the wrong place at the wrong time. Four pairs of eyes melted as they gazed with pure hatred at the smile on his lips.

Squeezing the Garbage

He squeezed the big black garbage bag with both hands, waiting for the feel of something promising, something like CDs or plastic containers. He listened for the delightful sound of glass bottles, maybe beer bottles or fruit bottles. The black bags could be like treasure chests with tubes of toothpaste only half used or jars of jam with enough left inside for four or five slices of toast. He never picked up the white bags with the exception of sometimes in the winter when he was wearing gloves, but he'd rarely ever found anything worthwhile in them so they weren't really worth the bother.

He loved his work. It was full of surprises. He loved climbing over the top of dumpsters and descending into a cavern of potential. He didn't mind if people saw him. He wasn't fazed by their looks of disgust or disapproval. Let them try to live off the measly income from the dole, or stand in line at the food bank. They wouldn't look so disgusted if they had to spend a night in a homeless shelter after a meal in the soup kitchen. But he, Charley Horne, wasn't homeless anymore and he hadn't eaten in a soup kitchen for over a year.

Charley Horne was a self-employed recycling activist. He worked in dumpsters, routing out the bottles and containers from the garbage of people who refused to recycle. Rather than buy new hygiene products that would lead to further use of plastic and other poisonous components, he finished off what was already bought and already replaced. He liked to think that he slowed the process of destroying the planet with garbage.

He felt something interesting in the bag, something square. He ran his fingers over it, pressing in and tracing the flat surface of a box. A box. Sometimes boxes were full of surprises. He'd opened boxes with brand new hand mixers and coffee grinders inside. His heart beat a little faster as his excitement grew. He tore a hole in the side of the bag and worked the box through the tear. He wasn't all that fussy about this. After all, everything in the dumpster was going into the dump truck whether it was in bags or not. The bags were just a means to get the garbage into the dumpster. But Charley was an environmental pro. He left as little a footprint as possible.

A rectangular box fell through the tear and onto a stack of bags. Charley's heart raced as he stared at the photo of an electric razor. Slowly, almost reverently, he lifted the box with both hands. It was heavy. Good. He opened one end and looked inside. His heart almost skipped a few beats when he saw the plastic wrapping. Plastic wrapping. That was always a good sign. Plastic wrapping and heavy box. Something new and maybe unused. As he pulled out the wrapping he saw the same electric razor as on the box cover. He stripped away the plastic and held what looked like a brand new razor in his hand. Holding the razor and box in one hand, he dug into the box with the other and pulled out accessories still wrapped in plastic twist ties. It *was* brand new.

He let out a whoop and stuck his head out the top of the dumpster to see if anyone was looking. Empty parking lot, no one peering down from the apartment windows.

He wanted to sing. He wanted to dance. His hands shook. This was his best find in ages. This was something he could take to the pawn shop and get some serious change. He kissed the razor. He kissed the box. He would have cigarettes and beer tonight. He would have a story to tell his friends, all of them recycling activists themselves. They would be in awe. They would be jealous. They would want to know which dumpster had yielded such a treasure.

They would want to know where.

And then they would come to this dumpster of dumpsters looking for treasure. Charley thought about this for a moment. He'd gotten so much out of this dumpster. He thought about the day a woman started calling out to him as she ran across the parking lot. He was just about to jump out of the dumpster and run when she yelled, "Can you do me a favor!" It turned out that she'd accidentally tossed out her wedding ring and it was in one of the white bags. But there he was, standing in her dumpster looking into her teary eyes. It took about ten minutes of feeling white garbage bags, some of which felt like they might have body parts inside. But he felt the ring in one of them, opened the bag, got a whiff of dead food stuff as he rummaged, found the ring and handed it to her. She thanked him and was back a few minute later with two six packs of empty beer bottles and a bag of plastic containers.

This was the dumpster that had made him a hero. But they would want to know where and they would press him until they knew. They might even follow him, especially Roy Connors. He was just the kind of sneaky son-of-a-bitch to follow him.

Maybe he should just keep the whole thing a secret. Maybe tell them he found some money on the sidewalk. A twenty dollar bill. Just lying there on the sidewalk and he'd said, "Your loss whoever and my gain," and he just scooped it up. That kind of thing had happened before.

But then there was the pawn shop. Ernie knew all his friends and they knew Ernie. He would tell them and they would want to know where he'd gotten it. He wouldn't be able to tell them that he'd found a brand nefw electric shaver on the sidewalk. That kind of thing never happened.

He thought about taking it to another pawn shop, but he knew that Ernie always gave him the best deal, at least twenty percent better than anywhere else. He'd be losing money taking it to another pawn shop.

He was stymied. What could he do? He was holding money in his hands, but he had to find a way to keep it secret. But there was no way. They would find out. They would question him. They would follow him. They would pillage his dumpster. They would take everything of value from it and leave him with nothing.

About the same time he was wondering if there was any solution in the world to his problem, the solution arrived in the form of the brightest light that Charley Horne had ever seen. The light was immediately followed by a torrent of energy that drove the dumpster across the parking lot with Charley's upper body flaming like he was a flaming ghost riding the dumpster into hell along with his secret.

Penguins Starving in the Full Moon Light

"And here's to the penguin cubs starving in the full moon light on a continent drifting off into the oceans."

Their glasses clinked. This was a matter of great importance to Waylon. Wine glasses had to clink. That was how you knew they were expensive crystal glasses. Clunking didn't cut it. Clunks were for cheap glasses with cheap blunt-tasting wine. Waylon didn't drink from cheap glasses that said, "Clunk." And he didn't drink cheap wine. The glasses they drank from contained expensive French wine and when Waylon's glass touched Jenny's glass, they said, "Clink" with an Austrian accent.

"Poor little penguin cubs," said Jenny. She sipped gracefully from her expensive cut crystal wine glass and savored the smooth fruity wine as it slid over her palette.

Waylon smiled as he reached his glass towards hers. "Here's to the human babies being blown to shreds by humans with bombs strapped around their bodies."

"To the babies!" said Jenny as their glasses said, "Clink."

They sipped and smiled.

"I think we were a mistake," said Jenny.

"A miscalculation in the abacus of evolution," said Waylon.

"A foul package left on the doorstep of an unsuspecting world," said Jenny.

"But the world took us in," said Waylon. "Took us in with a trusting heart."

"And we betrayed her," said Jenny. "Like an apple filled with razor blades."

"Like a fortune cookie laced with arsenic," said Waylon.

"We are ebola to Mother Earth," said Jenny.

"Here's to the last tree in the last rain forest," said Waylon, and their glasses clinked in cut crystal harmony.

"I wonder what they'll do with the machines when there's nothing left to cut?" said Jenny.

"They'll look for new things to kill and build new machines to kill them," said Waylon. "And they'll leave the old machines to die from rust in the forests they stripped to the bone."

"Bastards!" said Jenny.

"Bastards!" said Waylon.

Jenny thrust her glass towards Waylon's. A few drops of wine slipped over the rim of the glass and landed on the chesterfield. She giggled. Waylon giggled. "To the bones of the forests," she said, and their glasses clinked expensively. It was almost like a "click" with an undertone of "ink."

They laughed and sipped and Waylon said, "To the air getting thick enough to swim to the stars."

Click with an "ink."

"To the disappearing coastlines and the cities and villages soon to be underwater," said Jenny.

Click + Ink = Clink.

"To the primordial viruses newly awakened and ravaging the living of another time," said Waylon.

"Oh shit!" said Jenny.

"What?" said Waylon. "You didn't read about the…"

"I'm out of wine." She held her glass high and almost doubled over giggling. "I'm out of wine."

Waylon looked into his glass. "Me too." He laughed as though he'd just told the funniest joke in the world. He bent over and lifted a bottle from a porcelain bucket filled with melting ice and refilled their glasses, spilling wine onto the chesterfield. "Fuck," said Jenny. "It's all so…"

"…fucking pointless," said Waylon.

"We're so…fucked," said Jenny, and they both laughed. "By the way, what was I supposed to read about?"

Waylon thought for a moment but nothing came to mind so he thrust his glass towards Jenny's glass and said, "To all the flying insects that seem to have left the planet and the crops they left behind to die."

Their glasses clinked hard and more wine soaked into the chesterfield. They bent over with laughter. "Oh…oh…oh," said Jenny. "I have one."

"Let's hear it," said Waylon.

Jenny sat straight, almost to a sitting attention stance, and lifted her glass solemnly. Waylon followed suit. In a mock serious voice, she said, "And here's to blowing up in…" just as the nuclear tide tore through the living room and carried their particles off into a world bereft of flying insects.

A Thousand Sparkles

Tommy Kaplan lay under his bed again with a bottle of wine and a box of cheap facial tissues. He was always sure to call them "facial tissues" but he would never call them "cheap." They were economical. Unfortunately, it took two or three economical tissues to blow his nose without blowing a hole in the center of them.

He'd just blown a hole through three but what the hell...he was under his bed. Who would know?

"You blew a hole through your tissues again, didn't you?"

It was a female voice. Tommy turned his head and looked into Sally's big blue eyes as she peeked under the bed at him.

"You know," she said, "if you were to pay a few cents extra, you'd only have to use one tissue at a time and you wouldn't blow snot all over the bottom of our bed."

Tommy stared at her, not saying a word. His feelings were still hurt. He wasn't speaking to her until she apologized and he would stay under the bed until she did.

"I'm not going to apologize, Tommy." She lay the rest of her body down on the floor and set her chin on her hands. Tommy turned his head back to the bed and pushed the wine bottle up across his chin to his lips. He managed to pour about two tablespoons of wine into his mouth before he was pouring it across his cheeks. "And you're wasting a

237

lot of good wine, Tommy. Just because I was honest about your poem."

With tremendous effort, Tommy managed to bend his left arm just right so that he could wipe the wine from his cheek.

"You asked me to be honest. You said, 'I want your honest opinion. Don't hold back.' And that's what I gave you...my honest opinion. The poem sucked." She sighed loudly. "You're not a poet, Tommy. You write articles...fact-based, non-fiction articles about technology. And you're good at it, Tommy...better than most. You should be content with that. Stick to what you do best."

Tommy snorted. Sally pushed her right hand under the bed and poked him in the shoulder with her index finger. He tried to shrug his shoulder away from her finger.

"C'mon, Tommy," she said. "You're just going to get wine all over your shirt and snot all over the bed. And...well...maybe there was one good line in the poem."

He turned his head toward her and almost said, "Which line?" But he didn't. He wasn't speaking to her until she apologized. And he meant it. He had tissues and wine and he was good for the night.

"It was the second last line." She smiled. "Now, how did that go...? Right. A thousand sparkles of rain. I kinda like that. A thousand sparkles of rain. It creates a sort of magical picture in my head."

Tommy couldn't help smiling. The more he tried not to, the more it spread across his face. But he still wasn't talking to her.

"Ah ha! Looks like the ice man under the bed is maybe melting a bit?"

He tried desperately to reign in the smile but it was a no go. He'd created a "magical picture." She liked one line. All he had to do was make the other eighty lines create magical pictures. He could do it. He could be a poet. He'd always wanted to be a poet. He wanted to create magical pictures.

"Maybe if I read it again?"

He stopped smiling. Was she serious? Would she really read it again?

"But you have to say something first."

He squinted his eyes. Say something? He lifted the bottle to his lips and poured more wine across his cheek. He looked into her eyes imploringly. Was she serious?

"You have to tell me you love me."

He wanted to yell, "After you hurt my feelings! After you said my poem sucked! The poem I worked over a month on! You want me to tell you I love you?" But he didn't. She still hadn't apologized. He turned his head back to the bottom of the bed. His nose was starting to get stuffy again. He reached into the box by his side and pulled out a bunch of tissues.

"You're going to blow your nose again?" She pushed herself back about a foot. "Gross. You're going to put more snot on the bed."

That was the last straw for Tommy. She'd panned his poem. Then got his hopes up about the second last line. Then told him he was gross. Well, gross he would be. He stuffed the wine bottle into his armpit, put the bunch of tissue to his nose with both hands, took a deep breath and got ready to expel snot…just about the time the room began to shake and he felt a weird tingling. He turned his head just in time to see Sally shoot across the floor as though she were being pulled by some invisible creature. The bed flew into the air and against the far wall and Tommy's last thought was: A thousand sparkles…

Borscht Soaked Potatoes

Aleks Boback loved borscht. He could eat borscht until it dripped out of his eyes. He especially loved dipping boiled potatoes into his borscht, and the memory of doing that around the family table brought a smile to his face.

"What the fuck are you smiling about?" said Marina Gura, a beautiful woman with the charm of a broken window. Miles off to the right, Aleks heard the dull thud of an explosion followed a few seconds later by a tremor in the ground under him. "You think this is funny? You think we are on vacation here?" Marina's eyes were large, even larger when she was angry and in a mood to strike out at whoever was unlucky enough to be within fifty feet of her.

Aleks stopped smiling. Not because Marina questioned his smile in her bullying way, but because the bitch had broken his train of thought right before a bomb exploded. Visions of potatoes dipped in borscht evaporated from his mind and he was back in this stinking abandoned house that smelled like piss and fungus. A few stray beams of light made a weak appearance through the boards nailed to the windows.

"What the fuck is your problem now, Marina? You don't like smiling?" Aleks wasn't going to back down from her.

"And you think this shithole is something to smile about, Aleks Boback?" Her voice was sharp and venomous.

Aleks tightened his grip on his rifle thinking how satisfying it would be so put a bullet into Marina's forehead. Marina felt Aleks's malevolence across the ten feet between them and shifted the position of her rifle just in case.

"Fuck off, both of you," said Roman Zaleski, their commanding officer, who rarely spoke except to tell Marina and Aleks to fuck off. He sat with his back against a wall with bullet holes the size of eggs drawing a curve over his head. Aleks and Marina snapped their eyes towards him and then back to each other.

They simmered quietly until Aleks said, "Did you feel that?"

"What the fuck are you talking about now?" said Marina.

Roman snored gently against the wall.

Aleks looked around. "I'm not sure. It's..." Every chink in the wood covering the windows began to glow brightly and Aleks had just enough time to make one of his dreams come true. There was no borsht, so he put a bullet into Marina's head, and dreamed about borscht soaked potatoes as his body vaporized.

241

Ghosts of the Machine

"Yep, she's a beautiful sight indeed," said Murphy as he gazed lovingly at the machine with all its pulleys and conveyor belts and consoles. He turned to Johnson, grabbed his hand and started shaking it enthusiastically.

Johnson smiled wide enough to rip his face off if he sneezed. He stared teary-eyed at the machine. "It certainly is, sir, it certainly is."

"And you and your crew made this all possible, Johnson," said Murphy. "We'll never forget this, you know."

"I know, sir," said Johnson.

"Oh," said Murphy, "looks like Sinclair is going to say something." He looked in the direction of a man in a very expensive three-piece gray suit. He clapped his hands three times.

"Everyone!" said Sinclair. "Everyone! May I have your attention."

A hush fell over the room as seven men in very expensive three piece gray suits and five men in shitty mismatched suits trained their eyes on Sinclair. "We all know that progress is inevitable, that what is to come, will in fact come. We can't fight it. We can't stop it. We can only accept that things will change." He looked around the room into the eyes of each of the twelve men surrounding him. "And change they will. And I like to think…for the better. Things change for the better. And that's what's happened here. Things have

242

changed for the better. We...all of us..." He raised his arms in a sweeping motion to include everyone in the room. As he raised his arms and did the sweeping thing, not a wrinkle appeared in the arms of his expensive gray suit jacket. "...have embraced the future. And now the future is here." He pointed both creaseless arms toward the machine. "The future is here."

A loud cheer resounded in the room. It bounced off the walls and ceiling and swarmed lovingly over the machine. It was followed by a cascade or energetic applause as everyone in the room turned to face the marvelous machine that had been in the works for almost a year. And here it was...the future.

Moody smiled profusely as he stood by himself, happy with the news he'd received that day. All five of the production people had been given their walking papers. They were no longer needed. The machine would everything they did faster, more efficiently and, most important, cheaper. Much cheaper. In fact, cheap enough that all eight managers had, that day, received huge bonuses and raises in pay. Moody clapped his hands together hard enough to almost hurt them. Fucking idiots, he thought as he clapped and glanced quickly at Jones and Wallis.

Jones put his hand on Wallis' shoulder as he stared at the machine. Their suits, of course, were mismatched. Wallis turned his head to look at Jones, who turned his head to look at Wallis. "We did it," said Wallis.

"We sure did," said Jones. "And in under a year."

"Against all odds," said Wallis.

Jones squeezed Wallis' shoulders. "So…what next for you? Any prospects?"

"Nothing yet," said Wallis. "Didn't realize the job market would be this tight. How about you?"

Jones shrugged his shoulders. "Haven't really had time to get my resume together…with all the overtime and weekends here to get this working on schedule."

"Yeah," said Wallis. "Same here. But we did it, Jones, we did it."

Manfort shook Smith's hand firmly, maybe a little too firmly, as was his habit. "You people did a wonderful job, Smith. Wonderful job."

"Thank you, sir," said Smith, beaming. He loved getting praise from Manfort and the other managers in their expensive three-piece gray suits. It made him think that maybe someday he would be wearing one of those suits and filling someone's day with joy…just by shaking their hand. "It was a big job, but what can you say with a team like ours. It was all teamwork, sir, all teamwork."

"That's the spirit, Smith," said Manfort. "It's always the team. Always the team." He turned his gaze full on to Smith. "So, how long have you been with the company, Smith?"

Smith sensed an opening. He smiled wider. "Eighteen years, sir. Eighteen years last week. And every one of them a wonderful experience, sir."

"Well, Smith," said Manfort, "you've been a valued employee, and making this machine a reality must serve as a sort of culmination of accomplishments for you, Smith."

"It certainly does, sir," said Smith. "It certainly does."

"Granted it means that you and your team will no longer be needed here, but I'm guessing that you're all looking forward to new challenges," said Manfort as he smiled and nodded his head as though agreeing with himself. "And a much deserved break from eighteen years of the same-old same-old, right, Smith?"

"Right, sir," said Smith a little too loud. "Looking forward to new challenges."

Fucking idiot, thought Manfort as he turned and walked away from Smith, leaving the ill-suited man wondering what had just happened.

"Look at them," said Kingsley to Bingham, both wearing expensive three-piece gray suits. They're fucking happy. We just got them to build a machine to put them all out of work so that we could make more money and the fucking idiots did it…and now they're celebrating."

"Did you get your bonus?" said Bingham.

"I did, yes," said Kingsley.

"Did you get your raise?" said Bingham.

"I did," said Kingsley. "And I might say, it was not displeasing."

"They made us richer," said Bingham. "They're working class heroes."

"But they're all out of jobs now, Bingham," said Kingsley. "They replaced themselves with a machine and now they're all out of work."

Bingham thought a moment and nodded. "They're fucking idiot heroes."

Glowing in their expensive three-piece gray suits, Stansfield and VanHart stood on either side of Davis in his blah brand suit.

"This is going to make us all rich, VanHart," said Stansfield.

"You mean, richer, Stansfield," said VanHart. "This machine is going to make us richer than we ever dreamed."

Davis smiled sheepishly. Here he was, standing between two of the managers. He'd never stood between two managers before. It was like he was part of some kind of informal management meeting...two managers discussing things with Davis in the middle.

"Too bad about the team," said Stansfield. "All that work and now..."

"Just business," said VanHart. "We have the machine. We don't need them anymore."

For just a split second, Davis let a negative thought run through the train of his glory-moment standing between two managers, as though he were part of this important discussion about the machine. That was enough to abort the thought before it had a chance to turn into anything close to an idea. Besides, he had more pressing things to dwell on...like coming up with some kind of plan to find work and pay the bills.

Fucking idiots, thought Stansfield and VanHart simultaneously.

"Everyone!" said Sinclair. "I think it's time for the moment we've all been waiting for." Everyone

246

turned expectant eyes on him as he walked over to one of the control consoles. "I've been told that his machine is so easy to use...that even I can use it."

Subdued chuckles and laughter floated ingratiatingly toward Sinclair, who sat down at the console. "Apparently, all I have to do it press this button." He smiled and looked around at the smiles. He put his right index finger on a large blue button labelled START and pressed it.

They all felt it at the same time, expensive three piece gray suits and mismatched suits. For an instant they thought it was the machine, but when the walls flew at them and started shredding their bodies and heat began to melt the threads of their suits, it was the IA in the machine that had the last thought: *Fucking idiots*.

From the Dead

The divorce wasn't working. It wasn't doing a thing to stop the creepiness, that clear image of her eyes and what he'd seen in them. She was right. She was so right, but how do you accept something like that? It goes against everything you believe in, everything that allows you to get through each day with some semblance of sanity.

He stood in front of the washroom mirror staring into his own eyes. He saw the fear, the cold wrapper of doubt tightening around his world. He looked down at his skinny naked frame. He used to be overweight. He used to eat with such relish, savoring the taste of food, savoring the taste of life.

But that was long ago, before his wife had gone over the deep end.

Or had she?

He ignored her emails. He kept blocking her, but she kept finding ways in with new accounts and other methods. He'd had his cell number changed a dozen times but she somehow found her way to the new numbers. He didn't have the heart to call the police or take legal action. There was something inside him still attached to her, something cloudy and confused with questions that surfaced in some translucent pool of self-inflicted turmoil with questions, surfacing and sinking, surfacing and sinking. *Was it my fault? Could I have done something? Did I really have to leave her?*

He looked back into his sunken eyes. He wondered who he was, this skinny frame that ran. He should have stayed. He should have comforted her. He should have grieved for her. He should have helped her get through the days of her death while she was still trapped in the world of the living.

Sometimes he prayed for death, but it never came. He prayed now. And it came...at first, as a distant rumble just before the walls of his washroom swallowed him with fire.

In that instant, Clay Baker knew that he would be in death with his wife, Judy, and there would be no living to confuse things.

But the Coffee's Good

248

Cora Darling heard it on the radio. She wasn't sure whether to believe it or not. She turned on the TV to see if its news agreed with the radio's news. The screen scratched out static on every channel. She went to her home office and turned on her computer to see if the internet agreed with the radio. She frowned at the white screen with the block letters: You are not connected to the internet. She went back to the kitchen and sat at the table where steam still wavered over the top of her coffee cup. She picked it up and sipped. She had an assignment to deliver to a client in two hours. She could have done that two hours earlier but it was so beautiful out that she spent those two hours on the back deck admiring her view of the city in the distance, the light cloud of smog surrounding it, the glints and glitters from cars and buses and trucks streaming like metal water through the city streets and turnpikes.

And then it was time to get back to work. But first a fresh coffee made from the imported beans she'd bought online and had just arrived that morning.

She wasn't even sure why she'd turned on the radio. It was just there, on the table, facing her, unused for almost a year. She turned the dial and the radio face lit up and the news channel blared: We're getting reports of explosions in…

And then static. Most of the stations were static. Others emitted confused news reports. No one seemed to know what was going on. Two DJs joked about a weekend fishing trip one of them had "survived." One channel played classical music.

Cora thought that it sounded like Mozart. She left the radio on that station for now.

She'd had a feeling when she woke up this morning. She wasn't sure what the feeling was, but she remembered it being nothing good, like biting into a genetically modified peach and feeling the pit shattering around your teeth. Her back was to the glass doors leading out to the deck. She didn't have to look to see it. The wall in front of her suddenly burst into brilliant light. *I should have finished it and sent it off before taking a break.* The coffee cup was to her mouth. *And this is really great coffee.* The light from behind her was so bright it seemed to burn out everything in its path with sheer brilliance alone, and not just a wave of heat and angry energy devouring everything in its path, including Cora, who managed to get one more sip of coffee before she evaporated along with the coffee and her schedule.

Those Irritating Fireworks

Alvin screeched and shot straight up into the air, fur standing on end, claws tearing at the air and, oh, that awful cat-terror screech. This had a domino effect. Lucy poured half a cup of green tea onto her white blouse and Daniel's lighter missed his cigarette enough to set his mustache of fire. The walls of the Mueller home resounded with screeches of terror and pain.

Outside the huge Mueller living room picture window, the sky exploded with color. A burst of glittering red showered the sky with scarlet comets that in turn burst into a shower of smaller comets. Behind the red, a golden mushroom exploded into the sky with an ear-shattering BOOM. Not three seconds after Alvin landed on the floor, he was clawing up Lucy's tea sodden white blouse leaving a trail of blood spots where his claws tore through the blouse and into Lucy's skin. Lucy shrieked. Alvin crouched on top of her head, claws digging into her forehead causing tiny rivulets of blood to stream down over her eyebrows. Seven feet away, Daniel slapped his face vigorously, trying to put out the flame in his mustache.

Half an hour later, Lucy and Daniel sat in their cozy arm chairs fuming. The bandages on Lucy's forehead showed signs of blood spotting. The left side of Daniel's upper lip glistened with salve. Alvin crouched in a corner of the room, glaring at life.

"I don't understand what they get out of it," said Daniel, both arms prone on the arms of the chair. "They send a bunch of colored lights into the sky and make a lot of ungodly noise."

"It's what they do here and it's a...a nuisance," said Lucy, both arms wrapped around her chest, as though hunkering down for an attack. "A damn nuisance."

"They pollute the air with chemicals and noise," said Daniel indignantly. "Waste of time and money."

"And they do it every year."

"All that noise."

"And it can't be good for children's eyes."

"And their necks...all that looking up...straining the muscles."

"And the noise. Poor Alvin." Though, there was a trace of insincerity in Lucy's voice as she tightened her grip around her chest, still in pain from the clawing from Alvin.

"We may have to get help for Alvin." Daniel looked at Alvin, eyes fomenting sympathy. "I've heard that traumatic episodes like this can scar animals for life."

"And think of all the children...all those poor children waking up horrified from their sleep to the sound of that thunder. I don't even want to think about what it does to infants."

"Thank God it's just once a year."

"It shouldn't even be once a year. Maybe once every hundred years."

"On a desert island."

"Far away from here."

"Far away from the children."

"And the infants."

"And Alvin." Daniel cocked his head to the side and squinted his eyes.

"What is it, dear?" said Lucy.

"I'm not sure, my dear. Did you hear something?"

"I don't think so..." Lucy suddenly squinted her eyes. "I think..."

Alvin thrust his head up. His eyes widened into white circles.

"I think they've gone a bit far this time," said Daniel's mouth as it rocketed away from his head.

"The nerve of those…" said Lucy as her words evaporated into the rush of fire.

What the fuck now? thought Alvin in whatever language cats thought in as they turned into nuclear steam.

More Than Just the Candles

"Honestly, Amanda, this isn't what I had it mind." It was impossible to say where Wilbur's words came from, their source and their direction. Wilbur wasn't Wilbur anymore. Amanda wasn't Amanda. And it really didn't matter what Wilbur had in mind. Both were ingredients in a fiery stew of atomic displacement, their atoms reeling and doing things that were considered abnormal in polite society. But then, polite society was pretty much no more as well.

"This is not my idea of a good time." Amanda's words were equally as puzzling as Wilbur's. Where did they come from? Amanda is no more. Who was listening? Wilbur is no more. Didn't Amanda and Wilbur have bigger things to worry about? Shouldn't what's left of their words be wrapped around prayers or something?

"I wanted this to be a romantic experience for both of us," denoted Wilbur from everywhere and nowhere. "That's why I filled the house with candles. It took me half an hour to light them all."

"And now look at us." As though there was anything recognizable enough to look at.

253

"But, Amanda, I honestly don't think this had anything to do with the candles."

"Just like you, Wilbur, never take responsibility for your actions."

The disdain in Amanda's words burned into whatever flux of consciousness Wilbur had become like an existential slap to his disintegrating selfness. "But this is not what candles do, Amanda. Not even a house full of candles. This is not what it feels like to be burned to death by candles burning a house down. This is definitely something else."

"And how would you know what it feels like to be burned to death by candles, Wilbur. You've never been burned to death by candles. I would have known about it."

"No, Amanda, I've never been burned to death by candles. But I've imagined being burned to death by candles. I imagined it while I was a lighting all the candles. After half an hour of lighting candles, you begin to have odd thoughts. And I can tell you right know, Amanda, this is not what it feels like to be burned to death by candles. This is something else."

"This is YOU, Wilbur. This is another one of your failures. My mother told me you would do this some day. She warned me. "You'll just get burned if you...

For Laughing Out Loud

Life was stranger than he remembered. The people seemed different but he couldn't say what exactly was different. There was nothing he could point his finger at and say, "That's it!" But things were different.

Kayla was as beautiful as ever. She hadn't changed a bit. She lifted her wine glass and sipped slowly, savoring the subtle hints of fruit. Her pinky finger pointed out as she held the glass. Her eyes shifted to the stage where a bald man with a huge gut protruding under a dirty t-shirt unhooked the microphone from the stand and introduced himself: "Evening folks. I'm Larry." Deadpan flat voice. Not much of an introduction for someone billed as the city's most outstanding comedian. The dinner audience applauded. Politely. A deadpan applause.

Kayla smiled, her big brown eyes full of anticipation as she clapped her hands together, politely.

The applause died abruptly as though someone had hit the Stop Applause button. Larry looked around at the crowd, unsmiling, deadpan. He put the microphone up to his lips and said, "Ah gets ta thinkin'." He looked around some more, eyes serious, face expressionless. Some of the audience smiled. A few nodded their heads in agreement. Larry put the mike to his lips again. "Ah gets ta thinkin'." Chuckles broke out around the room as Larry surveyed the audience with his blank eyes. He put the mike to his lips. "Ah gets ta thinkin'."

Bursts of laughter peppered the audience. A few slapped tables and knees and Larry eyed them. He put the mike to his lips. "Ah gets ta thinkin'." The audience cracked up. One man spit out a mouthful of beer as he wailed laughter. People doubled over, slapping each other on the backs, pointing at Larry on the stage with his dirty t-shirt and deadpan stare. "Ah gets ta thinkin'." A woman at the table next to theirs laughed herself into a fit of choking. Kayla practically screamed laughter. The house bristled into a laughing frenzy. Two people fell off their chairs and writhed on the floor, laughing violently. Larry put the mike back on the stand and walked off the stage while the house went nuts.

What the hell?

Kayla doubled over in her chair, a thin line of saliva sparkled on her chin. He'd never seen her laughing like this. He looked around the club. He'd never seen an entire audience laughing like this, and Larry hadn't said anything remotely funny. Kayla looked at him and pointed as she tried to speak, "You…you…you…" She practically choked on the word. "You don't…you don't think he's…he's funny?"

He didn't know what to say. He played it safe and nodded. "Hilarious," he said. "Glad you're enjoying the show."

It took almost ten minutes before the audience calmed down enough so that eating, drinking and normal talk could resume. Kayla was one of the first to get it together. He was thankful for that.

"He's got to be one of the funniest comedians in the world," said Kayla.

"I guess," he said. "Lead-in and punch line all in the same sentence."

"He's a genius." Kayla sipped some more wine. "He's setting all new standards for stand-up comedy. Next week, he's starting a world tour. We were lucky to see him tonight. After the tour, we probably won't be able to afford to see him again."

"So...Kayla. What was your favorite part of his act?"

She thought about this a moment, sipped some more wine and said, "I think I like all of it. You know, the slow buildup of expectation and then the sudden reverse of events leading to something completely unexpected."

He considered this for a moment. "What were you expecting him to say at the end...the unexpected?"

She laughed, bent forward and reached her hand over the table to squeeze the top of his hand. "Anything, Alex, anything but what he said."

The lights dimmed and a spotlight beamed down on the area around the microphone. Chatter and clinking evaporated into the air. The curtains at the side of the stage parted and a short woman wearing a cowboy hat that seemed larger than her walked up to the mike and adjusted it to her height. Not a peep from the audience. The woman introduced herself as Mona. Her hat extended over the mike as she spoke and her face was barely discernible. After a brief round of polite applause the audience went quiet and Mona leaned in close to the mike.

"He's not a very nice person."

Titters and chuckles from the audience.

"He's not a very nice person."

Guffaws and knee slaps.

"He's not a very nice person."

Bodies bending with uncontrollable laughter.

"He's not a very nice person."

People falling off chairs, deafening laughter, glasses shattering as tables tilted.

Kayla's face turned blue. He rushed around the table and slapped her on the back a few times. She gagged for a few seconds and continued laughing. Mona had left the stage, leaving the room in chaos. Everywhere, white shirts were stained with wine and regurgitated food, evening gowns torn and spotted. A man sat on the floor with his head between his legs, hyperventilating.

Alex was stunned. Nothing Mona had said was funny. Nothing Larry had said was funny. *What's wrong with these people?*

After a few minutes, Kayla calmed down enough to talk coherently. "Alex, hun, where's your sense of humor. You used to laugh all the time...at just about anything."

"I guess I'm still trying to catch up on the reality of everything. It all seems so strange, like a monitor not quite in focus. Nothing to worry about, Kay."

Kayla looked doubtful and bent her head slightly to the left, just enough to signal thoughts going through her head, wondering if he really was OK. She sipped some more wine and relaxed almost immediately.

***

Doc Freeman was one of those men who was old for as long as you could remember, but never aged a day since you met him. He was tall and lean with a full head of gray hair—not a strand of which had ever turned white—and his blue eyes never lost their luster.

"You've been in a coma for ten years, Alex. These days, things change in a matter of months, sometimes weeks. After ten years, you're almost in another world. But you'll get used to it. Just give it time."

"OK, Doc...let me try something." Alex fixed his eyes on Doc Freeman. His face was deadpan. "Ah gets ta thinkin'."

Doc Freeman stared at Alex without expression.

Alex repeated, "Ah gets ta thinkin'."

Doc Freeman nodded slowly.

"Ah gets ta thinkin'."

"And your point is, Alex?"

"Ah gets ta thinkin'."

"It's natural for you to be thinking about things, Alex. In a coma for ten years...you have a lot to think about."

"You don't think that's funny?"

"Think what's funny?"

"Ah gets ta thinkin'."

"What are you getting at, Alex?

"The comedian, Deadpan Larry."

"Yes? I've heard of him."

"He said that four or five times and people were almost barfing they were laughing so much. But I just said the same thing to you and you didn't even crack a smile."

Doc Freeman thought about this, cupped his hands together and rested his chin on them. "I think it might just be a matter of delivery, Alex. Professional comedians…"

"OK, Doc…try this. He's not a very nice person."

"Who's not a very nice person?"

"Another comedian, Mona, said that a few times and brought the audience practically to their knees."

"Again…another professional comedian. It's all about the delivery, Alex."

Alex nodded slowly. "I guess you're right. Must just be stuff like a hangover from the coma."

"Now you're getting it, Alex. Things are going to seem strange for a while. But it'll all fit together in time. Just give it time and you'll fit back in."

***

He remembered coffee shops being bright cheerful places with ample window space and smiling high school students doling out the caffeine. The coffee shop he sat in was anything but. It was shadowy and windowless and the fixtures were shades of gray; the students wore dour expressions and were almost zombie-like in the way they stood behind the counter—not moving or talking until a

260

customer approached, and then they dished out unsmiling service.

Something caught his attention. It was the couple sitting behind him. The woman had said something and the man had laughed. He caught the tail end of the next thing she said: "...back atcha." The man laughed louder. The woman said: "Coming right back atcha." The man nearly cracked up. "Coming right back atcha." He cracked. Doc Freeman was wrong. Coma or no coma, there was something wrong here. After a couple of minutes, the man said, "They shouldn't be doing that." The woman giggled. "They shouldn't be doing that." The woman laughed.

Alex stood up and left.

***

City streets hadn't changed much. Cars, trucks and buses jockeyed like ants around a jar of honey. Horns blared, brakes screeched, thrush mufflers blared, drivers yelled. People jostled and rushed on the sidewalks. The air was bloated with the smell of fast food. Everything seemed normal. Except something he couldn't quite put his finger on. Something was different, something integral to a city street. He stopped walking and leaned against an ornate metal railing. He watched the traffic and the busy passersby, some alone and some in groups, some stooped over phones. *What is it*? he thought. *What's wrong here?* It came to him when he saw a group of six teenagers passing by. There was something out of place with them. He studied them as they walked by and realized that not one of them was smiling. They weren't even talking to each other. But they were obviously a group together.

He looked at others on the sidewalk. Nobody smiled. Their faces were, for the most part, neutral. They neither scowled nor smiled. Their faces were blank, expressionless. Everybody. He had a feeling that he was looking at a mass of mild-tempered zombies. He reached into his memories of sidewalks lining busy city streets. For the most part, he remembered determined faces, people going somewhere, having something to do and in a rush. He remembered animated conversations, anger, laughter, desperation…the whole gamut of human emotion flowing over the concrete. But the faces he looked at showed nothing. Even the ones talking into their cell phones seemed disinterested in their conversations, like nothing was really being said, nothing being heard.

He began to think that maybe he'd waked up on a different planet or some weird dimension far from where he'd made his last memories…long before the coma.

What the hell is going on?

***

He was sitting in another coffee shop with a laptop in front of him reading about Charlie Chaplan's definition of humor when he heard a familiar voice say, "Alex…is that really you?" He looked up and recognized the face instantly: Roger Pickford, his roommate from college. He'd gained some weight, but his face still had that chiseled look and his eyes were dark but bright. Before Alex had a chance to say anything, Roger was sitting across from him, smiling and exuberant. "Shit, Alex, you haven't changed a bit and how long has it been…fifteen, twenty years. I heard that you were in a coma but it looks like you're alright now and holy shit you look good. So you're out of that now. What're you doing now?"

That part hadn't changed about Roger either. Alex swore that he could talk for ten minutes without coming up for air.

"Christ, it's good to see you. You look good yourself."

"So what're you doing? It's been so long. So you were really in a coma? What was that all about?"

"Accident. Lucky to be alive enough to be in a coma, I guess."

Roger laughed. It was one of those laughs that permeated everything around him, bringing looks from people at other tables. "Always looking at the bright side. Cup half full. Looks like a few years out of it didn't change your attitude. How many years was it?

"Ten."

"Holy shit, ten years!" He swiped his right hand over his forehead as though to wipe away the disbelief. "Ten years! What's it like to be back in the world after all…" He looked down at the laptop. "I see…catching up on the internet. I guess that'd be the way. Things must've changed a lot for you."

"Not really, actually. Everything seems pretty much the same."

"The same? After ten years? You gotta be joking. After ten years?"

"Except one thing, I guess."

"And what's that, Alex?"

"OK...here goes." He straightened up and looked Roger full in the eyes. "Ah gets ta thinkin'."

There was a long moment of silence as the two men looked into each other's eyes. Roger waited to hear more. Alex just stared, waiting for a response.

"OK," said Roger. "You've been thinking. Thinking about what?"

"I gets ta thinkin'." Alex's eyes practically bled desperation. "Ah gets ta thinkin'! Ah gets ta thinkin'!"

Roger's eyes widened. He pushed himself back in his chair, away from Alex. "OK, Alex, OK," he said nervously. "I get it. So...what do you think about."

"No," said Alex. "I'm not really thinking about anything. It's a joke...Ah gets ta thinkin'."

Roger thought about this for moment, staring nervously at Alex the whole time. "I'm sorry, Alex, but I don't get it."

Alex's eyes flashed. "Right!" He learned forward, causing Roger to push himself back further so that he was pressed hard against the back of his chair. "I don't get it either, but everybody else laughed like crazy."

Roger seemed to calm down a bit. "Who laughed, Alex? Who's everybody else?"

"The audience, Roger, the audience." He leaned back in his chair. Roger relaxed a little more. "Some comedian named Larry got up in front of an audience and said 'Ah gets ta thinkin'' over and over and every time he said it, people laughed harder and harder until some of them actually fell off their chairs, some were in tears, some threw up. But this Larry guy didn't say anything funny. All he said was 'Ah gets ta thinkin'.'"

Roger cupped his hands on the table in front of him. His lips curled into a half smile. "You mean Larry, the comedian? The funniest man to hit stand up in years?"

"Yes, Larry, the comedian. But he's not funny. He just repeats some random slogan or something over and over and the people in the audience go nuts. There's no lead in, no punch line…just a stupid phase that means nothing."

Roger smiled as he shook his head slowly. "Alex, my friend, Larry's a genius…he knows how to tell a joke. I think you need to lighten up. You've been away for a long time. Things might have changed a little…"

"A little?" Alex's eyes flared. "A little? I walk around and see people all wearing the same vapid expression on their faces. No one jokes around. No one smiles. Everybody seems to be preoccupied with nothing. And they laugh at a stupid sentence that doesn't make any sense."

"Come on, Alex…people still laugh. We haven't lost our sense of humor in the last ten years. I think maybe being out of it might have had an effect on how you perceive things and…"

"How I perceive things isn't the problem, Roger." He pointed his finger at the other tables where people sat and talked, drank coffee, wrote in notebooks and buried themselves in laptops. "Do you see any smiles on any of the faces in here? Do you see just one person cracking a smile? The only people I've seen smiling besides you was a couple who left a few minutes ago and they did the same thing as Larry...they said nonsense and laughed. They laughed at nothing!"

Roger looked around and turned back to Alex. "It's Monday, Alex. People aren't usually in bright spirits on Monday."

"Monday, Saturday, Sunday...people smile and joke every day of the week. Look at that couple over there..." He pointed to a man and woman in casual wear facing each other in a booth by the window who seemed to be having a light conversation. "Neither of them have smiled since I've been in here. And it's the same with all the other tables. I've been here for over an hour and not one single person has smiled."

"Maybe you should go over there and tell them Larry's joke." Alex glared at Roger. "OK, OK...I was just joking. See...I just joked but you didn't laugh. Humor is still alive and well, Alex. You just have to see it. And be ready to laugh."

"But it wasn't funny, Roger. Larry wasn't funny. He just stated some stupid random thing and people cracked up over it. It wasn't funny. And nobody's smiling. Nobody's smiling!"

Alex's eyes glowed with desperation; Roger's eyes showed concern. Neither of them knew what to say until finally Roger said, "You know that humor is cultural thing, right?"

"What?"

"Humor…it's cultural. In some countries people will laugh at something while, in another country, you might be sent to jail for saying the same thing."

"What's that got to do with what I'm talking about?"

"Everything, Alex." Roger cupped his hands on the table and leaned forward. "You've been sort of *away* for ten years. During that time, people's sense of humor has changed. It happens all the time…something that was considered funny a hundred years ago might be considered tragic today. You were away from that progression for a decade. Things change fast these days, Alex. It's a cultural thing based on time and place. You just have to get with the times."

Alex stared at Roger in disbelief. His lips moved as though he were going to say something but the words smashed around in his head like bumper cars out of control. He took a deep, deep breath that seemed to take hours. He appeared to grow calm and his lips stopped quivering. He let the air out through his mouth. He looked over at the couple conversing quietly and said, "OK. Let's see what happens." He stood up and walked over to their table. The couple looked up at him, not smiling, but not frowning, neutral.

He looked from one to the other and said, "The turkey is out of the pan."

267

The two looked at him intently, as though wondering if they might be in some kind of danger and maybe they should run for it.

"The turkey is out of the pan."

The man and woman looked at each other. The crazy man hadn't attacked. Maybe everything would be OK.

"The turkey is out of the pan."

The woman shrugged as she looked at the man, who shrugged back. They both turned their eyes on Alex.

"The turkey is out of the pan."

The woman giggled. The man smiled.

"The turkey is out of the pan."

The man laughed quietly. The woman put her hand to her smiling lips and stifled a chuckle.

"The turkey is out of the pan."

The couple broke into outright laughter.

"The turkey is out of the pan."

They laughed hysterically, looking at each other, pointing at Alex.

"And you think that's funny? You think some fucking turkey being out of a fucking pan is funny?"

The laughter stopped abruptly. The couple shot each other confused glances between looking fearfully at Alex.

"What's so fucking funny about that!" yelled Alex. The room went silent. Everyone stared at Alex. Roger shook his head, frowning as he bowed his head into his hand. The couple at the table stared at Alex. Alex's face turned a light shade of purple. "What? What's so fucking funny?"

A woman three tables away said, "What did you say that was supposed to be funny?"

Alex snapped his head around and glared at her. "What!"

"What did you say that was funny?"

"Nothing!" he yelled. "Nothing! I said, 'The turkey is out of the pan.'"

A man a few more tables away said, "What was that you said?"

Alex glared at him. "The turkey is out of the pan! The turkey is out of the pan!"

Chuckles and giggles erupted throughout the room.

Alex looked around, staring in disbelief. Roger looked at Alex, smiling.

"What the hell!" yelled Alex. "The turkey is out of the pan!"

Laughter broke out.

"The turkey is out of the pan!" screamed Alex.

Chaos broke out. People slammed their fists on their tables, spilled lattes, slapped each other on the back and laughed uncontrollably until the noise was deafening.

***

A spotlight shone down on a lone figure on the stage dressed in ragged jeans and a torn t-shirt. The figure was unsmiling and disinterested, like a man waiting for a bus to take him somewhere he really didn't want to go. His head was bent slightly down, eyes focused on a spot halfway between the stage and the audience seated at tables in a half circle

269

before the stage. Slowly, he raised his head. He looked solemnly at the audience as though they were some minor irritant that he'd prefer to go away. He took a deep breath and said in a flat, lifeless voice, "She wore a green dress."

The audience tittered.

"She wore a green dress."

Pockets of laughter broke out across the floor.

Kayla smiled. Roger smiled. Doc Freeman smiled.

Alex focused on their table as he fought against smiling, a gesture that would have blown the act now that he finally knew how to tell a joke; in fact, he could tell a joke so well that he'd supplanted Larry as the most important comedian of the day, and he was so glad to finally fit in.

A Room Without a View

For the third time today, Jasper wanted to kill his computer. He wanted to punch it hard in the monitor, kick the shit out of its CPU, spin the mouse by its tail and smash it onto the surface of his desk, pull the letters out of his keyboard and set them on fire.

But he didn't.

He sat at his desk staring at a screen where everything was suddenly dormant, his cursor frozen over a Word document, his web browser refusing to surf, his keyboard disabled, not even Ctl Alt Delete working so that he could close all the programs and start over again. And it was against company policy to do a hard shutdown by pressing the On/Off button. He'd done that shortly after he'd started working for xTLan Tech and he'd found himself surrounded by two inquisitive geeks from Tech Services and an annoying manager asking him if he'd read the policy manual, quoting from it, offering to send him printouts of the relevant passage. He'd felt like he was auditioning for a sequel to Office Space.

In a situation like this, according to the policy manual, he was supposed to send an email to Tech Services. It had to be an email so that an automated Job Number could be assigned to the request for services. It couldn't be a phone call. It couldn't be a face-to-face request. It had to be an email. There had to be an automated Job Number.

Which was impossible.

His computer was frozen. Useless. A piece of junk. A high tech paper weight. There was no way out...he had no choice but to accept the inevitability of his situation. He stared at the monitor and, dead pixel by dead pixel, the solution presented itself in all its wonderful and inescapable glory.

He punched his computer monitor so hard he broke his hand in four places.

**

Unemployment really sucked, just like everything else in Jasper Proud's life. He was forty-two years old, single, and hadn't had sex in three years. He wasn't bad looking but he was no whatisname...that guy in the movies. Jasper was the other guy...the one nobody remembered. He lived by himself in a flat with windows facing the concrete block wall of a four story furniture outlet. His flat was on the second floor and he had to turn his lights on in the daytime and he had to keep the window open to let out the killingheat and the stench of rotting things in the walls. He had no savings. His credit cards were maxed out and to top it all off, he hadn't shit in three days.

Stress had that effect on him.

"Fuck the world," he said. The bitterness bleeding out of his voice soured the air around him and made the gray concrete buildingscape on the other side of his windows all the' more depressing. He craned his head upwards and told God to fuck off. He guzzled another mouthful of beer. His chair could have been salvaged from the bottom of a landfill but it matched his mood and his life. He used his left hand to guzzle beer because his right hand was wrapped in a cast and it hurt like hell. He stared at his reflection in the forty inch flat screen television that he'd accidentally poured water on while he was watering his dying corn plant because he wasn't used to watering it with his left hand. Maybe he shouldn't have watered his corn plant when he was drunk. Maybe he should have just stayed in bed. Maybe he should never have been born.

No TV tonight.

***

His alarm clock went off late, but that was OK…he didn't have to get up for anything. He was unemployed and incapacitated. The alarm could go off anytime it wanted. But he was pissed anyway. "Fucking clock." For just an instant, the thought crossed his mind that maybe he should slap the clock off the bedside table, but it was the kind of thing he would do with his right hand and he'd already done that kind of thing and now he was unemployed and had a broken right hand. He reached out and pressed his index finger on the button to turn the alarm off.

"Fucking stupid clock." He rolled over and faced away from his stupid clock. He stared at the concrete blocks of the furniture outlet and it occurred to him that he was the only person in the world who could see that portion of the outlet's wall unless he had friends over, but he had no friends.

Not even his landlord, who never visited the flats he rented for fear of contamination, would see it. The view was Jasper's and his only. All that dark grey concrete. The parallel lines where concrete cemented on concrete. All his to enjoy.

"Fucking wall."

Or not enjoy.

He stared at the wall and the longer he stared, the angrier he grew. He wasn't sure exactly what he was angry about. He was unemployed, broke, maxed out on his credit cards, his television was broken, his hand was broken, he was in pain, his clock was stupid, he was out of beer and he still had to shit. That was a lot to be angry about, but it wasn't really what he was angry about. There was more. So much more. There was his whole life and what he was going through now was no more than a replay of his life for as long as he could remember…like a bad song stuck in a loop.

"FUCK OFF WORLD!"

He suddenly went quiet. He raised his eyebrows. He lay motionless, thinking: Did I just scream? He thought about this for a moment. It sure did sound like he'd screamed. His voice had been loud like a scream. It had been full of anger and remorse and pain and pissed-off-edness like a scream. His throat was sore, as though he'd just finished screaming. He was frozen motionless, except for his eyes, which darted around the room at the walls, the window, ceiling, the door. No complaints from the neighbors. No pissed off bangs against the floor, ceiling or walls. Maybe he didn't scream. Or maybe no one gave a shit. Maybe everybody was at work or sleeping off hangovers or too high to notice anything but dust motes floating just beyond their noses.

"FUCK OFF WORLD!"

He held his breath, listening for a response, an echo, a complaint, a confirmation, but a dead silence clipped his words the instant he finished mouthing them as though he hadn't said a thing. As though his anger at everything didn't exist. As though it had been taken away from him by the silence like everything in his life had always been taken away from him and making him almost afraid to ownanything including his own life…and that just pissed him off more. He wasn't going to let the silence silence him. He would have his words. His words would resound. His words would crush the silence.

"FUCK OFF WORLD!"

What the fuck…not even an echo? Where's the echo? He looked around as though maybe the echo was hiding somewhere in his bedroom. Where could it be? Behind the cheap faded imitations of famous pictures with their cracked frames and broken glass? Was it under the bedside table? Maybe it was hiding behind the dresser with the drawers that didn't close all the way because the plywood was so warped. There should at least be something for a second or two. It doesn't have to be an echo…just something…for a second or two. But there wasn't. There was nothing to confirm that Jasper Proud had just screamed.

"FUCK OFF WORLD!"
"FUCK OFF WORLD!"

"FUCK OFF WORLD!"

Nothing. Not even a scared roach scurrying away from the crazy man's screams. And still no complaints from the neighbors. He jumped out of bed and ran, naked, to the livingroom. He screamed at this water-logged TV.

"FUCK OFF TV!"

He stood in the middle of the room, back bent forward, arms dangling, staring into silence. He screamed at this mismatched couch and arm chair.

"FUCK OFF COUCH!"

"FUCK OFF CHAIR!"

He screamed at the beer-stained coffee table.

"FUCK OFF TABLE!"

He screamed at the yellowing ceiling.

"FUCK OFF CEILING!"

He screamed at time-flattened carpet.

"FUCK OFF CARPET!"

He screamed at the open window with its magnificent view of concrete blocks and parallel lines.

"FUCK OFF WINDOW!"

He stopped short. He stared at the wall. He held his breath. What was that? He cocked his head to the side. Was that an echo? He listened. Nothing. He listened again, this time a little more intently. Still nothing.

"FUCK OFF WORLD!"

And there it was again, somewhere in the distance of the concrete and the parallel lines:

fuck off world

It wasn't much, but it was there. It was an echo, an anemic feeble half-hearted echo (sort of like his life) but it was an echo.

It would do.

He stood in the middle of his living room, bent forward, arms hanging. He'd just accomplished something. He wasn't sure what but he knew that something had just happened and it was a positive thing that just maybe didn't suck. Maybe. He walked to the window and stopped directly in front of it. Another foot and he would be outside falling into the void between buildings. He braced himself, took a deep breath and…

"FUCK OFF WORLD!"

fuck off world fuck off world fuck off world

An echo.

A wave of exaltation rampaged through the very cellular structure of Jasper's body. Every molecule in his biological composition vibrated with exoneration. Jasper DeLong was a man. He was a man with an echo.

"FUCK OFF WORLD!"

fuck off world fuck off world fuck off world

He forgot about his broken hand. He forgot about his broken TV and his broken life. A wave of beatific relief spread through his body and tears saturated his lashes with hope. A wonderful thought raced through his mind.

I think I can shit.

He spent about an hour in the washroom, shitting gleefully. He became acutely aware of the human body's profound ability to hold vast quantities of excrement. Without exploding.

He also thought about the echo. It wasn't all that big a deal. It was just an echo, his own voice bouncing off the walls in the narrow space between the two buildings. He wondered why such a small thing made him feel so good. He wondered how it could possibly have made him shit.

He stayed on the toilet long beyond the time he'd emptied every ounce of shit from his body. His hand didn't feel as painful and his bowels felt like they could float away. He hadn't felt this good in years. He hadn't felt this good in his entire life. For the first time in ages, he smiled. It was a crooked, uncomfortable smile, something lacking experience and practice. But it was wide and scary.

He wiped his ass and flushed, pulled up his skivvies and pants and left the washroom without washing his hands. His place, his germs, fuck off world.

For the first time in his life, he felt like he was on to something. For the first time ever, he felt like he had control over something. He wasn't sure what it was yet, but he could feel it, feel the sense of empowerment. After all, he'd just had the most intense shit of this life. Now that was control.

He walked to the window and kneeled down. He stuck his head out and looked up. A slit of blue sky hinted that maybe there was more to life that his tiny apartment and the furniture store's wall. He looked down. Despite the sunny day, the ground between the two buildings was dark and overgrown with shade-loving weeds. He screamed.

FUCK OFF WORLD!

fuck off world fuck off world fuck off world

He smiled. Sort of. He would need ample practice on that front. But the overall sense of wellbeing felt good. He pulled his head back in and stood up. He wondered how he could apply his newfound sense of elation to something more productive than shitting. There had to be something else he could do with it. He sat down in his ragged chair and pondered. He made faces as he pondered, faces that reflected thoughtfulness, inquisitiveness, puzzlement, excitement, calculation, disappointment, criticism, lightheadedness…but not a glimmer of conclusiveness or decision.

FUCK OFF WORLD!

fuck off world fuck off world fuck off world

No decision, but he did have to shit again.

***

Three days after Jasper started shitting again, he passed out on the living room floor. He'd eaten everything edible in his refrigerator and cupboards, mostly condiments like catsup and relish, a couple of withered apples, freezer-burned veggies and a piece of chicken. He found a couple of bags of crackers that may or may not have had traces of mold but he covered the suspect spots with scrapings from the bottom of a peanut butter jar and a raspberry jam jar.

He had no money and he hadn't been outside his apartment in a week or so. He couldn't leave. He had to stay inside until he reached some sort of decision. What could he do with his new sense of self? How could he apply his new found positivity in a positive way? What was his next step?

That's it, he thought as he stared at the cracks in his ceiling and a metal fan that had likely stopped fanning before he was born, *I need to decide on a next step. What to do after I get up off the floo*r.

He sat up and put his head between his legs. He was dizzy as hell but he finally had one clear thought: What do I do next?

Sitting up was a good start. He waited until some of the dizziness passed and stood up. He walked to his chair and sat down. What's my next step? He'd never thought like this before: thinking in terms of 'do this' and then 'this' and then 'this'. He'd never had any kind of chronological order in his life, a checklist for living. He'd always simply jumped into the day and let it take him wherever. When he was working, he did whatever came at him, finished it, and went on to the next thing. He couldn't remember ever having written a list. When he went shopping, he bought what he came across. He paid his bills as they came in. He did laundry sometime after he couldn't stand the smell of things he donned. There was no order in his life, no progression from here to there. He was always just here. And right now, here wasn't a good place to be. He could starve to death hanging around here too long. He needed food and there was no food here. He needed to just get out and about, do the social thing. Go out and shop or something, with emphasis on the "or something" given that he had no money, no credit and no job.

Where would he go? What would he do?

Maybe he could apply for a new job, pass out resumes, look for Help Wanted signs in store windows, check the Want Ads or go to the library and use one of their computers to find a job. He wasn't sure what he wanted to do...anything but what he did at the last job...data entry. He didn't like computers and they didn't like him. They spewed strange messages about esoteric errors and pages not found and they broke down when you needed them most.

He looked across the room at a metal telephone stand with a phone on it that hadn't been used in ages because the bill hadn't been paid in ages. But it wasn't the phone that caught is attention...it was a large book with a yellow cover: The phone book on which the phone rested. He grabbed it desperately, almost knocking the phone onto the floor, and curled up in his chair with it. The yellow pages were bursting with possibilities. He turned the pages and scanned. The book was heavy and his broken hand hurt like hell but he ignored the pain as he scanned each page for an escape from his life.

There were restaurants and plumbers and auto sales and signs for your truck and stuff for your pets that he would never be able to afford for himself.

His mind spun with the possibilities. With all this, there had to be somewhere where he fit in, somewhere without idiotic error messages from computers, somewhere he could just work and be happy. Could he sell flowers to love struck young men and be happy for them? Could he flip a burger and take pride in grilling it to perfection?

A notice slashing downwards on one of the ads caught his attention:

LOOKING FOR A NEW START?

It went on to say that they were always on the lookout for new talent. No experience was necessary.

No startup expenses. No experience. He was qualified. This job was cut out just for him. A thought blazed across his mind: *What is this job that I'm qualified for?*

It was difficult to tell. The ad was written in a confusing way. He thought it might be some kind of delivery service. He could deliver things. Maybe they would give him a car. Or maybe it was some kind of referral service. He could refer. And he didn't have any experience in that. They would train him, teach him to refer like an expert, make him a referral wiz. And they would pay him. He could buy a new TV. Beer. He could buy a case of beer to drink while he watched sit coms on his new TV. All he had to do was refer.

Or deliver. He didn't care much either way. Deliver...refer...it was all the same. He would have a new TV and a case of beer. And maybe even a car. He would like that. He smiled. He scratched his groin. He eased back in his chair. He'd never felt so exuberant before. He almost couldn't breathe.

The following day, he woke with a new sense of purpose. Today would be the starting point in a life bursting with meaning and satisfaction. He snatched the phone book up quickly and turned to the pagewith his NEW START. Still naked from bed, he walked into the kitchenette and copied the phone number. There was a pay phone in a drug store just down the street. He would go there and make the call that would change his life.

***

Jasper sat on a park bench staring into the street. He wore a blue plaid full-sleeve shirt, navy blue slacks and black leather shoes with newly fortified soles, fresh with glue from that morning. His face was blank, his eyes unfocussed. His lips trembled. His new sense of purpose had been thoroughly doused with a single phone call.

The woman on the other end had asked, "What do you want to do with your life?"

Without thinking, he'd replied, "I want to refer. It's always been my dream." To cover his bases, he'd added, "And deliver. I've always wanted to deliver."

A silence had followed. He'd waited seemingly forever with his new sense of purpose gasping for air in the silence until he'd begun to lose patience. "Why did you ask that?"

"I beg your pardon?

That did it. He'd heard that line before…too many times before. "Why did you ask me that stupid fucking question?"

At the exact instant that he'd realized that was the wrong answer, there was a click at the other end. The call was over. His new sense of purpose fizzled. He'd hung up the phone and stared at it for several minutes before trudging down the street to the park bench.

It was a bright sunny day and passersby were animated in the brisk sidewalk traffic. He wanted to kill them all but his hand was still recovering from killing the computer monitor. He wanted to tell them to shut the hell up…there was nothing to be so happy about. He wanted to stick his foot out and trip them. He wanted to sink into the bench and disappear from the face of the planet. Or maybe he could just stand up and walk into the street as a bus passed. But he wasn't ready to die.

And he wasn't ready to live.

Killing Assholes

I'm not a bad person. Not really. I pay my bills on time. Like, I'm a goddamn fanatic when it comes to paying bills. I'm not one of those dickheads who runs up a tab and then says, "screw it, I got better things to do with my time and money than pay for something I already used." I don't do that shit. I pay my bills. My parents did. I do. It runs in the family, like almost a genetic thing...you owe money, you pay it off. And I'm a considerate driver. I mean, I don't take any shit when I'm driving. I mean, some asswipe cuts me off, I give him the finger. It's a woman...hey, I'm all for equal rights...I give her the finger too. But before I lost my license, I stopped for pedestrians. I stopped and let people out at intersections, even if it meant that the prick behind me honked his horn and I had to give him the finger. Or her the finger. Makes no difference to me. I'm that fucking considerate.

I'm not some kind've sexual deviate. I haven't had it in a long time and, you know, like I've done some arm wrestling with the Big Snake, but I don't bop hard bellies...nineteen's my cutoff and no younger no matter how big their tits are. And when a lady says back off, I back off. No's no in my b\ook, same as hers. And I don't watch porno flicks or read those expensive hardcore magazines. Playboy and Penthouse. That's my limit.

I don't cheat on my tax forms, even if I knew how to do that. I don't steal. I don't lie, at least unless I really have to and then it's okay because I really have to. You know…life's gray sometimes. I don't talk about my friends behind their backs. I don't do that ever, and I've smacked a couple of dicks in the head for doing that in the past. No excuse for backstabbing your friends. No excuse at all. I don't cut into lines if I see somebody I know near the front of the line. I hate it when people do that! I don't play my music loud. I figure my music is my choice and it might not be my neighbor's choice, so I keep it to myself. That's kind've a choice I make for everybody so, like, being considerate can even be empowering sometimes. I don't give the check-out people in grocery stores or department stores a hard time when their computerized cash machines fuck up or the bar thing on the merchandise doesn't work and makes the computer fritz out. I don't give innocent people a hard time. Innocent people get a hard time from every direction…but not from me. I don't do that.

But there's one thing I do…and I gotta say that I really love doing it.

I kill assholes.

About one a month.

***

What finally broke the camel's back was one day when the guy in the scabby t-shirt spit on the sidewalk. That was it. Shit. I was sitting on a bench eating a sandwich. He saw me sitting on the bench eating my sandwich. And the cocksucker spit…I mean, a big white stream of white gunk, the kind that's thick and sticks to the sidewalk like dirty lard.

286

I mean, what kind've asshole does a thing like that? And he was looking right at me when he did it. Like his eyes were saying: "Enjoying that sandwich, chump? Here, enjoy this." Hack. Pitchu. White gob piled up on the sidewalk right in front of me. And I lost my appetite.

So I followed the prick.

Yeah, followed him. Really surprised myself when I did that. Just stood up and went after the dumb prick. He didn't see me...didn't even suspect that somebody was walking behind him about thirty feet away and sticking to him like a shadow. Probably all wrapped in thinking who he was gonna gross out next. Prick.

I followed him for most of the day...and what a prick he turned out to be. Like, right after grossing me out, and I mean, this was only about a block away, about two point zero minutes after grossing me out...he shoved a kid.

A kid.

Like, he was walking down the sidewalk all wrapped up in asswipe thoughts, probably laughing his brains out about grossing me out a block and two point zero minutes back, and he's not even looking where he's going and there's this little girl in a sort of white and blue sailor's dress and she's just standing on the sidewalk right in front of this prick with her back to him. I dunno, maybe waiting for a cab or something...maybe waiting for a friend. But the prick I'm following comes up behind her and instead of just moving a few inches to the side and walking around her, the jerk reaches out his hand and pushes her. Just pushes her! Knocks her

287

right down on her ass. And just keeps on walking. I mean, the little girl didn't start crying or anything…just got back up and made a nasty face at the guy's back and went back to waiting or whatever she was doing. I would've stopped and asked her if she was okay, but I didn't wanna draw any attention to myself, following this prick and all, you know. So I just kept on walking and, shit, it didn't take long before he was into it again.

This time with a dog tied to a street sign in front of a music store. It was one of those ones you read about a lot, attacking kids and stuff. Not a Doberman…the other one, with the flat ugly face. But it was all tied up to the sign and it wasn't growling or dripping stuff or anything, just lying down all curled up and looking like any normal dog, but the guy I'm following slows down and looks into the window of the music store and looks to the other side. Prick didn't look behind himself so he didn't see me, but he suddenly bends over and scoops up a piece of red brick that was littering the sidewalk from construction on the building next to the music store, and not thinking that anybody's watching him, he just ups and throws the piece of brick right into the poor dog's side, and the dog takes to yelping and growling at the prick but it's tied up to the street sign and the dumb prick I'm following walks around the dog just far enough to be out of biting range.

And what happens when the owner comes rushing out of the store after hearing his dog making all that noise? Old guy in one of those hats. Even wearing suspenders. The prick turns on the old guy and starts giving him shit for having a vicious dog and says that he oughta call the cops. Fucking nerve! The old guy just stands there looking between the prick and the dog and not knowing what to say, just looking kind've old and confused and worried about his dog...maybe even afraid that he's gonna lose the dog if this creep calls the cops. But the prick just turns around and keeps on walking.

And I keep on following him.

By now I've got this guy sized up for a real creep. He's about medium tall, real short hair like he's one of those punk guys but he's not wearing those fruity red boots or anything. He's wearing a dirty brown t-shirt, faded blue jeans, and Jesus boots with no socks. I always hated those fairies in sandals. Think they're cool, but they're just a bunch of fucking fairies. He's got squinty eyes and a long nose. Hate those too. And his mouth is kind've pinched up like he spends a lotta time sucking on his thumb or something.

And then he does it again.

Prick gobs another big white pile of spit on the sidewalk like something he's been saving up at the back of his mouth for a long time. Even looks down at it and I swear he was smiling, thinking about the people who were gonna walk by that pile of shit and gag or barf or something. Cocksucker.

I followed him for another hour, watching him gob and strut and act like a prick, like when he went down a whole block with a key scraping the sides of parked cars. Shit, one of them was a '78 Firebird. In immaculate condition! Prick should have his hands cut off for something like that!

That's when I knew that I had to do something, something that was gonna really put him in his place, something that would, I dunno, even the score or something. The prick spit again on the sidewalk and it was, like, all this white froth blowing out of his mouth and that's when it came to me. That's when I knew what I had to do. That's when I made up my mind that I was gonna do it.

I followed him home. I found out where he lived, at least what apartment building he lived in, and it was a real dump. No surprise in that. The sidewalk had all kinds of garbage piled up. Even the steps leading up to the doors of the buildings on his street had fuck graffiti painted on them. Just figure what the buildings looked like...and his was the worst on the block. But I knew where he lived. I knew where to find him. And that's just what I was gonna do...find him every day for the next few days and follow him.

Prick wasn't working so he just walked around every day with me following him and him doing the same messed up stuff every single day...spitting all over the sidewalks, scratching cars, stealing everything that wasn't nailed down and hanging around with a bunch of losers just like him, but he didn't spend much time with them...seemed like they didn't much like him either. Seemed like they cussed him a lot and said things that pissed him off, but then they looked pretty pissed off all the time. Buncha bald-headed leathered-up weirdoes is what they were.

But here's what I did. I followed him and I carried a big empty Vitamin C bottle and a butter knife. And whenever he spit on the sidewalk, I waited until he got a good distance away and then I went over to the spit and scraped it up with the butter knife before it could sink into the sidewalk or dry up. Sickening shit that was, but I did it. And I didn't barf once. Came close a couple of times, 'specially at first, but I kept my cookies down. And I followed the prick around for nearly a week…until I had a full bottle of his gob. Man, it was starting to stink like something dead when I opened I up to put more in. You can bet I was glad when it was full and I wouldn't have to be smelling that shit anymore, at least, not for more than one more time…and it was good that it smelled bad for that one more time.

If it smelled that bad, then it must've tasted twice as bad.

I think it was something like the fourth or fifth day that I was following him that I was ready. This time when he walked up the steps and through the door and into his building, I followed him right in. Not really close…just close enough that that I wouldn't lose sight of him. But, hell, I wasn't really all that worried about his seeing me anymore.

Nothing was gonna stop me now.

He looked around when I came through the door and he gave me a look like I was maybe the most unimportant thing in the universe let alone his life and he just looked away and started walking up the worst set of rickety-rackety steps I've ever seen in probably the worst looking stairwell on the planet. The walls looked like the people that died in World War III…like, when it ever happens. I followed him up the stairs and the prick never even suspected he was being followed, just walked up the steps real arrogant like and I followed him up to the third floor. The hall was the shits…I mean, the walls here were painted with bad smells instead of paint. He stopped at a door. He just turned the knob and walked in. Didn't even keep the door locked. Man, I could hardly wait to see what this place looked like.

It was a dump. Just like the hall. Just like the prick I was following, and he was looking at me now…still with that fucking arrogant better-than-you look, but I could tell that he was worried about seeing me coming through the door with a big Vitamin C bottle in my hand. I could smell the worry, like he was sweating it or something.

"Who the fuck are you?" he said.

"Got a present for ya, prick," I said.

That's when he got really worried…soon as I called him prick. He knew I wasn't no friend, and now I could really smell the sweat coming off his asshole body.

"Take your fuckin' present and get the fuck out of here," he yelled. He still had that arrogant look, but I could smell the sweat.

"But I put a lot of work into this present for you," I said.

Now he looked a little bit puzzled like he almost wanted to know what the present was, 'specially thinking that a lotta work went into it, but I could smell that he was afraid of finding out what it was…probably got a lot of rocks and dog shit wrapped up as presents when he was a kid. He sure didn't look like the popular kind. Not like me. I was popular…or else.

"I don't care how much work you put into it…take your fuckin' present and get the fuck out of here now!"

That's when I just dove right at him. I'm one fast motherfucker. People don't expect that in someone my size, but it's true…I'm like pig fat on a freeway. I took the cocksucker by surprise. Works every time. People don't expect people to just attack that sudden. Catches them with their guard down, even if it's already up. I was on him and he was on the floor and I was on top of him and I had one hand clutching his throat, squeezing the life out of him. His ugly hairless face was kind've bloated like and now he looked more pissed off than arrogant, but I could smell the sweat in his eyes like it was rotten hamburger. He tried squirming his body around, but I was too heavy for him. He was trapped. I pushed my face right into his ugly face and I said: "I spent a lotta time on this fucking gift for you and you're gonna take it. You ain't got no choice, ya prick."

He just stared up into my face, gagging and turning purple, while I wedged the big Vitamin C bottle on my hand that was squeezing the prick's throat and used my other hand to untwist the top. I tossed the top away and took the bottle in my free hand and held it right over his mouth.

"You ever hear the old expression, what goes around comes around, prick?" I said. He just gagged and looked confused. Dumb fuck. "I'm the guy who

293

was sitting on the bench last week, remember? You ruined my lunch with this stuff!"

And then I jammed the top of the bottle into his mouth and watched the shit inside pour slowly into the prick's mouth. Watching that thick shit emptying into a human mouth almost made me puke but I watched. I mean, it was like I had to watch, like it would be some kind've crime against God if I didn't. So I watched. And when the bottle was empty except for the stuff sticking to the insides of it, I pulled it out and, really fast, I put my hand over his mouth so's he couldn't spit the shit out. That part felt really right. He was stuck with his own gob in his mouth and couldn't spit it out. Stuck with himself, sort of.

And then something really weird happened. At first it made the hair all over my body kind've stand up or something, it was that weird, but then the weirdness kind've melted away into something else.

I mean, I couldn't see his mouth because I had my hand over it, but I was looking right into the prick's eyes and it almost looked like he was smiling. He wasn't struggling or anything, just lying there with his mouth full of scraped-up gob and me sitting on him and his eyes were smiling. And then his eyes kind've went really dull, like, what's that word? When something looks not as bright…luster! They lost their luster. And he still wasn't moving, not struggling or anything, just lying there with a mouth full of gob and all the life drained out of his eyes. And that's when I realized what was so weird.

Prick was dead.

***

I walked around for the rest of the day just thinking about that prick, what an asshole he was, how I followed him and scraped up his spit, watching him and getting to know what a complete asshole he was and then making him eat is own gob. But mostly I thought about that look in his eyes just before he died. And about the way he just sort've gave it all up and stopped struggling before he was dead, like he didn't give a fuck, like he didn't even want to go on living, like he was almost happy or something. I mean, that smile in his eyes…

I thought about the way that made me feel. It was almost like some kind've freed up feeling, like a lot of stuff was being lifted off my shoulders…or like some kind've cosmic vacuum cleaner sucked a shit load of crap out of me. It was like God himself was in my arms, in my hands, making it all happen, making it all come to some kind've close. It was like I was the last chapter in that asshole's life.

I was the happy ending.

It made me think about assholes in general, about all the people in my life…in everybody's lives…who make living more of a hell than it really is. I thought about those assholes who call you up on the phone…on your own fucking phone…and try to sell you something you don't want and don't need. I mean, one of those dumbasses dragged me out the shower when I still had a phone and I was dripping water and soap all over the floor while some idiot asks me if I want to buy gardening equipment and I'm telling the prick that I live on the third floor of a fucking apartment building but he says that it's on sale and they're never gonna be selling the gardening stuff at this price again, whatever the fuck it is–I don't know dick about gardening–so I should buy it or I'll miss out. "I live in a fucking apartment building!" I screamed at the prick. "The back yard's a fucking parking lot!" And the prick still tried to sell me gardening shit. I hung up. I would've killed the prick. I would've jumped right through the phone line and killed the prick if he would've called back.

That's what I mean about assholes in general. Like the people who make those automated telephone answering systems that send you around and around, asking for this option and that option, and sending you to this place and that place, and then they send you into some fucking dead end with dead end music like the shit they play in elevators or in some doctors' offices. I think it's supposed to calm you. It just pisses me off. And I really get pissed off at the ones that say: "Your call is important to us. Please hold." If my call is so fucking important, then pick up the phone and turn off that goddam music! Almost seems like phones breed assholes.

* * *

My second asshole had a cell phone.

I hate those things. Don't know how many times I've come a pube hair away from being run over by some asshole talking away on a phone while he's, or she's–and it's really easy to be

296

sexually orientated fair on this one–driving along yakking away on the phone, all wrapped up on the cell phone and not watching where they're going, so god help anybody who gets in their path because they're gonna ram their front bumper up your ass and probably just keep on driving and never even know they killed anybody. If assholes had uniforms, they'd probably have cell phones hanging all over their jackets like soldiers have grenades hanging there. Fucking grenades probably do less damage.

So there I was...about a month after killing Mr. Gob-a-Lot...sitting in this place having a coffee and chocolate dip donut or three, and there's these two guys sitting about four seats away from me and they're talking away. One of them is small with dark hair and he's like mostly listening to the other guy, who's kind've big–maybe about one ninety-five or thereabouts–and they're talking for about five minutes, mostly the big guy talking, like I said, but I'm kind've of studying them. I do that a lot...just sort've look at people and try to figure them out, see if I can guess what they're about. Think maybe someday I might, you know, write a book or something. I think I got a lotta stories I could write about. But I'm thinking that these guys work together or something. I mean, they're both wearing white shirts and ties and it looks like they just sort've dropped into this place for a coffee break to talk business maybe. And right when the little guy starts to say something, the big guy holds up a finger to shut him up and pulls out a cell phone and starts talking into it.

What the hell is the world coming to! I've seen this a million times. The big guy just starts yakking away on the phone as though the other guy doesn't even exist, as though as soon as the cell phone rang or buzzed or whatever they do, the little guy just disappeared into some other world, like he existed only when the big guy wasn't talking on the cell phone. At that moment, I could've gone right over to their table and grabbed that phone and shoved in right down the prick's throat. "Fucking message on hold!" I could've yelled while he choked on his call. I watched for about five minutes and the whole time the big prick didn't even look at the other guy...yakked away on the phone. The little guy looked kind've like he really didn't give a shit at first, just sipped his coffee and sort've looked around the place, but after five minutes, he looked like he was starting to get a little bit irritated, and if the big guy had given a fuck about anything else but talking on his cell phone, he would've seen that the guy he was sitting with was getting just a little bit pissed.

I kept watching. By this time, I could've just started smashing the phone over the big guy's head until I cracked his skull open. The little guy was starting to get fidgety. He took a business card out of his shirt pocket and started reading it and flicking it with his thumb. I wanted to just yell at him to just get up and walk out of the place and leave the prick with the phone sitting there talking all by himself. But he stayed and the longer he stayed, the madder I got. The more he flicked that fucking business card, the more I wanted to kill the big prick with the phone.

So that's exactly what I did.

Not right away though. Not right then. In fact, as soon as I made up my mind that I was gonna to kill the prick, I calmed down. I wasn't mad anymore. I was determined. I was determined that the prick with the cell phone was gonna die, so I just sat there all relaxed and drinking my coffee and watching the two men for about another ten minutes while the big guy yakked and yakked on the cell phone. I mean, there's assholes and there's assholes...making anybody wait that long while you just ignore the poor bastard while you talk on a phone sitting right in front of the guy so that he can't do anything but try to not interrupt your call and pretend that his time is worth dick-all while the other guy just yaks and yaks. The little guy was getting more irritated. Like, it showed in the way his eyes were all over the place like he was looking for some place to escape but always coming back to the card he flicked with his thumb because there was no way out...except maybe to just get up and walk out. But he wasn't gonna do that.

And that made me think...one of the biggest things that assholes have going for them is the fact that the people they fuck over don't do anything. They just sit there and take it, just like the little guy was doing right now. Just sitting there wanting to get up and just walk out but glued to his chair because he didn't want to look like an asshole by walking out on the other guy. I mean, shit, that might interrupt the prick's phone call. They got all those books on etiquette and doing and saying the right thing, but somebody should write a book about when you don't have to be considerate anymore, about that line that people cross over where you don't have to treat them like humans anymore and you can just tell them to go fuck themselves. Maybe some day I'll write that book. I got a lotta thoughts on the subject.

And then, wonder of wonders, the big guy finally finishes his call and puts the phone back in his pocket and, get this, he just like starts talking to the other guy like nothing ever happened, like he didn't just spend nearly half an hour ignoring him and making him waste his entire coffee break listening to some fat tub of cell phone yakking machine blatting to some dumbass somewhere else who's probably doing the same thing at that end. He didn't even say he was sorry. I could see it in the way he looked while he talked. It was like the little guy was nothing more than some kind've stage prop in a play all about the big guy and everything that he didn't have time for was just supposed to disappear but be right there when he paid attention to it again.

Yeah. This guy had to die.

I waited a bit after they left and then I got up and followed them. They were walking. That was a sign. It meant the big guy had to die. I mean, if they were in a car, I wouldn't be able to follow them, but they were walking. They walked down the sidewalk about a block away to a discount furniture store. I was right…they worked together…probably furniture salesmen. The store was pretty shabby looking: big dirty windows with cracked tiles under them, and the top part of the building looked like it had cheap apartments and probably needed paint for the last fifty years. But there seemed to be a lot of customers inside looking around. Must be good prices. I walked by the door and slowed down just enough to read the sign with the hours listed. They closed at nine.

Nine.

That's when the big guy would be mine.

I was parked across the street when the store closed. I was kind've split between which was the bigger high...killing the asshole with the phone or using a stolen car. I was fucked if I was caught at either of them, completely fucked if I was caught at both. But what the...with my record, I was already fucked. No loss!

He was the first out. That figured. Probably left all the paperwork for his skinny buddy. And, holy shit! He was walking out of the store with his cell phone jammed into his ear. But that was good. Meant that he wasn't looking around, wasn't seeing me waiting there across the street for him. He was all wrapped up in something that had nothing to do with here and now. And I was here and now.

He walked into a parking lot around the corner of the store and disappeared for a couple of minutes. Then his car pulled out of the lot and onto the street. He was driving away from me. Great! I didn't have to do a ninety-degree, or whatever they call that thing they do. He was driving a Toyota something or other...no patriotism...but that figured. And the prick was still talking on the phone. Took the turn onto the street wide. Not paying attention. Not here and now, where I was waiting for him. I started up the car and followed him. Prick was all over the road, head bobbing up and down while he talked, not paying any attention at all to his driving. Pissed me off so much, I almost hit an old guy who came right out of nowhere on a crosswalk.

He finally pulled up in front of a small single-floor house in a sort of nice neighborhood, like the kind've place where there's no bars on the doors or windows, but there's all these signs that the place is close to bars...paint peeling on just about all the houses, garbage on the curbs that looks like it's been there a while meaning that the city's starting to give up on this street, same with the burnt out street lights and the street signs painted over with "fuck you" for god knows how long.

This is where the dumbass lived. This was his house. The lights were off. He lived alone...or the others were out. But I figured he just lived alone. Only real people in this prick's life were at the other end of his cell phone.

His next call was gonna be a wake up call from reality.

Reality was parked across the street from his house, watching him, and noticing that there was no basketball net over the garage door. Something unnatural about that. Reminded me of when I was a kid.

I waited for the deep dark, the time when everybody's probably in bed, even the dogs. I got out of the car and walked real casual-like up to his yard and looked around. Nobody was looking out the windows of any of the other houses, so I ducked into a clump of bushes and made my way up to the house. Fucking prickly rose bushes in there somewhere. Hate those things. There was light coming from a window at the side of the house and that's where I went. I looked in and there he was, sitting in a recliner chair, watching TV, eating something from a white bowl. That's when I noticed how big the prick's gut was. Must wear a girdle or something in the daytime. His arms were big, but they didn't look hard. I could take this guy…I knew it. I made my way around the house, peeking into all the windows I could see into, and it looked like he was alone.

It was time to kill him.

I went to the front door and knocked. Just like that…I knocked on the door and stood there like I was just any old visitor dropping by at two o'clock in the morning to pay a visit or something. Who the fuck knows, these days. Prick just opened the door. Didn't even ask who it was. Cocky bastard, this one. He said: "What the hell do you want?" I just ran right into him. Pushed upward on his upper body and lifted him right off his center of gravity and down he went onto the floor. I kicked the door closed with my foot and then punched him a couple or three times with my fists until he stopped struggling as much. He could take a beating…but soon as he quieted, I jumped up and brought my foot down into his chest as hard as I could. I could hear bones snapping. Ugly sound, but this prick needed it. I looked around and saw just what I needed.

He was sort of squirming around on the floor with a dazed look in his eyes, or at least the one that he could still open. He must've farted, 'cause the air was filled with something that smelled like burning sulfur. He was moaning with a kind've gurgling sound. I didn't have much time. I jumped across the living room and grabbed his cell phone from the TV table beside his recliner chair and then jumped back fast to where he was just starting to push himself up on his elbow. I let him have it in the side of the head with the cell phone. And then I let him have it again with the cell phone…this time square in the face. By this time, he wasn't making any more noises and I wasn't saying a word. It was just the two of us, looking at each other and the only noise was the sound of the cell phone smashing into his face until I was sure that the cocksucker wasn't ever gonna talk on the phone again while some poor bastard had to wait for him.

* * *

Walking home from his place, I did a lot of thinking. I guess killing people does that to you. I thought about what a fucked up world telephones were making the place. I remembered when I still had one…assholes calling me up and asking me to buy all kind've crap I didn't want. One time, this bitch calls me up–although I know some guys who're bitches, just to be fair with the sex thing– and she starts asking me questions about what kind've shit I buy and I said: "I don't do shit over the phone. Take me off your fucking list." And she says: "I'll do that, sir, but first, can you tell me how many children you have?" I hung up. Phones make it easier for assholes to be assholes. They make it possible for the assholes to come right into your home and fuck you up. Best thing that ever happened to me was losing my phone.

* * *

It was just a little over a month after that that I killed another asshole.

Started in a movie theater this time. I was watching a movie, minding my own business, and this skinny prick sits right down behind me. Lots of other empty seats in the place, but he sits right down behind me. Place was so empty I could almost hear the dumbass breathing. Prick even knocked my chair a couple of times. People should have their feet cut off for doing that. Then I heard some kind've crinkling noise, like paper or something. And then I heard it...the one sound that I really hate coming from another human being.

He was chewing gum. With his fucking mouth open! Making all kinds've snapping and cracking noises, bouncing the wad of gum off his tongue, wrapping it around his teeth, and making sucking noises with his lips. Whole theater with empty seats and this prick has to sit down right behind me and chew his gum with his fucking mouth open.

Big mistake, asshole.

And there was the feeling again...once I knew that I was gonna kill him, I calmed down. The sound didn't bother me anymore, just fed my resolve, and I kind've enjoyed it now. I sat right through the whole movie listening to him chewing and smacking his lips together. Prick went through three pieces of gum. I turned my head sideways once and saw him putting the chewed-out gum under his seat. That's why I never touch the bottom of a seat in a movie theater ever since I was a kid and put my hand right smack into a pile of sticky gum that I had to wash off in the washroom and miss half the movie. Man, would I like to run into the dumb prick who put that gum under the seat now. Right fucking now. But he's long gone. Probably choked to death on a wad of gum.

But the prick behind me was here. Still chewing. With his mouth open. Right behind me. Pretty soon...pretty soon, prick wasn't gonna be chewing gum anymore. I can't even remember any of the fuck scenes in the movie...just remember trying to think about how I was gonna handle this one.

It had to be gum. Just like the prick who spit all over the place. This asshole had to die by gum. Fuck, that meant following him around for the next week, hoping the prick would spit out the gum where I could get it. But if the guy had to die by gum, then that's the way he was gonna die and I would follow him around and I would pick up the slime ball's gum wads and save them for him. This thing had to be done right, and I was gonna do it right.

I'm that much in tune with my inner balance.

The movie ended and they started playing the credits–credits for a fuck movie...yeah, sure–and the five or six people in the place stayed and watched them, maybe waiting to see if they were gonna give out the phone numbers of the sluts in the movie. Or maybe they just didn't finish whacking themselves. But the guy behind me got up about a minute into the credits. I stayed where I was, just sort've looking over to the side to get a good look at him. Skinny, just like I figured, blond hair growing down over his ears, wearing a blue sports jacket with a wide white line going down one side. Prick wasn't half bad looking and I wondered what he was doing in a movie like this when he could've probably been making it with the real thing. I waited until he was well up the aisle and almost to the exit before I stood up and started following him.

The sun was bright when I walked outside, but these movies were too dicey at night, especially leaving the building. Besides, I figure it's good to work up your appetite for the nighttime just in case a little action comes along at night. Not much likely to happen in the daytime. I looked around and saw him almost right away. He was on the other side of the street, walking south. Hey, this was looking to be a cooperative asshole...that's the direction I was gonna go. I crossed the street and followed him.

This neighborhood was a dive. Used to be kind've a nice place when I was a kid. Like, the stores used to have big picture windows with lots of neat stuff right up close where you could grab them after smashing the window with a brick. Not anymore though...like everything was barred up and some of the stores even had cashiers inside bulletproof cages with little slots all around where they could poke a shotgun out and like blow your head off. It was a lot easier to get away with things around here when I was a kid.

Two minutes into following the prick from the movies, and like doesn't he just spit a big wad of gray stuff out of his mouth. Well, Mr. Gum Chewer, looks like you go out the same way as Mr. Gob-a-Lot. I looked around and saw an old cardboard coffee cup by some garbage on the sidewalk. I scooped it up and kept following the prick. I looked around. There were other people walking and standing around doing nothing, but nobody was paying any attention to me or the prick I was following, so when I came to the gum, I scooped it up with the cup. It must've still been wet because it didn't stick to the pavement or anything. This guy was making it too easy for me. Gotta love it when that happens.

I followed him for about three blocks before he came to a door between two storefronts. He unlocked it and walked in without looking around. I went to a restaurant across the street, Dixie's Diner or something...the words on the big glass window were faded and peeling. On one side of the front, I could see one of those sliding steel grate things that they slide over the front of the place when they close up. Like people just don't trust people in this neighborhood anymore. Makes it impossible to pull anything. I went in and sat down where I could keep an eye on the prick's door. Waitress was right on my case to buy something, so I ordered a coffee. Looked like this prick was going to be expensive to kill. Thought that maybe I should save receipts or something and claim them on my taxes the next time I ever filed the fucking things. Position: Asshole Killer. Expenses: One coffee at Dixie's Dive.

About the same time the waitress was getting in my face again for taking too long to drink the coffee, the prick came out. I gave the waitress a dirty look and left. As I passed by the window, I saw her at my table picking up the cup and looking around for a tip. She looked up and saw me and gave me a dirty look. Watch it lady...I might start following you, so just shove your fucking tips down your throat till change for a buck comes out your ass.

I followed the prick for about a week...took that long to get enough gum saved up. Couple of times, people saw me scoop it up in the old coffee cup and looked at me real disgusted like, but I didn't hang in this area much anymore anyway, just came around sometimes to check out a fuck movie or three.

This prick had a sort've girlfriend he dropped by to see whenever he felt like it. I mean, he spent most of his nights at a pool hall doing a lousy job of sharking...dumbass couldn't bank worth shit and made about every fourth combination. Sometimes I stayed for a while after he left and got the gum he stuck to the bottom of the table. Had to be real careful about that...fuckers in this place see you doing anything weird and you ain't walking home...you're lucky if you can still take a cab home. But the cup was finally full...or about as full as I could wait for it to get. It was time to kill.

I knew about what time he was gonna get home on Monday nights–just before dark–so I was waiting by the pricks's door when he got home. I had my back to him, leaning against the building like some kind've homeless bum or a drunk. I heard the key clinking in the lock and the door creak as he opened it. I half turned my head and watched him go in through the corners of my eyes, and when he was inside, I stepped closer to the door and put my foot out to stop it from closing completely. I stepped right in front of the door and looked up a whitewashed stairway. The prick was nearly at the top of the stairs and he wasn't looking back, so I scooted in. At the top of the stairs, he turned left into a hallway so I hurried up, trying to be as quiet as possible, like trying not to creak any of the rotten floorboards with my weight.

Dumbass was waiting for me.

Right at the top of the stairs and at the beginning of the hall. Came at me with one of those Karate or Kung Fu kicks, kind that goes around in a big circle and smacks you in the side of the head. Fucking kick did hit me in the side of the head…last place in the world that's gonna do me any harm. So there he was with his leg still off the ground and me pissed off because the dumb prick just kicked me and almost made me drop the coffee cup filled with gum. I punched downward with my left fist right into his dick and then I brought my right fist– squeezed full've the coffee cup and gum–flat down on the top of his head as he doubled up. Prick hit the floor like he was filled with lead. I went down on one knee and grabbed his neck and pulled his head up. I had the gum ready to jam into his mouth, but there was something weird about the way the prick's head kind've just hung in my hand and his eyes were open but not seeing anything. Dumbass was dead.

I stuffed the gum into his mouth anyway.

But I didn't feel too good about that one…left a kind've unfinished taste in my mouth, like there was still something I was supposed to do but I didn't know what it was. Maybe I was supposed to say something to the prick before he died, or maybe he was supposed to say something to me. Maybe he was supposed to taste all that gum that came from his mouth. I dunno. I thought about it for a while and it didn't make any sense…so I stopped thinking about it.

* * *

Instead, I started thinking about all the kinds of assholes there are in the world. I mean, it was kind've of scary at first. I was hearing all these voices, not God's voice or voices from demons: I'm not crazy or anything…I'm just as normal as you. The voices I was hearing were the voices of all the pissed off, fucked over, dragged down, and tired people of the entire fucking world. You know who I mean…the people just like you who're like sick and tired of people who call you up when you still had a phone and it's the wrong number but they just hang up without saying sorry or anything, just hang up as though they're pissed off at you for being the wrong fucking number. And I heard about the pissed off people who put shit up on bulletins boards in super markets and Laundromats and then come back a few days later and see that some jerk has pinned a notice right on top of theirs so that nobody can even see it.

* * *

That did it! I started hanging around the bulletin board at the Washing Green Laundromat. Just waiting…waiting. Like, it didn't take long. She was one big, mean looking woman. Big with frizzy brown hair that looked like she dried it in the microwave or something. And she had on too much makeup. She looked like some kind've frigate in a parade. Like, right away I knew that she had a mousy little husband who said things like yes dear and yes dear. And she was dressed just the way you would expect…a plain top that didn't say anything about how big she was, and pants that showed her flat ass. Like, I don't wanna be prejudiced against fat people or anything, but how could this woman sit down with all that weight on that no-ass and not damage nerves or bones around that place where the rest of us stack our fat. I mean, she had her cushions in all the wrong places.

And then I saw her do it. Fucking bitch (and not all fucking women are bitches, but this one was) took a pin out of one of the ads on the bulletin board and pinned her ad right on top of it. Like, her ad completely covered the other ad…and she was using the other ad's own pin! Man, that's like beating somebody to death with their own tire iron.

I mean, who would even see the ad underneath her one? They wouldn't even know to lift hers and look under it for some kind've hidden secret message or anything. Whoever put the ad up that she covered was just wasting their time and their paper! I hate it when that happens. I mean, I try to see this from the eyes of the person who wrote the ad she covered. I mean, this is some poor slob who needs money and has to sell something because they can't afford to pay the bills or some other thing and that's why they had to put the ad up in the first place. And then some fat bitch with no ass covers it.

Fat bitch had to die.

And to seal it even more, the bitch looks right at me as though I'm some kind've dirt...like maybe I'm some kind've criminal scum or something. Like, she was gonna pay for that. I waited until she left and then I went over to the bulletin board and pulled her ad off. Some dumpy woman with a hamper gave me a dirty look. I told her that the woman who just left pinned it on top of somebody else's ad and she said: "And that makes it alright for you to tear her ad down?" If I wasn't such a fucking gentleman, I would've slapped the bitch right in the chops, right there by the bulletin board. But being a gentleman, I just told her to fuck off and walked away with the ad. It's people like her give the assholes so much power, like those pricks who say jailbirds should have rights and all that shit. Nobody cares about the victims anymore.

When I got outside, I saw her car pull away, big new Buick. Bitch didn't even need the money. I looked down at the ad. It was for some kind've church thing, a bazaar. It had an address. I knew where to find her. It had a date and a time. I knew when to find her. No phone number, though. But that was all right...I wasn't the kind of weirdo who would play games with the people he was gonna kill.

I was waiting outside the church when she drove up in her big fat Buick. I hate Buicks; they're for nose-up-their-asses old people who don't wanna have anything to do with the rest of the world. That's why every Buick on the planet has tinted windows...just like the one pulling into the church parking lot now. I was standing in a dark area not far from the front doors to the church...just waiting. She got out of her car and walked across the parking lot. I should've been waiting there, right in the parking lot, but I was by the front door. Fucking bitch went in a side door. Shit, I had to go in. Had to pay two bucks to some old cow who looked me up and down like I didn't belong there or something. Figured I might come back for her some day...you know, people who pass judgment on others...biggest assholes of all.

There were tables all over the place, loaded with old used shit that people didn't want anymore. Some of it was even new shit. Saw an electric wax buffer still in the box for ten bucks. Could've used one of those at one time. Then I saw a set of steak knives for a buck. Those, I could still use. I bought them. Then I started looking for the Buick Bitch.

She was at the other end of the room, giving orders to a bunch of old ladies standing around a table with cakes and cookies and other baked shit.

She was looking at the old ladies with that same better-than-you look that she gave me at the laundromat. I ran my thumb across the blade of one of the steak knives. This was going to be sweet. I stayed at my end of the room...well away from her...just in case she might've recognized me from the Laundromat, and I watched her for about twenty minutes. That was about all I could stomach. I don't like watching fat old bitches like her pushing sweet little old ladies around. But she wasn't gonna be doing that for much longer.

I looked around the room. It was a big room. I saw a door about halfway down the wall on my right...and another one on the same wall, but all the way down at the end, where the Buick Bitch was still yakking out orders to the old ladies, getting them to rearrange the cookies and stuff as though making different patterns on the table was gonna make the fucking stuff sell better. I mean, a six-foot long table with cookies and cakes. How much bossing around can anybody on the planet come up with for six feet of church hall real estate? I figured it was the far door, the one closest to the table. She would've stormed right through it, taking the old ladies by surprise and making them piss their diapers. Wouldn't be too hard to find it from the outside.

That was where I was gonna wait for her. As I walked back through the front door, I made sure the old cow at the admission table saw the steak knives. I smiled at her and she looked away from me as fast as she could. Not so fucking uppity now, old shit cow.

315

I walked around the side of the building to the door at the back and waited in the dark by some high bushes. I wasn't worried about her coming out with other people. She wouldn't. I wasn't worried about her coming out in a crowd at the end of the bazaar. She would leave early, after she got bored pushing people around. And leaving early would just drive in the fact that she was above the others. Come in late...leave early. Stick around just long enough to make life miserable for a bunch of feeble-brained old ladies. She wasn't gonna be doing that much longer. Not after tonight. Not after meeting my bargain steak knives.

I waited there for about two hours. About a couple dozen people came out, some in groups, some by themselves, but they didn't even suspect that I was standing over by the bushes, waiting in the dark. Too wrapped up in their little church thing and their little church thoughts. Made me think about the time when I was a kid and I went to church every Sunday like I really believed or something. But I went. Until one day I went to some kind've teen thing, a teen dance and activity thing. There was gonna be a lot of knock-out church girls there, the kind that tease your balls off and never give more than a handful of tit...with their fucking bra still on. But I wasn't getting much of anything anywhere else at the time, so what the fuck, me and my friend Earl went to the dance. Problem was, Earl was a Catholic. The teen thing was in an Anglican church. They told him he couldn't come in. I told them to take their fucking cock tease dance and stuff it up their ass. Never went to church after that, fucking discriminating assholes.

The door opened.

And there she was, all alone, looking like she was disappointed or something with the whole world because it didn't live up to her standards or something. I mean, like the whole fucking world was supposed to stop breathing and listen to her breathing so that it could pace her or something. Man, was her breathing in for a big change of pace.

As soon as the door shut behind her, I walked out of the dark by the bushes and walked right up to her. She gave me that same better-than-you look that she gave me in the laundromat. "Remember me?" I asked. She looked really angry and went to say something but saw the knives in my hand. "They're for you," I said. And before she could say anything, or scream, I drove one of them right into her throat. Her eyes opened up really wide, like you see in horror movies where some bitch gets killed by some kind've murdering psycho. Right away, I shoved another one into her stomach. She tried to look down, all wide-eyed, but could just bend her head a bit because of the knife sticking out of her throat. Now her eyes started to narrow as though she was confused or something. I stuck another knife right into her chest. It didn't go in far though. Must've hit a bone, one of her ribs. Her eyes winced as though that was the first one she felt. Now she was looking at me, right into my eyes. I didn't like that. She wasn't uppity now, just confused and looking at me with one of those "why me?" looks that people get when shit they started comes back and bites their ass. I pushed another one into her chest. This one went in, right between the ribs and must've hit something important because now the Buick Bitch's eyes were wide again...not as wide as before but wide, this time with fear. I reached into my pocket and took out the ad that she put up on the bulletin board and showed it to her. She looked at it and gagged. "Remember this?" I said. I shoved the last knife into it and pinned it straight into her forehead. It went in smoothly for going through bone. Good knives. Her face twisted really weird, like she suddenly looked really vulnerable and fragile. I almost felt sorry for her as she fell down with that fragile look all over her face.

* *
*

I thought about that look all the way home. It was like, just before she died, something that was inside her came to the surface...like what she was until then was some sort of cover or disguise. I started thinking that maybe she was really unsure of herself deep down inside where we all know ourselves better than we think. Maybe she wasn't such a bad person after all, I thought. Maybe all she needed was for somebody to dig through the shit on top of her personality and get to know her inside and maybe then she would've seen that the shit inside her wasn't so bad after all, and that she didn't have to be bossing around little old ladies and giving people like me better-than-you looks...and covering other people's ads with her own. And maybe she would've driven a Ford.

318

Or maybe she was just afraid of dying. Maybe all bullying assholes like her are really just a bunch of cowards under the surface, and now she's a dead coward. It didn't take me long to stop thinking about the Buick Bitch.

* * *

It was the next asshole who stopped me from thinking about her.

I was sitting in the living room, staring at the wall, thinking about the Buick Bitch…you know, a relaxing evening, quality time with my thoughts…and suddenly it was like there was a minor earthquake or something. I could feel the floors and walls shaking and I could hear this booming sound coming from outside and it was getting louder and louder. I stopped thinking about the Buick Bitch and went to the window.

Fuck, it was like, when one asshole went down, they passed the baton to the next asshole, and there was the next asshole down in the parking lot in a big black Camaro, from the eighties I was guessing. Fucking million watt stereo pounding out that yappy ghetto crap where people who can't sing just yell and swear a lot, sort've like barrio country music. The sound went something like boom boom boom boom fucking boom boom boom and it filled the whole air around the block with boom boom boom and the dumbass's windows were all up! Guy must be deaf or something. He turned off the car engine and the music stopped. Then he got out. Young guy with short blond hair and a stunned look on his face. No fucking wonder. Probably deaf from the booming. He walked past a heap of garbage on the sidewalk and ducked into the building with the balconies. Some kind've rich deaf dumbass? He can afford a balcony. I didn't remember seeing him around before, so he must've been new to the block.

He should've moved somewhere else.

Every night for a month, I listened to his fucking boom boom. He woke me up with it in the day. He dragged me away from my wall at night. He interrupted my thoughts. He disturbed my meals. He pushed his music into my life and backed me up into a corner. For a whole fucking month.

A month.

It was time. I didn't even hear the boom boom boom that night...not once I decided it was time to kill him. It was like, when I decided to kill them, they were already dead so they couldn't bother me anymore, and anything they did after that was just fuel, like throwing another log into my resolve. I waited until the next night...right in front of his building. And I had the perfect weapon. I picked it up as I walked by the garbage heap...a broken CD, sharp and shiny. I waited by the door. I didn't care if he saw me. He didn't know me from dick anyway.

I could hear him coming from blocks away, the boom boom boom in the distance, getting closer, getting louder, until I saw his car lights first and then saw his car. I could feel the air pounding into my face from the booming pushing it. Nobody has the right to force their music onto everybody around them the way this prick was doing. But he wouldn't be doing it much longer. I ran my thumb over the sharp edge of the CD behind my back. It reminded me of something, but I had to stay focused on the prick getting out of the black Camaro. The music stopped. He banged the door shut–no way to treat a vintage car like that–and he started walking toward the door and me. I looked right into his face. He was younger than I thought, clean shaven, skinny. He was wearing some kind've band t-shirt, Prison, or something, and faded blue jeans. He looked at me looking right into his face and looked as though he was trying to figure out who I was or if he knew me or something.

Just before he reached me, I looked around…nobody watching. It was just me and him. He started to say something to me. That's when I walked right at him and brought the CD up and slashed it across his throat. He looked shocked. It made him look even younger. I slashed his throat again. He just stood there, looking like he didn't believe what was happening. Blood was spurting out of his throat. I slashed again and he sank down onto his knees. He looked right into my eyes as though he was trying to figure out why I was doing this to him. I said: "I'm the volume control." He gave me a really confused look then and it made him look really really young, and then I realized that this guy couldn't be much more than sixteen, and maybe he was just sixteen. Maybe he wasn't new to the neighborhood. Maybe he was living in this building for a long time with his parents and he just got his license and the Camaro was his first car.

He was just a kid. He fell forward onto his face, dead. Blood from his throat started to spread out onto the sidewalk. He was just a kid.

I figured maybe I should cool it for a while.

* * *

And I did. For a month. And then I killed a litterbug...followed him for a week, picking up his litter. A month later, I killed some asshole who was standing in the middle of the sidewalk yakking to some other asshole about nothing. Dumbass saw me coming and just stood there so that I had to step into the street to get around him. I had to follow him for eight days before I got a chance to push him into an oncoming truck. It was like they kept passing that baton from one asshole to the next. Right after the sidewalk hog, I started tracking two dumbasses who threw a Frisbee back and forth right in the busiest section of the park, right in the place where everybody takes their kids and spreads out blankets for picnics and shit. They kept bumping into kids when they ran after the Frisbee and then they threw the Frisbee right into the middle of people's picnics...and one day the Frisbee hit a little girl in the head and made her bleed. From that one I learned that a broken Frisbee cuts just as well as a broken CD. No sooner were they dead than I stepped into a pile of dog shit on the sidewalk. Got the dog, too. But that was the last time I followed anybody around picking up their shit. About a month after that I just jumped right into this woman's car. Jumped right into the passenger's

322

side, right beside her. She was talking to another woman right in the middle of the street, yelling out their windows at each other, just ignoring all the people honking their horns at them to get out of the way. Just as soon as she finished talking and started driving away, I jumped in. Pushed her and her car over a cliff outside the city. Long walk back but it gave me a chance to think about things.

* * *

I thought about all the kinds of assholes in the world, the assholes who don't flush the toilet and leave shit floating around or just piss all over the toilet seat so you get your ass wet when you take a crap, the assholes who give bartenders and store clerks a hard time just because they know they can get away with it, the assholes who speed up when you try to pass them in a passing zone and then slow down in the no passing zone, the assholes who draw underlines in library books or tear out the pages like I used to do, the assholes who draw fucked up graffiti on the natural beauty of bridges and freeway underpasses, the assholes who leave chewing gum under tables and chairs in restaurants so that you get their gum all over your fingers when you're putting your gum there, the assholes who call you up when you had a phone and tell you that you've won something but you know fucking well that you haven't, the assholes who make the phone systems that make it impossible to talk to a real human being even if that real human being is just gonna lie to you anyway.

323

I thought about all the assholes like shitty bosses, child beaters, wife beaters, animal beaters, terrorists, murderers, bankers, scam artists, politicians, thieves – especially the petty ones who steal from people who have next to nothing, like pensioners and welfare bums – pedophiles, lawyers, bad cops, used car salesmen, bullies, striking government workers, other religions, television holy rollers, cults, obscene phone callers, stalkers, rapists, tobacco companies, dictators,

I thought: "Man, I've got my work cut out for me." It took me until dark to get home, but that was okay…like I said, I did a lot of thinking. Maybe too much thinking. I thought about all the assholes that I took out. I thought about the looks on their faces before they died. That first one, the prick who went around spitting all over the place. The look in his eyes before he died…like he wanted it. But the kid with the boom boom boom didn't look like he wanted to die. Even the Buick Bitch looked…like whatever it was coming out of her before she died. I tried to make sense out of it. They should've all been happy to die…their contribution towards making the world a better place to live for people like me. They should've seen it as a species quality thing. But some of them seemed like they really wanted to go on living. It was those ones that I thought a lot about while I was walking home. They all looked so confused, like they couldn't believe that it was really happening. They looked afraid. They looked pathetic. They weren't assholes for those few seconds before they died…they were just people dying.

I don't know how many assholes I've killed. Lots. About one a month for a long, long time. And now I'm tired, especially after that long walk into the city, and all that thinking. I figure the thinking is what was more tiring than the walking. It drained me.

It kind've scared me—all the killing left to do. By the time I got home, it was like this giant wall standing in front of me and I was standing under it with a slingshot, and I couldn't even see the top of the wall.

* * *

And now I'm home, staring at my living room wall, my bare feet bleeding and cooling down in the night air coming through the window. It smells like somebody's cooking chicken somewhere. I'd go out and get something to eat, but what's the point? I'm not hungry anymore. I'm not thirsty, even though I haven't eaten or had anything to drink since this morning. Jumping into that car was a mistake. People saw. But even that's not important anymore. And none of the assholes who stare at me frightened, relieved, or confused…stare at me in my own mind, right into the backs of my eyes…none of them are important anymore. Only one thing is important now—that one last asshole.

That one last asshole.

About the Author

Biff Mitchell is bald and has no idea how to use his cell phone. In spite of this he taught writing workshops through the University of New Brunswick's College of Extended Learning for a decade. He's also given workshops on science fiction, humor, mystery, horror and publishing through the Maritime Writer's Workshop, the FogLit Literary Festival, Culture Days Canada and the Muse Online Writers Conference.

Biff has managed to trick publishing companies and magazine editors into publishing several novels, numerous short stories and novellas, and even some poetry. Poetry. A few years ago, his ebook *eMarketing Tools for Writers, 2nd Edition* was a bestseller in the business section of Fictionwise for over a year.

Biff is also a world famous photographer in his daydreams and has taken a few passable pictures that he displays on his photography website biffmitchellvisuals.com.

You can learn more about Biff at biffmitchell.com.